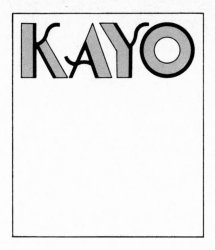

Also by James McConkey

The Novels of E.M. Forster

Night Stand

Crossroads

A Journey to Sahalin

The Tree House Confessions

Court of Memory

Chekhov and Our Age (editor)

To a Distant Island

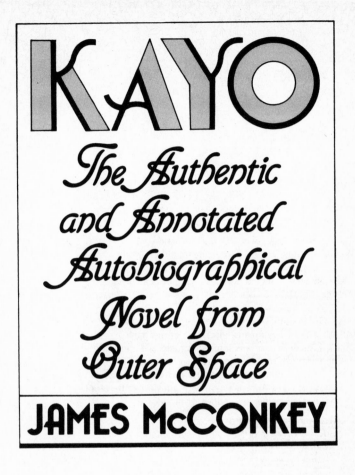

KAYO

*The Authentic
and Annotated
Autobiographical
Novel from
Outer Space*

JAMES McCONKEY

E. P. DUTTON · NEW YORK

Copyright © 1987 by James McConkey
All rights reserved. Printed in the U.S.A.

PUBLISHER'S NOTE: This novel is a work of fiction.
Names, characters, places, and incidents either are the product
of the author's imagination or are used fictitiously, and
any resemblance to actual persons, living or dead, events,
or locales is entirely coincidental.

No part of this publication may be reproduced or transmitted
in any form or by any means, electronic or mechanical, including
photocopy, recording, or any information storage and retrieval
system now known or to be invented, without permission in
writing from the publisher, except by a reviewer who wishes to
quote brief passages in connection with a review written for
inclusion in a magazine, newspaper, or broadcast.

Published in the United States by
E. P. Dutton, a division of New American Library,
2 Park Avenue, New York, N.Y. 10016.

Library of Congress Cataloging-in-Publication Data
McConkey, James.
Kayo: the authentic and annotated autobiographical
novel from outer space.
I. Title.
PS3563.C3435K38   1987   813'.54   86-19921
ISBN: 0-525-24505-7

Published simultaneously in Canada by
Fitzhenry & Whiteside Limited, Toronto.

W

DESIGNED BY MARK O'CONNOR

10 9 8 7 6 5 4 3 2 1

First Edition

The publisher attests to the authenticity of the following narrative "from outer space," at least to the degree that it was printed directly from diskettes made from the hard disk of a "long-humming home computer" found in the Finger Lakes farmhouse of one Professor "M." Any unusual typographical characteristic is a consequence of the publisher's desire to present a faithful, untouched transcription of this remarkable document.

CONTENTS

PART TWO

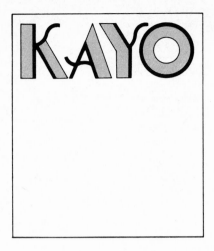

The Scribe's Prologue

1

Let me admit, at once, the nature of my crime: about a year ago, I intercepted—snatched with my right hand—a message from space intended for a fellow professor at Corinth, the well-known astronomer Frank Duck. In the following days, I so managed to ingratiate myself with the sender of the message that he forgot entirely he had wished to contact Professor Duck, who, poor man, had been anticipating such a contact for many moons, decades even; retentive readers of the daily papers and news magazines will recall that it was in the nineteen-sixties that Professor Duck, then director of the radio telescope observatory at Coal Bank, West Virginia, inaugurated Project Alice, the attempt to communicate with beings on another planet who by the very fact that they could both decode and answer our signals would be more advanced than we, their civilization having managed to survive the perils that still promise to decimate our own. According to the article in Newsweek announcing the start of Project Alice, the first questions the astronomer wished to pose to the intelligent beings, once communication had been established, were "How did you conquer cancer?" and "How did you overcome war?"

It is, of course, a violation of professional ethics for one person to steal the results of the research of another, which in a sense I did, on that memorable winter evening I looked over my shoulder while descending the slippery slope of the A.D. White House, home of the Society for the Humanities, on the Corinth campus, in the attempt to see the constellation Orion, and saw instead, either at the moment I lost my balance and fell on the driveway or while I was sliding downhill on my back, a blinding flash in the heavens above the Space Sciences building, separated by only a fence from the garden of the White House; and further saw, in the diminishing light of a now spectral glow, a small parachute slowly descending toward the flat Space Sciences roof. A slight breeze, errant or (I sometimes like to think) intentional, sent that parachute on its own slippery glide through the frigid night air in a direction destined to intercept that of the comfortable toboggan of my plush-lined overcoat. A luminescent rock, ragged and misshapen as an overgrown Idaho potato, swayed in the tiny harness of that parachute, gleaming with such uncanny power that I saw it even with my eyelids tightly shut as a protection against the inevitable moment of collision. And yet I was not frightened in the slightest. Indeed, the gay abandon with which that rock-bearing parachute and I were falling toward each other made me giggle; at the moment before impact, I reached upward with my hand (I have no idea if my eyes were open or closed) in the way a baby reaches for a star or a bauble over his crib.

Whether or not I caught that rock, I cannot say, for neither it nor the parachute possessed substance; I felt simply a warmth—in my eyes as well as my hand—which seemed to me friendly, but which nevertheless etched into my brain like a brand the following letters, though each of them was reversed: OHCNASBEBEDBUMAMAOOTIEMTCATNOCYHWKN-ABFBAED.

Since rock and parachute were nearly as evanescent as the silent celestial flash from which they came, I was left only with that assemblage of backward letters burning away in my mind like the afterimage of a sight that has dazzled the retina. With a gracefulness that in other circumstances would have surprised me—I am, after all, in my sixties—I bounded to my feet the moment they found purchase against the bend in the driveway curb my slide had brought me to, gave that characteristic <u>Homo sapiens</u> jump programmed by our genes following any stumble or harmless mishap (is it to let a predator know we are capable of a fleetness it can't match?), and, in my mad dash across the street, sent a little sports car that had braked to avoid hitting me into spirals on the icy pavement.

"Goddamn the fucking absent minds of all fucking neolithic professors," the driver shouted at me from the sidewalk where his car now illegally rested, the adolescent squeak with which he twice pronounced the obscene participle betraying the freshman status that made his driving of the car on the campus another violation of the rules, even as his easy reference to the Stone Age suggested he was destined to join the ranks of the unemployed, as an archaeologist. "Stuff it, kid," I cried, resorting to a quickly transmitted vulgarism of my own in my hurry to get to my basement office across from the White House. How could I stop to apologize while my mind carried its precious and perhaps ephemeral baggage of letters? In the sanctity of my untidy little office, beneath a humming fluorescent tube, I transcribed onto paper those backward letters, each of which obediently blinked off in my brain as I wrote it, proving beyond doubt the etching had been intended for this purpose. After some puzzlement, the letters having been slightly garbled by a time warp or space woof (it pleases me to imagine the latter, for in my fancy it places that intelligent being—who in all subsequent communication refused to inform me of the location of his planet even though he was otherwise effusive in his expressions of friendship— somewhere beyond Sirius), I decoded that message intended for Professor Duck.

To keep it from him until this moment in which I make public not only it but the entire lively account that Ohcnas, talented but obscure novelist and memorialist from another planet, poured upon me as if from a dipper (could that be a cruder clue to his whereabouts?) is, as I have already confessed, a culpable act, one for which the perpetrator might have his tenure revoked—especially in these days in which the salaries of senior professors, at least of those not at the "cutting edge" of research in their fields, are a burden to chairpersons, deans, and provosts. Much as I would like to reveal my identity, prudence (a virtue that certain classics of literature have taught me to cherish) dictates that I use as nom de plume the name given me by Ohcnas for my humble role as scribe.

Though the document that follows will convince all but the most skeptical of readers (chairpersons and other administrators typically have a frame of mind bent that way, from a series of collisions with the speedier wits of their so-called subordinates) of its authenticity, it strikes me that those with the deepest belief in it will still suspect some kind of subterfuge—that, for example, Professor Duck, cautious of his reputation, cannily invented a fictitious scribe of a lengthy narrative he himself truly received, perhaps years ago while he was still in West Virginia. Such a conjecture, if accepted, obviously would get me off the hook, galactic or otherwise, so my vehement denial of it suggests something about my character.

And let me hasten to add that there has been no collusion whatsoever between Professor Duck and me in the preparation of this manuscript. I barely know that astronomer. As a young man I taught in a region of Appalachia not far from Coal Bank, but my residency there preceded his. In the hills of that remote corner of America, the stars shine in a voluptuous manner, and I would gaze at them with no doubt the same fixed intensity of his later radio signals. The grand and wheeling constellations spoke to me of the soul's liberation in the infinite plane of truth and radiance and union that lies beyond our normal consciousness. The hamlet in which my family lived was seventy miles of treacherous mountain roads from the nearest hospital. Returning from that hospital late at night on the October day that had blessed my wife and me with a son, I knew nothing but elation for the miracle of tiny fingers and toes, of a warm little stranger sleeping at a loved one's breast. My midnight journey was an easterly one; again and again (at the crest of a mountain, or through the **V** of a deep and forested hollow), I saw the lovely Orion, the fateful constellation I was searching for a year ago when I slipped on the ice. The precious jewels that outline the mythological figure enchanted me in a manner they never had before; they seemed to be silently telling me something I had yearned all my life to hear. I was so drawn into communion with the three stars of the giant hunter's belt that on one occasion I nearly drifted into an oncoming truck, as if the glare of its headlights or the colored lights on the cab roof would bring me truly home.

Though Ohcnas was to have some sharp words for me on this score, I sometimes think that time is a meaningless human construction, an attempt to measure the eternal present. If so, Professor Duck and I were in the same region at the same "time"; but it is only a beguiling thought on my part to imagine that certain messages I received from the stars in happy and receptive moments of my salad days were answers of a then wordless sort to the signals the young astronomer was sending into the heavens.

Anybody who would bind me to Professor Duck would find but the flimsiest tissue of coincidences. It is true that he and I both left Appalachia for the same university in upstate New York (both of us arriving long before it was celebrated in a brilliant novel of manners or had achieved legendary status among the knowledgeable as the actual locale of the fictitious Wordsmith University in another, more fabulous, work). Yet it is also true that I first saw him neither in Appalachia nor at Corinth but in the sky. A number of years ago, when my children were small, my wife and I took them camping in Ontario. In driving through Toronto, I became lost, a not uncommon experience of mine. Whatever else I may be accused of, I do not possess, as even my detractors agree, an irascible temperament, and so on this as on earlier occasions I simply permitted my car to slide in and out of traffic patterns, as if it had the guiding spirit of a Rocinante; it chose to rest in a parking spot just opposite the planetarium. A happy choice, for it gave me an opportunity to let others, aided by technology, lecture in a comfortable setting to my children about the sights of the universe—my own enthusiasm on frigid nights for red giants and nebulae having made them perversely resistant to anything further from me about such celestial glories.

The theme of the show that nothing but circumstance and a rusty Rambler had brought us to was a question, "Are There Intelligent Beings in Space?" Readers impatient for this prologue to end should pause to consider my astonishment when, as the room slowly darkened and pinpricks of infinitude appeared above us, I saw on that vault none of the constellations so familiar to me since Appalachia but rather a visage of my fellow communicant from that region—Frank Duck himself! For that was the identification made by a resonant voice that spoke from the heavens at the moment the starry face became clearly visible. Though over the years we must frequently have passed each other in the decrepit corridors of Goldwin Smith Hall or both been in attendance at one of those crowded faculty meetings dealing with parking problems on campus, I had not known him at all, and so in a sense that seems very real to me I first met him when he was high above me in a Toronto planetarium that was honoring him as a pioneer in extraterrestrial communication.

Then, several weeks before I was to be introduced to the corporeal Professor Duck, my wife and I drove downtown in our most recent car, a Volkswagen convertible.[1] The day was balmy, the top was down, and my wife and I were relaxed and happy. Suddenly over the roof of Rothschild's Department Store, later to go bankrupt, appeared a vast object from outer space. Its skin glowed, and it trailed smoke. It was traveling most leisurely, in a direction that suggested the imminent destruction of Corinth's most impressive landmark, the library bell tower on its hilltop location, whose carillon at that moment was pealing the alma mater. Apparently my wife and I were the only ones to see the alien object; the pedestrians talked to each other as if the world were not to end, the line of

[1] It is another of those coincidences that only in certain moods I find to be inexplicable and even eerie that Professor Carl Billions, a colleague of Professor Duck's, presently owns the reincarnation of that very vehicle.

6

motorists behind us honked peevishly at our neat little car for not moving ahead when the traffic signal changed. At the last moment, the ghastly intruder, perhaps charmed by the sentimental tune, spared the campanile; it headed on a northwesterly course, disappearing into the more conventional spectacle of flaming clouds at sunset.

I said to my wife, "I won't tell anybody if you won't," for I had long since learned the folly of trying to win belief from the downcast multitude about what anybody can observe simply by <u>looking up</u>. How many of my readers, I wonder, have seen tiny but colorful horseshoes soon after dawn in a cloudless winter sky? Though I have seen countless numbers of those splendid emblems of good fortune, and though science attests to their existence as "icebows," the morose colleagues of my department with whom each morning I exchange words in the Temple of Zeus, a coffeehouse close to my office in the basement of Goldwin Smith Hall,[2] don't believe in the reality of any sign that doesn't portend doom. They ridicule me each time I approach their table with a smile that speaks of the joy I know will come to me that day. "Oh,

[2] When America had its Baedeker, Corinth, N.Y., had a single star— awarded for a museum of plaster casts, of which only those that duplicate the figures that once decorated the west pediment of the Temple of Zeus at Olympia remain; this museum, of course, is the present coffeehouse. You readers may think I've blown my cover in revealing the proximity of my office to the temple of that god who took on a number of disguises himself in order to populate the heavens with his offspring; but a similar identification applies to the offices of a number of other members of my department. Any one of them might be the scribe, for all of them meet the following criteria: (1) superior imaginative and writing prowess; (2) sufficient knowledge of another, such as his residency in Appalachia, the cars he has owned, the horseshoes he has seen, etc., to insert details that hint at his culpability; and (3) the motive, however misguided, to gang up with the administrators in a devious scheme to get him canned. That motive also exists for the medievalists in the office at the far end of the basement corridor that was refurbished for them after having served for many decades as a men's rest room. On any number of occasions, your authentic and absent-minded scribe, whoever he may be, unzipped his fly while hastily entering a sanctum whose long-since-stripped plumbing had always seemed to him medieval; from this innocent but repeated act the basest rumors have spread, intensifying his insecurity.

God," one or another of them will interrupt his obsessive recounting of the preceding night's unbearable television news to say, "he's seen another of his goddamned horseshoes in the sky." They accuse me of being a manic-depressive because I don't exist in their state of perpetual and bitter melancholy.

Professor Duck is not of their petty sort; indeed, the notion of him as deity having been, as it were, implanted in me in advance of the party at which I met him in person, I was worshipful enough to blurt out, before the hostess had finished introducing us, the kind of news I thought would win his approval. He was interested, all right! Truthful though I am, I may have exaggerated certain details concerning both the trajectory and the dimensions of the amazing object, simply to please him; for, after I finished, he said, "Now please tell me again, as accurately as you can this time, the appearance of the object. Did it resemble anything you've seen before?"

"An overgrown Idaho potato," I said. "It trailed smoke, like an exhaust, and there were flames where the tailpipe belonged."

"Did anybody else see it?"

"Yes, sir," I replied promptly. "My wife was with me."

"May I speak with her?"

"Of course." And I immediately took her, in midsentence, from the conversation she was listening to. When Professor Duck asked her to describe what she had seen in the sky, she said, "A long cylindrical object, quite smooth; something like a red-hot and smoking cigar."

What a disappointment for Professor Duck and what an embarrassment to me! My wife believes that my emotions sometimes distort what I perceive, and that she, because of her background in science, possesses the greater objectivity. I gave her a sharp poke, my signal that once again she was wrong, and should here reconsider what was obviously a vivid phallic fantasy; she retaliated with a poke of her own, though I failed to perceive what conceivably might make a potato suspect. Professor Duck sighed, putting away in his breast pocket the little pad on which he would have jotted down our observations, had they jibed. "It's always this way," he said.

"One requires corroborative evidence for sightings of this sort, but two people never agree on what they've seen."

Though I was not at fault, I felt that I had let the astronomer down; it so humiliated me that to this day I dart into anybody's office when I see his now familiar shape waddling toward me down the corridor. I have become acquainted with a number of interesting colleagues in Hebraic Studies, Russian Literature, Economics, etc., thanks to Professor Duck, and pray that this personage, who may not even choose to remember our single encounter, is as just and as infinitely forgiving as I take him to be.

Since the document about to unfold is to my knowledge the first of its kind, and no doubt will arouse an intense curiosity in the scientific community as well as the general public,[3] it occurs to me that for the sake of these two groups and for a third that falls between them (I refer, of course, to the psychologists), I should describe my state of mind as I left an overheated lecture room in the A.D. White House for that cosmic catch.

The lecturer I had been listening to was a cocky young male of the Derridean persuasion—an adjective that always trills in my ear as if a policeman were blowing the whistle on all that I most cherish. Normally, the laws these sophisticated cops try to enforce in their journals and public addresses are incomprehensible to me, a confession that ought to win the sympathy of the masses, whose knowledge of this subject is no doubt even more limited than my own; and it is to the general public alone (the psychologists may also wish to lis-

---

[3] Once I met a publisher who, in the process of letting me know that he was regretfully rejecting an effort of mine on the grounds that it would appeal only to the most discriminating audience imaginable, became ecstatic over a novel his firm had just accepted. It purportedly had been written by a prisoner in a Soviet-bloc country who had managed to secure the freedom of at least his manuscript by means of a trained pigeon that came each morning to the bars of his window for another beak-sized portion. "What's the novel about?" I asked. He said impatiently, "Who cares what it's about? The story that counts is the one about the pigeon. Just imagine the impact in the media!" All that fuss over a novel composed by a convict on our own little planet and transmitted by a common and probably flea-infested avian, however smart. I say no more.

ten) that I now speak of what I know about that group loosely banded together as poststructuralists, a term that immediately imparts to the uninitiated the anxiety of wondering about the group that came before them. Let us ignore that question to consider the essence (a word they deplore) of their belief or nonbelief.

You and I and Professor Duck may have souls that bind us to each other and to the stars, but not these poststructuralists—most certainly not those of the dominant Derridean subgroup. They do not await with beating hearts a celestial message; it is doubtful if they have ever seen the larger moons of Jupiter, or for that matter even own the cheapest of binoculars for the purpose of bird-watching. Do you know where they search for messages? On the paper just under their bifocals, in language itself, that's where! If, as they postulate, God is but a human construction, then words can possess no Absolute referents, and are nothing but the curious or banal signs of a specific culture. True communication, as the individual expression of one unique person to another (I trust my readers have the courtesy to find me unique; in the past, I have always found them to be so), obviously is impossible. Language becomes a series of signs in a single and hermetically enclosed cultural text, and nobody's use of words is more valuable than another's. Freud, you psychologists may be interested to know, is exempted (other than for his embarrassing male chauvinism) from cultural bias and imprisonment within the text and is used as a further blade to cut down all writers to the same size.

General reader, did you ever wonder, as a college student, if the scholars who taught you about Shakespeare and Milton and Dostoevski and Father Hopkins were really atheists who hated the books they professed to admire? You would not be surprised to discover how quickly some of these scholars found in the readings of their new Gallic masters (Derrida is not the only insouciant Frenchman involved) the key that liberated them from "the tyranny of the author," and joined the butcherous ranks of those at the "cutting edge of research."

To return, then, to that stuffy lecture room, where that youthful Derridean was blowing his whistle at my beloved

Wordsworth. I admit that Wordsworth, in his elevated moments, can get pretty foggy ("a sense sublime / Of something far more deeply interfused," for example), but I know what he means. Writers once gloried in the imprecision and ambiguities and odd resonances of language, finding in them the entrance to the spiritual realm that lies beyond words; but if scholars and critics are impervious to the charms of that realm, what fun they can have with the language of one who is not, and in particular with such a poet as Wordsworth! "Willy" was the name this brash young scholar, not yet fully schooled in the polite subtleties of the new philosophy, called that senile babbler he confused with the majestic poet.

What, you may ask, had drawn me to such a lecture? In truth, I was asking myself that question, for, as I always do at these perverse inquisitions in which the believers are tortured by the blasphemers, I was keenly aware of the language of my own seedy clothes and untrimmed hair. I worried about what these acolytes of French theory—capable as they were of using semiotics to take apart reputations as well as texts—might be theorizing about me from such signs as my worn corduroy jeans held up by a wide leather belt bejeweled with fake emeralds, my old cowboy boots, and a hairstyle that placed me among the hippies of a now defunct generation. It gave me some consolation to realize that Frank Duck and such a fellow astronomer as Carl Billions weren't the smartest dressers either, with their turtlenecks and the like.

Still, at the wine-and-cheese reception after that ghoulish rite of Gallic deconstruction, surrounded by the new generation of intellectuals wearing conservative clothes but speaking in tongues so radical as to be unknown, I felt melancholy, and hastily drank a number of small glasses of a wine whose bouquet resembled moldy burdock. Had I been deluded by my decades-old feeling of communion with the stars? Was I but an ignorant and elderly mystic, a believer in the kind of signs that no longer exist? Fastening the few remaining buttons of the plush-lined overcoat that had been my first purchase upon my discharge from the army in 1944, I left that gathering (nobody smiled regretfully, nobody even noticed) for the exhilarating air of winter, and looked at once for the cold and mysterious comfort of that mythic hunter in the celestial vault, a figure no doubt as lonely and as déclassé as I.

Was it circumstance or fate that first took me to the lecture, and then away from it <u>at the precise moment</u> necessary to intercept a message intended for Professor Duck in the adjacent building? Sometimes, I think my life is charmed; I know for a fact that on all occasions in which I have been most desperate for a transcendent sign, that sign has come. No wonder I felt no fear, and even giggled, as the luminescent rock drifted toward my raised hand!

Perhaps the cleverest among my readers have perceived that in transmission each of the <u>R</u> letters in that message somehow became a <u>B;</u> perhaps they too have held the jumble to a mirror like the little one on the bookcase in my office (I am vain enough, I admit, to look for a bit of egg or danish on my lip before dashing off, late, for another class) and have already decoded it by separating it into words:

DEAR FRANK WHY CONTACT ME
I TOO AM A MURDERER SANCHO

A majority of the signs that have come to me are, at least initially, a bit cloudy, and I had no idea that night as to what this one really meant. Frank Duck is certainly no murderer, so the message had to be taken with, as they say, a grain of salt. Who was this distant "Sancho," and who or what had he killed? In the following pages, the reader will find the answer to this and many other questions that as yet he has not sufficient knowledge to ask; but first he must discover how I established such rapport with a being elsewhere in the universe that I cannot conceive of him as (in the lingo of those preposterous sci-fi inventions) an <u>alien intelligence.</u>

2

Over the past year, my life became so enmeshed with Ohcnas' (he resists the reversal of the letters of his name into an English he considers backward) that I often found it difficult to distinguish one from the other.[4] It is as if the first-person narrative he composed—and how well that confessed murderer writes!—weaves me, the necessary scribe, into the very fabric of its touching and yet diabolical plot. I think that sometimes he wanted me to become him, thus releasing him from the onus of his guilt; at other times, his obvious pride took over, and I became no more than the servile amanuensis who traditionally is permitted to interrupt his faithful word taking only when he feels it necessary, for the welfare of his master, to question revelations that strike him as dubious or scandalous.

For some days after I had decoded that original communication, I felt feverish. In my mind I kept hearing a high-pitched confusion of syllables, much like the sound a magnetic tape makes when run backward on its spindle. At 3:00 A.M. one morning, I suddenly awoke in a sweat; I found myself trying to recapture a voice that had been shrilly calling to me as I slept, but it was transformed at once into the twinkling strands of the skyrocket or shooting star or cloud of fireflies that constitutes my earliest memory. Stealthily I left the bed I share with my wife, and padded outdoors—where my alert bedmate, who had been feigning sleep, caught me as I stared heavenward, a hand cupped to an ear.

Neither of us should have been concerned by my nakedness; it is not my custom to wear pajamas. Nevertheless, she implored me to see a doctor; on an earlier day, I had nonchalantly mentioned to her my fall on the driveway, and she assumed I was still suffering the aftershocks of a concussion. Given her suspicions, I obviously could not reveal the reason I was standing outside like that—the first time in my life that I withheld the truth from her. It was my second recent bit of deviousness, and, like the first, beyond my control. Perhaps slowly but surely—who can ever say about such matters?—I was being prepared for my long and revelatory association

---

[4]Sometimes our involvement made me an erratic lecturer, though no more so than many of my colleagues, who also have been known to forget to come to their classes, and who also have confused one text with another. I do wish, though, that I had not been teaching Don Quixote in those frantic weeks that I was nearing the end of my transcription!

with sly Ohcnas. It goes without saying that from the moment of his first message I fervently desired intimacy with him, and yet had no idea as to how I might achieve it.

I seriously considered consulting a psychic, for I am acquainted with one whose abilities are beyond dispute. Her "office" is a table at a boisterous country tavern not far from my home. She is known throughout the region as "the Grotto witch"—the Grotto being the name of the tavern, which is partially built into the base of a forested hill. Though I could give many examples of her prowess, a single (if extended) one will suffice.

After putting the pastoral desire into the head of my Appalachia-born son (he is too bright to have committed such a folly unaided), this psychic sold him her small herd of goats, for her hands had become too arthritic to permit her to continue milking them. The thirst of these goats—they needed much liquid to wash down all of the evergreen plantings and garden produce they daily were filching—caused our well, always stingy, to go dry. Having been apprised of the situation, apparently through mental communication with a parched-tongued Daisy, the spoiled favorite of her former herd, the psychic came at once to our door, a freshly cut forked branch in hand; on that hot July afternoon, she led me a merry chase through blackberry brambles and patches of poison ivy, while pointing out delectable fungi on the rotting logs we hurdled. In a little clearing three-eighths of a mile from the house, she grunted and skidded to a stop, holding with all her might to a branch that wanted to pull her underground.

"Damndest place for a well I ever seen," the boorish well-digger growled, upon squeezing his rig through the rough trail I had made to the clearing after two days' sweaty misery with machete and chain saw. "Did you let some witch find it? You so-called intellectuals with your fat salaries are the most superstitious suckers that God ever created to be a pain in the ass to common laborers like me."

I am glad to report that his rig got stuck in the mud made by the water that gushed up under incredible pressure when he hit the subterranean Mississippi <u>at the very depth</u> the psychic had foretold.

How often I sat in my car before the Grotto tavern, contemplating with pounding heart the possible consequences of a consultation with the "witch" within! If she <u>were</u> able to establish contact with Ohcnas, couldn't she claim legal right to everything he revealed? Furthermore, what proof would the skeptical world possess that she wasn't inventing the content of his messages? Whether we like it or not, we live in a technological age, one in which primitive "thought waves" are undervalued by a practical-minded public. Sitting in my car and pondering these matters while listening to the raucous laughter and country-and-western music coming from the tavern, I reluctantly decided that I was in general agreement with professors Duck, Billions, <u>et al.,</u> on the need for modern technology if we are to communicate, on a regular basis, with inhabitants of a planet in another solar system (especially if we are to gain wide acceptance of the authenticity of the intercourse).

Despite this clear rationale, my readers may find it difficult to believe that such a staunch traditionalist as I would suddenly purchase a home computer of the most sophisticated sort. Let me explain, as best I can, the circumstances that led to my decision.

It was less than a fortnight after the White House lecture, with its remarkable aftermath, that I saddled my quarter horse, Smoky, and went out for what I took to be a therapeutic canter through the Finger Lakes countryside. Winter or summer, the peacefulness of this land nurtures the soul; and on this mild day the sun was shining on the distant blue-gray hills, and water glittered in nearby brooks freed for the moment of their icy armor.

Years ago, I would mount Smoky while my wife would climb into the saddle of her half-Arabian Tammy, and with Ben, our Irish setter, companionably frisking along nearby, his tail a gallant red plume in the golden oats or among the blossoms (dependent upon the seasons) of chicory, day lily, jewelweed, or phlox, we would ride for hours on end. In those days we dreamed we might someday pack the saddlebags with food and camping gear and ride our horses on a circuitous route past deep gorges with their sometimes slender and sometimes broad waterfalls, around the shores of various lakes where the Iroquois once had encampments, and along dark forest trails, our ultimate goal being an enchanted chapel—a miniature Gothic cathedral, with flying buttresses and stained-glass windows, built much earlier in this century by a wealthy and grieving and splendidly quixotic father for the son buried nearby—that is situated on a steep and wood-covered slope near the tip of an isolated peninsula separating the two arms of the loveliest of all the Finger Lakes, the one whose head is a wide basin holding water of the deepest blue and decorated to its rim with immaculate rows of wine grapes.[5]

Alas, Tammy threw my wife in a fright over a chipmunk and the bruise ended her enthusiasm for horseback riding; we never made our expedition and now Ben is dead and the horses, like their owners, are too old for such a strenuous journey. Their long relationship as stablemates has made them inseparable, a fact I neglected to take sufficiently into account on that mild winter day I was cantering along the road, enmeshed almost as much with nostalgia for now impossible dreams as with strange current matters about an Idaho potato; but a prolonged and anguished neighing from the paddock when I was a quarter-mile away caused an always dervishly inclined Smoky to whirl around three times with such rapidity that he broke the brittled leather of the reins. Twenty years old though he was, and fat from a lack of exercise, my gelding galloped homeward to his mare with all the fanaticism of a young thoroughbred stallion. Having lost the stirrups, I was bouncing up and down as rapidly as I was cometing forward, and I have but the haziest recollection of overtaking a small white truck whose driver may or may not have taunted me with the words "Can't control a horse? Get a computer" as I sped past his window. In any event, after I unsaddled Smoky and gave him a smack on the rump he would long remember, I simply acted on impulse (whether it came from within or without is a question I cannot answer) by jumping into my car and driving off to Corinth to buy one! From all the competing makes, I immediately chose the one whose name—Rainbow—best coincided with my spiritual preoccupations.

[5] My descriptions of the Finger Lakes countryside, however expansive my affectionate sentences, never failed to fascinate Ohcnas in the early days of our contact.

I knew there was something strange about it from the first moment I sat before it, for my heart began to beat rapidly. It made odd beeps and whirs without any intervention on my part, some of them shrill sounds of the sort I had heard in my head. I realized at once that Ohcnas—I was still thinking of him as "Sancho" and of course was far from finding the diminutive, or familiar name, that would unlock his file for me—must somehow be within it, perhaps imploring me to give his original message, made at some extraordinary expenditure of psychic energy, to its rightful recipient. At first his signals were more deeply coded than that first message, signifying that he was on his guard. I tried to be casual (O difficult task!), allowing my mind almost at random to pick one little thing or another about myself to win his confidence. I told him, for example, that I was of fairly slight stature, for a human male, and anything but athletic; that I despised warfare and guns, never went hunting, and that yet in my fantasies while making love imagined myself a mighty hunter armed with a sword, and that my beloved was a divine and ravishing huntress who had killed me with her bow so that we could love each other in the heavens forever. In reply, on my screen, I got nothing but fragments. Once something like the blinding flash that had produced the parachute and rock illuminated the screen, and it is likely that I had a subliminal awareness of those two connected objects; then everything went dark. Thinking I was on the verge of contact, I desperately pressed button after button, to get at last a despairing response: LOST: FOUR CLUSTERS ON SEVEN CHAINS.

Immediately I phoned the emergency number, printed in my manual, of the manufacturer in Massachusetts. A calm voice told me to perform a number of tests, none of which apparently worked, for that voice asked for my address, and promised that a serviceman would be sent. I knew, of course, that my machine was unusual, but it really made me tremble when an immaculate white truck appeared before my door in less than half an hour and a serviceman, clothed in a uniform just as white, came whistling into the house. My readers already must have a pretty good idea as to where I live, in a Finger Lakes farmhouse at a remote crossroads; not only am I far from Massachusetts, but my address is one that gives problems to the most experienced UPS route man. Even if the truck just happened to be the same one whose driver conceivably had instructed me to purchase a computer, its return must be accounted hardly less of a miracle. O Ohcnas—my sometimes moody but yet fun-loving Kayo! I'm sure you want all this to be part of your document, to demonstrate your psychic powers and your ability to play with me! Your so-called serviceman fixed my computer in a trice to receive your messages, gave me a wink, and vanished as quickly as he had come.

My readers know as well as I do that life sometimes seems strange, even hallucinatory. More than once I've considered the possibility that not only the universities but all the nations of the world are simply freaky Disney-type theme parks, set up to amuse, "instruct," or terrorize us with their illusions. On the present occasion, though, I wondered if the figure in white—however competent and "real" he seemed, plying his single tool, a Phillips screwdriver, with its star-shaped tip, into the intricate viscera of the console—might have been but a construction of my own now wildly stimulated imagination.

But somebody, or something, had obviously worked magic with my computer, for it began to operate in a new and startling way. That is to say, it hardly needed me at all. As if both it and I were entranced (were those my fingers touching the keys?), I began some further chitchat with Ohcnas, my mind making nimble associations vaguely connected with the lingering effect my recent visitant still had on it. My general subject was mental transference. I told him about a recent television-viewing experience of mine in which I had switched channels from a PBS documentary about the great white shark—a program that kept focusing on the monster's teeth—to a heartwarming account of human determination and caring, but the smiles of all those compassionate characters revealed fangs that any instant might become bloodied with still-living flesh. In playing such a trick on me, was my mind trying to tell me something about all creatures great and small? I was chattering on like that when Ohcnas suddenly interrupted me with a question of his own. Controlled though he was, that question carried the weight of his compulsive need to tell _me_—for at last I had completely won him over!—his entire story.

"Tell me, Sid," he wrote on my computer screen, "do you think I have teeth like that?"

Except for a cursor pulsing like the blood through every artery of my body, the screen soon went black as sin. Whatever my excitement, I knew from the ever-beating cursor that Ohcnas was waiting for me to find the file name that would be our indissoluble link. I will not weary my readers as I wearied myself in the attempt to find the name for our file, the KAYO perhaps inserted by the mysterious repairman as he adjusted my machine. With a mockery mixed with affection, Ohcnas had referred to me as "Sid," a diminutive in English that also is a bastardization of the Arabic word for "lord," a title owned by the ostensible scribe of the book that has been such a favorite of mine since childhood that the story—especially, as I age, the second part—sometimes seems my own, and so naturally I teach it even in courses where it might seem inappropriate. One of the fragments that over and over had earlier appeared on my screen was the single word _Nod_—which is, of course, a reversal of the title of the Spanish knight who is the protagonist of that pioneering novel.

Agile as my heightened sensibility continued to make my thoughts, it took me much too long (perhaps because I was working from such recondite clues) to realize that (1) I was in contact with a playful intelligence on a planet that in many ways was such a mirror image of our own that the inhabitants revered literary classics similar to our own; and (2) my correspondent, as indication of our friendship, wished me to discover either a similar mock title for him or a diminutive of the reversed name he had chosen for himself from that _very novel_ (or one remarkably like it) I have cherished for decades. I tried any number of phonetic variants of the first syllable (the barbaric Ohc) of his name, asking him if one of these guesses might be okay; vivaciously, he responded, "That's _Kayo_ to me, Sid!" Thus did I discover the historic file name (so I assume it will be) that thenceforth bonded us on screen and hard disk.

Having triumphed over the final obstacle, I now was

ready—my readers have been ready for quite some time, I <u>know,</u> but nearly everything I've dutifully reported (including certain details that may seem to cast me in a foolish light and that a less scrupulous scribe would have deleted) will prove to have its own odd bearing—to receive the following narrative, presented in the clear and yet always beguiling style that characterizes my dear but dangerous Kayo.

SID HAMETE

PART ONE

CHAPTER I. Butchery at the Kayo Corral

On the sixth day of the fifth lunar month of our year 5891, calculated from the birth or maybe the death of our Allah,[1] a small but dedicated group of fun seekers, alerted by the church bell tolling out the thirty-first hour, began to assemble on the front porch of the general store of the Kayo Corral, that re-

[1] So Kayo begins his narrative—in medias res (or even later), as the reader will discover; perhaps this is a conventional "narrative hook" of authors on his planet. The flippancy he accords his Deity may be the swagger of a man who already acknowledges himself damned, or simply of one who wishes to express his freedom from the morality of the masses. In either case, Allah, on a planet that in so many ways is the opposite of ours, would likely be a liberal and compassionate figure: note, for example, that apparently He is worshiped in a (progressive and quasi-Christian?) church.

All subsequent footnotes, though uninitialed, will be mine, and will constitute my only voluntary intrusion into a text become another's. —S.H.

construction of a frontier town whose synecdochical name of course (secretively!) honors me.

That the spectators at this staging of an event of our myth-haunted past—a duel to the death between two of our legendary figures—were few in number was no disappointment to me; it simply meant that our citizens on holiday were flocking to one or another of my newer entertainments for them, all of them conceived in a single moment of far greater inspiration than that which produced my tawdry namesake. The Kayo Corral had been authorized as a pilot study by our president, always cautious in small matters. The corral was to be built in my region on an extensive piece of rocky and hilly land so unsuitable for modern agriculture that many decades ago it had reverted to the national government through non-payment of taxes. Declared a <u>land-use area,</u> meaning it was up for grabs, it had been frequented in winter mainly by skiers and in summer by hikers and all year long by both for trysts— in short, by people who sent no money to federal coffers so empty that the dropping of an occasional coin would have reverberated against the metal walls were it not for the mattress of IOU notes. In his quest <u>to balance the budget,</u> a quaint term we use for any saving of a few pennies,[2] our president (known to an intimate group of advisers, of which I am far from the least in importance, as Teddy) would have sold the whole parcel to a favorite for a pittance, had I not quickly interceded with my first theme-park proposal, the predecessor of those enormously successful federal undertakings that I will describe in due time.

Once a mecca for camera freaks from a distant nation of islands, as well as for citizens of our own ASU[3] bearing cam-

[2]Since it was apparent that Kayo was clogging the flow of his narrative in the attempt to explain the peculiar word usage of his planet, I interrupted him here to say that <u>I followed his drift</u> (a phrase he understood at once), and that further definitions were unnecessary. So much for your "hermetically enclosed cultural texts," Monsieur Derrida and company! At the very least, why not "infinitely reflecting"?

[3]In response to my query, Kayo told me that these initials stand for <u>Assorted States United.</u> He quickly added that the "proud motto" of his country is <u>Assorted We Stand,</u> and that the national bird is the

eras of a less sophisticated make we had imported from that far-off archipelago, the Kayo Corral had come, except for weekends, to resemble an authentic abandoned frontier town. That is to say, its deteriorating saloon, blacksmith shop, bordello (candy and soft drinks were sold there), general store (high-priced souvenirs, including imported chaps and toy holster sets branded with my logo for the kiddies), opera house (docudrama about the Winning of the West,[4] a region separated from the Kayo Corral by a paltry couple of thousand miles), and church (box lunches served in the pews on rainy days) brought so few paying customers that <u>absolutely false</u> reports were spread concerning certain well-paid and often absent employees who were blackmailing an unspecified high governmental official. On weekends, though, the dedicated fun seekers arrived, drawn both by the games of chance in the saloon (free beer helped to provide some exciting betting) and the duel (especially popular with the children) between the Good Avenger and the Desperado. I have lingered too long on details[5]; let me get back to the church bell that I left tolling its measurement of the hour as the spectators leisurely gathered.

At the thirty-first stroke, for the first time in the history of this event, nothing happened. The perspiring sexton, think-

passenger pigeon, "whose extermination proved for all time that we are a nation of ever-vigilant sharpshooters." Could he have been serious? I fear so.

[4] Having given a small indication of what it would mean to us Earthlings to live in a mirror world, I have decided here and henceforth to reverse the majority (but not all!) of Kayo's geographical and chronological references, etc., in order that the reader may feel less disoriented in an environment peculiar enough without this problem.

[5] A characteristic of Kayo greatly responsible for his success. As he told me in an aside, his Teddy could always trust him, however sticky the problem, to come up with an imposing list of selective and frequently bewildering statistics for the use of the presidential press secretary, all of the items calculated to satisfy the public's demand for "accountability." And, of course, the details upon which he has been "lingering" above, and indulgently will return to, are nostalgic embodiments of what once were fresh and fond schemata in his own entrepreneurial mind. Clearly he is not so dismissive of his first-born as he likes to pretend.

ing the actors had somehow missed their cue (a possibility as unlikely as that recorded in one of our minor literary classics in which a flock of Indians, perched in the boughs of trees overhanging a canal, misjudge the lethargic progress of a houseboat as long as a football field and so fall helplessly into the water at the stern of the vessel whose pale-faced passengers they had intended to scalp),[6] began to toll the hour all over again. At the nineteenth stroke of the second try, with the aged sexton[7] more than ever at the end of his rope, an unseen horse neighed in apparent anguish at the eastern edge of the settlement, to be answered by a similar neigh at the western edge; and at last the two riders appeared, from the respective alleys in which they had been concealed. The rider to the west was an appealingly fat little figure, dressed in white buckskin with fringes on his jacket, and white boots; he wore a white mask for disguise, but of course his costume identified him at once as the Good Avenger. (The one bizarre element of his attire was a huge pair of old-fashioned and badly damaged binoculars that dangled by a strap from his neck.) He seemed unable to get his loudly neighing horse to budge, possibly because of the gentleness of his kicks. Meanwhile, the rider to the east—dressed in a black costume decorated with countless little mirrors glittering in the sunlight, his face disguised (as is proper for any Desperado) in a black mask—was having problems of his own. That is to say, his mount whirled about three times and then

[6]A duplication of this botched massacre occurs in one of our own nineteenth-century classics, and is made fun of by one of our greatest humorists. Regional pride causes me to mention that the writer of the first work lived by a lake only a few hours away (by pleasant back roads) from my present home, while the latter wrote his most famous novels in a gazebo even closer. As is well known, the humorist was both brought into our world and carried out of it by a comet, but only an addled reader of the present text would believe that this historical fact is responsible for the similarity between that novelist's riposte and Kayo's.

[7]A distant relative of Kayo's, who suffered from chronic shortness of breath; as it turns out, all of the park employees but one, a cousin of the president's with a drinking problem, were members of Kayo's extended family.

began to charge toward the other horse at an incredible speed.[8]

The confrontation was supposed to take place near the general store (a smart decision made in advance of the very opening of the park, in order to encourage the purchase of merchandise both before and after the spectacle), but all that the spectators could see as the Desperado flew past was the cloud of dust raised by those furious hoofs. Led by the youngsters, the crowd, delighted by the change in the routine, pursued as fast as it could that cloud roiling inexorably onward. Fortunately for the children, the cold-blooded murder, committed at point-blank range while the two horses were nuzzling each other, took place a couple of hundred yards in advance of the fleetest pubescent, her view of it obscured by the settling dust.

It is no wonder that the eyewitness accounts of what actually took place are confused and contradictory. Though the spectators agreed that the Avenger didn't resemble the actor who normally played the role, they had difficulty believing that anybody who took the part of a such a good man—in our history books, a true patriot—would actually have planned that heinous act; and yet, according to the television commentator on the public channel (the one reluctantly underwritten by the federal government), the deed had obviously been premeditated. The television truck, cameraman struggling to keep his footing on the roof, almost ran down more than one innocent in its wild attempt to catch up with the Avenger's horse.

On the slow-motion segments of the film shown on the news hour that night, viewers throughout our land could see and hear the harmless explosion made by the blank cartridge of the Desperado's starter's pistol, and observe that the Avenger was untouched, except for a smudge of burned powder on a

---

[8]My first inkling that Kayo might be incorporating my own experiences into his narrative. Nobody likes to be ridiculed; the reader can imagine my indignation at learning that my seeming ineptitude at horsemanship, whether I was identified by name or not, was perhaps being broadcast throughout the universe. Needless to say, at least to a trained reader, neither this spoof nor other future references to me in any way discredit the deeper truth contained within the work.

jowl; they could see the Avenger tugging away at the butt of his revolver, finally managing to extract it from the holster, whereupon in his nervousness or haste he caught it in the strap of his binoculars. Barely had he disentangled it when it went off with a genuine roar and here—permit me to switch tenses—the camera goes out of focus and wavers across the landscape as it invariably does on catastrophic occasions. The blur resolves into a close-up view (how quickly do our cameramen adjust these days to assassinations!) of the Desperado on the ground, the blood actually <u>leaping</u> from a chest wound too gross for me to describe without offending the reader. But how strange to see that dark crater, that fountain of blood, while the rest of the body glitters like some joyous and ethereal creature! Divine and airy as it might at first glance seem, the body, thin at the waist and hips, broad in the chest (but oh! that wound), is that of a male in the virile summer of his life. In an agonized attempt to gather air for his poor, demolished lungs, he rips the mask from his face. And now the mirrors on his tightly fitting black suede jacket and pants begin to dance (myriad dazzles of tiny suns) as the whole lovely body shudders in that fleeting, yet ultimate, paroxysm rarely caught on television; alas, he soon is still, forever! (I admit to such fascination with this gruesome and yet heart-rending sequence that, having obtained a tape of the film, I still replay this segment over and over.)

The Avenger leaps from his steed, tearing off <u>his</u> mask for a better view or to let the world know who has committed this villainy. The camera pans to the oncoming horde, quickly finding (what a pro that cameraman is!) the faces of the wide-eyed tykes, and catches a view of a burly accomplice, mercilessly knocking those kids down in his rush to demolish the camera, his hairy arm reaching upward to grasp the tripod—the last bit of action to be caught on film before the dizzying topple that ends it. Is the Avenger a terrorist in the employ of one of the tiny but fanatical countries that oppose ours? Or is he a spy (as suggested by his binoculars) of one of our larger and more implacable enemies, a secret agent who suspects the nearly derelict Kayo Corral to be the cover for a laboratory engaged in research on a new poison or weapon? Is the "Desperado" a disguise or fetish of the brilliantly mad scientist in charge? Nobody can say; perpetrator, corpse, accomplice, and horses seemingly have vanished into the dust-and-smoke-laden air before the first adult reaches the scene.

But the murder weapon, an authentic six-shooter with one cartridge fired, remains on the bloody ground, along with the harmless weapon of the deceived opponent, tangible evidence, if the film was not enough, that the violence has not been spectral or the consequence of some mass hysteria. All that the commentator can report is that the killer has been identified through police records as an outlaw bearing the cryptic name of Nod, and that his victim is none other than one Ohcnas, a.k.a. K.O., a.k.a. Kayo, a shadowy figure known to be a confidant of the president on crucial matters of state—in other words, the corpse is that of both the founder of the park and the very teller of this tale!

CHAPTER II. *Kayo's Formative Years*

To explain the mystery of my apparent death, as well as to prepare for the comradeship that bound Nod and me up to the moment of his dying (no subterfuge there: dear Nod lacked the cunning), I must begin with a number of details about myself alone.[1]

---

[1] Something of obvious appeal to our narcissist. Probably the reader should be wary of accepting everything that Kayo reveals about himself in this crucial chapter. Like you and me, Kayo is both titillated and appalled by recollections of his earlier days—his growing sexuality, the hissing fuse ready to explode his nuclear family, etc.—and is as capable as anybody on Earth of manipulating the past to justify the darker side of his own nature. (We have already noted his mischievous distortion of a certain small experience of my own.) At any rate, as an assistance to the reader as he journeys with Kayo past the tricky shoals of the latter's infancy and youth, I have bracketed and starred (like a comforting buoy) those words of his that to me have the shine and resonant clang of an authentic and deeply felt personal truth.

Surprising as it may seem to inhabitants on the Earth with a cultural assumption about all <u>Sanchos</u> (as you call us), I am not a "peasant" born into a family subsisting on goat's milk and pig's feet and porridge. Quite the contrary: even before my mother, a former film star, or at least a <u>starlet,</u> had weaned me from her lovely breasts, she trained my salivary glands to respond to a crystal bell gently tinkled in the paws of the giant Vladimir, a longtime family retainer of dubious loyalty who spoke fluently in seven tongues. That little bell was an <u>objet d'art</u> given her by a former lover, the potentate of a small but romantic island kingdom, whom she'd met quite by chance in a ramshackle roadside diner on the rarely traveled <u>Old Dixie Highway.</u>

The ambiance of our family dinners was certainly one of refinement: silver candlesticks, linen napkins, gold toothpicks, etc., the candle glow dimly lighting the immense painting (the work of one of our nation's most celebrated <u>Leonardos</u>) of an aluminum soft-drink container, as well as the bald pate of my silent father. For he in cheerful modesty admitted to being such a <u>crude materialist</u> that he felt it best to refrain from speech during the dinner hour, reserved as it always was for genteel conversation. After supplying, at Vladimir's signal, what passed for our ritualistic grace (my conjugation each day of a new irregular verb in one or another of the more socially acceptable foreign languages, usually <u>Gaulish:</u> a stinging slap on my wrist from V.'s whiplike fingers if I got anything wrong), I too lapsed obediently into silence.

Our typical menu included your <u>vichyssoise,</u> your <u>co-quilles St. Jacques,</u> your <u>petits chaussons au Roquefort,</u> and so on and so forth, <u>ad nauseam.</u> Believe me, a kid born to wealth and culture sometimes longs to be with the less privileged waifs, munching on a <u>chien chaud</u> dripping with <u>moutarde</u> while reading a comic book! If my skill in foreign tongues has never amounted to much, whatever the early start my lessons gave me, the reason lies, at least in part, in my unspoken sympathy with my monolanguaged father (<u>Papa,</u> as Vladimir instructed me to call him, with the accent, of course, on the second syllable), especially as he reached furtively under the table for the quart-sized bottle of ketchup he kept between his shoeless feet, and which he used to blanket his veau. That drippy red mess on his plate (dread omen though it turned out to be!) comforted him as if it were a kind of couverture de securité whenever Emmamae, my melodiously murmuring Maman (a name also chosen for my use by V.) stretched her diamond-braceleted arm across the table to stroke our imperious butler's broad but finely manicured hand, or playfully to pluck the elastic band of the fancy imported watch she had bought him.

Yes, unconventional as it sounds, Vladimir, our butler, sat at the table for all our meals, and was the one who curtly ordered Dilsey, our frightened cook (she was the truly loyal family retainer), to "explain herself" if a dish lacked the subtle fragrance of a particular herb, the one who finished the last piece of meat on the table without even a glance at Papa, the materialist, who might or might not have his fork poised to spear it himself. If Maman was the rare beauty who should have married a prince, Papa was "old shoe." Every inch of him was a patriotic Unitedian. Whatever the wealth he had inherited, the multinational corporation he headed (if titularly and at a remove), he remained as egalitarian as any poor slob in our nation, by Allah! And so Dilsey had her place at the table, too, though she was rarely at it: she was up and down, ever scurrying into the kitchen at Vladimir's arrogant bidding.

Despite Maman's wheedlings and V.'s unconcealed disgust, we lived not in a penthouse suite in one of our major economic centers, not in the mansion of one of those vast estates whose emerald lawns are riddled with swimming pools and tennis courts and the droppings of blooded animals of various sizes and shapes, not even in one of our more modest suburbs with their split-level houses, above-ground pools wrapped in vinyl, and metal sheds for garden equipment. [Rather, we lived in a comfortable but wholly unostentatious crossroads farmhouse in our Northeast Lake District, that old house of classic proportions in which my stubbornly egalitarian Papa, like his father before him, had been born.]*

Corporate headquarters of the bottling firm that Papa had inherited were in a southern metropolis. On his first visit there following the death of his father, that whirlwind trip arranged so that he could accept the symbolic reins of command from a grateful management team, my Papa, middle-aged by then

31

but still boasting a brushed-forward garden of long blond hairs, courted and won his southern belle and movie actress Emmamae, that Emmamae of centerfold fame. She had been hired as lead dancer in a revue (bankrolled by the corporation as part of the festivities in his honor) that ended with each scantily clad maiden splintering bottles of the major competing soft drink against the wooden noggin of the clever effigy of the rival board chairman, said to be in his dotage.

While I recognize that I risk credibility in any brisk summary of such details, I swear that they are commonplace enough: if not everywhere on our planet, at least in the portion that we so rigorously defend. In particular, I insist in all honor on the prosperity and homespun good nature—one supporting the other—of my father and grandfather (the one celebrated for devising the modern shape of the bottle bearing our Aznap-Cola brand). Such qualities, I am told, have characterized the family at least as far back as the pharmacist ancestor from the deep South who invented the first addictive formula—and probably distinguished even the writer from distant times for whom I was named, author of a folksy epic beloved by all Unitedians, The Authentic Adventures of Kayo Aznap. I emphasize such details simply to illustrate a basic truth of our country. Though one or two "Sanchos" of the generations of practical-minded and inventive Aznaps of bygone ages may very well have been peasants (the male descendants, the ones who hand on the illustrious name, have always been glad to acknowledge our humble origins), it doesn't take shrewdness long here to become top rail; bottom rail always belongs to the introspective, moony-eyed, spiritually inclined Nods.

It was only to be expected, then, that I would attend the best prep school, the most prestigious college, my acceptance quickly achieved by the promise of those handsome gifts that resulted in Aznap Halls at both academies—though my graduation from the latter was delayed a year through my failure to pass a foreign-language requirement (later waived). I attribute my dismal performance not only to my love for Papa but to my hatred of the wrist-slapping, mother-snatching, Papa-destroying Vladimir, that poisonous viper in our ménage à quatre, that perhaps necessary snake [in our Edenic region of shimmering waters, leaf-dappled hills, and wines of a yet-to-be-acknowledged subtlety of "nose."]*

Obviously, Vladimir was not your typical manservant; in fact, he was the only aristocrat among us. Scion of slaughtered princes (hence a prince himself, if bloodlines count for anything), distant cousin of a beheaded czar, he had concealed his noble lineage successfully enough in his native country to gain a handsome salary (with the notorious fringe benefits that Commie states typically provide for their chosen ones) from the Ministry for the Free Dissemination of Truth. His was the cultivated radio voice that beamed the virtues of that so-called workers' paradise around the world in six languages (the seventh, of course, was his glottal native tongue, one that makes the sputum fly). A jealous underling in the ministry who had been taking a crash course in one of those six languages in a desperate attempt to hold on to his job (if one can believe V.'s sardonic account of his own forced exile for being a <u>decadent bourgeois sympathizer</u>), tattled to the fifth minister from the top that Vladimir's words contained a subtle attack on the very workers he was ostensibly praising.

In any event, <u>Maman,</u> during one of her frequent solo visits to the nearest cultural hub (<u>Papa,</u> of course, hated the ballet and his corns kept him from the museums), found out the current address of an elusive employment agency that specialized in newly arrived foreigners whether they were legally admitted or not. She snapped up her V. from the pathetic lineup the minute she saw his massive torso and lambent eyes as well as the tarnished medal, token of a nobleman, that dangled conspicuously from his ill-fitting coat. (<u>Maman</u>'s flaw, the human weakness that adds to my vexed adoration of her: she falls for princes.) Vladimir became our butler before I was born, and so of course I thought him part of our little family. Indeed, I so resemble him in physique (same admirable torso) that I considered him as something like an uncle, though once when I called him that he gave me his profile in the cruelest, most aristocratic, manner. Unlike my own dear, short-limbed, pudgy, bald, bespectacled, and sometimes embarrassingly flatulent <u>Papa,</u> Vladimir bore me no love whatsoever.

I was an only child, but my early years were not solitary

ones, for <u>Papa</u> gave me almost as much attention as he gave the stock-market reports. Often, when the latter were favorable, he played ball with me, sometimes managing to coax bangle-jangling <u>Maman,</u> disdainful Vladimir, and wary-eyed but obliging Dilsey into a scrimmage, however inept all of the adults were. Only twice did V. verbally expose his true feelings toward me. On the first occasion—I was a young adolescent by then—he cried out, "You little bastard!" just after a line drive from my bat caught him in the groin. (I'll get to the second occasion in due time.) As for <u>Maman,</u> well, she certainly took precious hours from her primping, her perusal of diet books, her earnest consultations and vanishings with V., to toy affectionately with me; my earliest pleasurable recollections, which I'm sure she considered me too young and too innocent to remember (if indeed they did take place, and were not nostalgic fantasies of my older self) must of necessity be veiled from the reader. I can only say that tender references to me as her "little prince," or her "princeling," were mixed into her baby talk to me. All too soon, she would hand me over to the more restrained but always reliable Dilsey.

In addition to such contacts with my parents, [I had, of course, the beneficent natural world everywhere about me, and soon learned to imitate the movement of the gentle creatures of the wild, hopping like a rabbit and bounding like a roe.]* But I would be lying if I said I was without loneliness. [Writers on my planet perhaps are born from families such as mine.]* From an early age, in moments of solitude, I began to scribble—implausible stories about greedy monsters (wearing crowns but named only by an ominous initial) whom the little hero finally manages to decapitate with the righteous frenzy of a newly anointed revolutionary.[2] Gradually I learned the craft that was to lead to small literary successes here and there, despite the fact that my major preoccupations increasingly were in that more powerful game of politics. (Though it brought me no fame, it delighted me to be able to combine these two interests in ghost-writing Teddy's hefty autobiog-

[2] Kayo's oblique reference to an early infatuation with the "Marxism" once rampant on his planet, an irrational phase of his growing-up never alluded to elsewhere in this document.

raphy.) But enough of this pleasant bypass into the laurel groves of what, from the standpoint of economic returns, has always been but an amusing hobby of mine.

As delicately as I can, let me touch upon the family tragedy. After more than two decades of Vladimir's intrusion into our daily lives, during which time at Papa's own gallant egalitarian insistence this "butler" had thrice daily buttered his bread at the table, our breadwinner's jealousy finally was aroused. That is to say, his deep concern with mergers, coupons, financial and business magazines, the reliability of brokers, annual reports of corporations including his own, etc., was no longer enough to keep that decent man from suspecting that something out of the ordinary realm of finance might be going on in some other wing of our many-roomed country farmhouse.

And yet I cannot believe (having already indicated his discomfort at certain observed hand contacts) that Papa was too stupid to be unaware that lewd scenes, dumb shows of relentless passion, just might be taking place in the pantry, one guest room or another, within the excessive humidity of the basement and the dry heat of the cramped attic, perhaps even in Maman's perfumed boudoir. Allah knows how often I lay in my stuffy dormitory room at college, unable to sleep because of my raging imagination, wishing to murder that seven-tongued Rasputin who held my still-lovely Maman in hypnotic thrall! No, in some far room of his own capacious mind, Papa knew, I am convinced. Perhaps his pursuit of an ever-greater golden hoard gave him a satisfactory, quasi-sexual, release. Perhaps he had been intimidated by the presumption of cultural superiority in a servant he considered his equal, as he considered all humankind. Perhaps he had sufficient reward in his affection for me, his son and heir, the next chairman of the board of Aznap International.

For Papa, the devastating blow fell during one of the religious holidays that brought me home from college. While the five of us were at table, V., who even at this late date subjected me to the indignity of an investigation into my scanty wardrobe of slippery foreign verbs, shouted at me the second of his revealing cries: "Dolt!" That explosive noun carried the well-known sound of parental rebuke. In fact, it reverberated in the room as if Vladimir were disowning at that instant and forever a male child who obstinately refused to take advantage of his cleverest genes.

Dazed and embarrassed as I was by the thunderbolt of a revelation whose truth I had only conjectured as a dim possibility, I still had enough of my mother wit left to see Papa looking from Vladimir to me, as if he were noting something fishy about the two of us for the first time in his life. Then, with great concentration, he tapped his fingernail six times against an incisor, a habit of his that gave Maman the creeps and at which Vladimir always smiled, smugly; and then, without the smallest attempt to disguise his movements, he reached down for the bottle of ketchup. He showed his only real loss of cool by harmlessly kicking a discarded shoe through the open doorway to the kitchen at the sight of the tears pouring down Dilsey's sweet cheeks. I dared to look neither at Maman nor at V., for fear my glance would be judged a conspiratorial one.

What power a single word can have, if expressed with a particular intonation! I cannot say that the insight that simultaneously came to Papa and me means anything more than that the two of us in certain ways were remarkably similar, suggesting indeed (despite our physical differences) that I was his son. On the other hand, the thought that I might be a prince nearly unhinged me. Dark secrets, the stuff of tragedy, flit like dust balls across the drafty and wide-planked boards of almost any old farmhouse.

All that I can say is that poor Papa, from this moment forward, was an homme dérangé. (Did I spell that right? Damn that V.!) Perhaps it was the sense of being unmanned at home that gave him a desperate and unwarranted machismo beyond it. (Machismo is a word from another foreign language, one that Vladimir spurned to commit to memory, possibly because of its omnipresent usage by an ever-increasing tide of other illegal aliens, all of whom in his opinion had washed up on our shores amid the flotsam of their serfboards. I should also point out that it is the language of our distant Aznap forebears, as V. well knew.) Papa took control of his corporation by phone and unannounced trips via his private jet to the corporate headquarters. He either fired his best officers or they fled to the embrace of the hated rival. He ordered quite uncalled-for changes in that profitable and staid corporation, one so beloved by our whole nation that it was almost as emotional a symbol to us as our flag itself. Reluctant as I am to do so, I must confess that yes, it was Papa alone—but a Papa made daffy by Prince Rasputin—who ordered the infamous alteration in the secret formula of our most famous carbonated beverage, and who then had the further witlessness to make a public announcement of the fact.

With Aznap International leading the decline, our entire stock market fell, presaging what might have been a worldwide depression (reliable indicators had long since pointed ominously downward) had not a valiant Teddy (whom I had not yet met) infused the economy with generous orders for a whole panoply of new, hastily designed, defensive weapons. Too, the despised competitor of Aznap International chose this moment of great weakness on the part of Aznap to stage a successful unfriendly takeover that managed, in forcing poor Papa out, to save the day, the nation, and, in a manner of speaking, the entire free world. Believing himself cuckolded at home and in disgrace throughout the globe, watching his vast fortune melt away, Papa—how I hate to reach this bitter moment!—blew his brains out with his grandfather's revolver amid the cobwebs of the part of the house that Maman had not completely redone, the homely woodshed.

As a hasty conclusion to this disagreeable account, I sadly admit that Maman ran off with her V. even before the notoriety settled, and with barely a peck on the cheek for me. You can guess who got whatever remained of Papa's cash: Vladimir! That sinister alien used it to purchase outright a major advertising agency. He put himself in charge of three prime accounts, and to this day, he still plans the worldwide campaigns, and writes the copy in various languages, for a snobbish vodka made by his vulgarized motherland, an overpriced sake, and a luxury Pilsner. (The first is a product of our major present-day enemy, though once our staunchest ally, while the latter two are made by the criminal foes we not long ago smashed and who now are listed, quite properly, among our dearest friends.) Oh, with what dark fascination do I continue to follow in the admiring prose of the glossiest of our business magazines, the upward drift of Vladimir's mobility! Of course I love my <u>Maman,</u> and exonerate her completely, while acknowledging her feminine weaknesses. She apparently is happy in her thralldom, and thinks it best if we never see each other again. We no longer write or otherwise try to communicate with each other, not even in the lonely silence following her throaty enunciation of her maiden name, Emmamae Mammalia, and the ensuing beep on her personal answering machine.

Much is to be learned from anybody's childhood, however sad and tragic it turns out to be; so here let me put down, for whatever help it may be to the young Scouts on Earth, the lessons of my childhood experiences:

1. Don't trust foreigners.

2. Be especially wary of princes and other aristocrats, whether deposed or not.

3. On the other hand, don't carry your egalitarian notions too far. (Actually, I have some mixed feelings about princes.)

4. Don't be cowed, or unduly impressed, by pretentious cultural artifacts (books, fancy ballets, operas, paintings, etc.) <u>even if they're being praised by somebody who is at home in a variety of languages.</u> (In my own writings, I am simplicity itself and always strive to make a good <u>read.</u>)

5. On the other hand, diligently study the irregular verbs in a foreign language yourself. The superiority provided by fluent command of even <u>one other</u> tongue can advance an otherwise lackluster career. (I say this however deficient my own capabilities in this regard or whatever my murderous hatred of any glib son of a bitch whose relationship to me long was uncertain.)

6. Chew your native foods; eschew foreign ones.

7. Don't marry. (I never have.)

8. Under no circumstance allow your inherited good sense, your shrewdness, to become rusty through disuse in any aspect of your life. Whatever the extent of your present fortune, try to outwit somebody each day of your life.

9. If you suspect another of unfair dealing, don't dally: get the bastard before he gets you. (Long ago I would have slit V.'s throat, had I not possessed a healthy fear of the next prince to take over the conjugal bed.)

10. In the manner of a wiser and disillusioned Gatsby, recite each of the above rules daily; make them part of your instinctive behavior.

[While setting down this list, so familiar to me, I found myself, much to my surprise, daydreaming of the poignant Sundays of my young life, those serene mornings in which Papa (whose bad example taught me almost everything I know) rose early from his bed in order to give Dilsey the rest she never demanded. He loved Readi-Mix pancakes, thick and chewy, drowning in good old-fashioned imitation maple syrup, and served with a generous portion of those little sausages on ample display in the frozen-food section of our supermarkets. Oh, that quintessence of everything native, that marvelous Unitedian Sunday morning feast! Wearing his absurd chef's cap, standing at the doorway of a kitchen full of smoke from his pair of overheated griddles, he would tinkle the little crystal bell, gift of Maman's first princely lover, and call out, "Good morning, Emmamae. Rise and shine, Kayo. Breakfast, Vladimir. I'll keep some warm if you want a leetle more shut-eye, Dilsey." (No doubt that leetle betokened his brotherhood with all "serfs.") And then shyly, after a pause, "Well, the crêpes are ready, folks."

[From this sudden memory, so strong that I weep as I tell of it, I must add an eleventh rule, perhaps the most important of them all: Blot out the past, if you can; if you can't, don't ever let it turn you into a sentimental fool.]*

CHAPTER III. An Interrupted Lesson

At any designated location in your nation, Sid,[1] you have, as I understand it, two possible times, one "fast" and the other "slow." The difference between them is but <u>one hour,</u> and yet what confusion it throws you into, whenever you must change from one to the other! ("Hey, Ma, do we <u>spring</u> forward or back? Which way are we supposed to <u>fall</u> tomorrow?") How astounded you would be by the varieties of time we employ on our planet, differences in chronology that give us no difficulty whatsoever!

First of all, we divide time into two categories, one <u>personal</u> and the other <u>political.</u> Personal time is much like your time, whatever our more generous quantity of hours. It is by this time that we measure our lives, make our appointments, etc. I need to say little about a time so unexceptional except to insist on its limited use, as a convenience to the private citizen. Though we have our seasons, much as do you, we don't monkey around with personal time, shifting it forward or back, for as a <u>cohesive political society</u> we don't find it very consequential.

Political time—zoneless, national in scope—is a different matter. It consists of two antithetical parts. That our citizens smoothly follow both <u>without even consciously being aware of them</u> suggests that our minds possess a much more sophisticated mechanism for chronological adaptation than do yours. Listen very carefully to what I am going to say: it is of

---

[1]With what a shy grin did I respond to this first use of my assigned diminutive within Kayo's actual narrative! We (by that I mean the wide public as well as the spectrum of specialists earlier alluded to) know that one of the crucial questions any writer must answer to his own satisfaction before commencing any manuscript is this one: <u>For whom am I writing this poem, story, advertisement, technical treatise</u> (or whatever it is)? I was both humbled and elated to realize that Kayo was telling his extraordinary tale for me alone!

utmost importance to the story of my political advancement. For my part, I will keep in mind that I am addressing what on our planet would be a child of conventional IQ, if that. You will have the opportunity to prove yourself more intelligent than I suspect you are; for, as part of the learning process, I am going to address some questions to you. When you see the A on your screen, respond to the best of your knowledge.

Q.: Ready?
A.:
Q.: I asked, <u>Are you ready?</u> My, you <u>are</u> slow-witted, Sid.[2]
A.: Ready, sir.
Q.: The difference between our two types of political time is, in the final analysis, a <u>philosophical</u> one. Do you know what "philosophical" means? In this context or any other?
A.: A reference to something that exists as a quality or value rather than, say, as a physical phenomenon?
Q.: Be careful, Sid! Do you believe that a quality really can be said to <u>exist?</u> That it has a life of its own? The implications are enormous.
A.: I realize that, but of course I so believe. Absolutely. For example, the human soul—
Q.: Obviously you consider philosophy to be inseparable from metaphysics and moral issues. You're still in the Dark Ages. Here we're far from such meretricious thinking. Here the word <u>philosophical</u> refers to questions or concepts (some simple, some abstruse) of language itself. Think of philosophy, if you will, as always concerned with a particular <u>manner of speaking.</u>
A.: Then the difference between your two types of time doesn't really exist? I don't mean to be the one who asks the questions, of course.
Q.:
A.: I've always found it easier to ask questions than to answer them, myself.

[2] But of course I had no idea in advance that I was going to be a pupil in a cosmic classroom! Is Kayo here turning me into his childhood self, so that he can play the brutally contemptuous Vladimir?

Q.: Does time itself exist?

A.: Only as a manner of speaking, I suppose.

Q.: Well said! And doesn't it follow that if your very subject exists as a manner of speaking and (as you say) only as a manner of speaking, you can separate it according to the parts that constitute that manner of speaking?

A.: Philosophically, that would be so.

Q.: Philosophically, then, we classify our two types of time as "conservative" and "radical." Consider your little problem solved. What is the difference between conservative and radical?

A.: Am I permitted to use some examples?

Q.: Only if you must.

A.: Well, when I was a little boy, Republicans were conservative and Democrats were radical. That was because the Communists didn't really exist, except as a manner of speaking. I mean, those atheists were generally somewhere else, like Russia. But some people thought they must be in our country, because the Democrats supported the labor unions, which were organizations of the working class. You see, both Russia and our country are classless societies—again, as a manner of speaking. That is to say, everybody in Russia belongs to the working class, which never has existed in our country, where everybody belongs to the middle class. Since our class is higher on the scale than theirs, it made lots of people mad that the Democrats would support a lower class that existed only in Russia. That's what made the Democrats so radical. I'm still speaking philosophically, of course.[3]

Q.: Maybe so, but—

A.: The people who got maddest were those the Democrats said they supported, for they weren't atheistic Communists even in the philosophical sense. They all left their unions en masse and joined the Republi-

---

[3]I'm aware that I may sound ridiculous here, at least to some ears. But in my attempt to impress Kayo, I was desperately trying to conform to the definition he had made the condition of our discourse.

cans. But that was only later, after things got confused.

Q.: Perhaps you mean <u>more</u> confused?

A.: Are you trying to trap me? I know that <u>confusion</u> is a quality. Doesn't it have to exist, like an apple pie, if we are to have more or less of it?

Q.: Yes. No. I'm not sure. I may have erred in permitting your use of examples.

A.: <u>Confused</u> isn't a strong enough word for what I meant, anyway. Later, you see, things really got <u>fucked up</u>.[4] I hope you don't mind a vulgarism if it's used in the philosophical sense. For a time (though <u>your</u> time doesn't include it as one of its parts) we had a group known as <u>liberals.</u> They were hated so much by everybody else that even the radicals believed in their own existence. I guess hatred, even if it doesn't exist, gives you a pretty good sense of your own identity. Maybe the problem with the liberals was that they didn't hate anybody else enough. In any event, economic conditions and wars (some of which existed only as a manner of speaking, although lots of people got killed) did the liberals in. Now we're a unified and prosperous society, whatever our party allegiance. But we're still fucked up in the sense that ever since the liberals' disappearance we haven't really known who we are or what we ought to be doing. You could only consider us to be conservative if you take the position of yet another group, the poor, but they don't exist except in a manner of speaking. Try to help a nonexistent group and you make a whole society dependent upon handouts. You know, Kayo, until you led me to see that politics are nothing but the parts of time, I couldn't make sense of politics at all. No wonder you've done so well in that field!

Q.:

A.: Kayo?

Q.:

A.: Did I say something wrong?

[4]This obscenity is not part of my normal vocabulary.

Q.:

A.: Kayo? Listen, I have a confession of my own to make. I really don't have the slightest idea as to the difference between <u>conservative</u> and <u>radical.</u> Maybe my difficulty has something to do with my particular time and place, or with some primitive mechanism in my mental clock, but the terms seem interchangeable to me. Tell me the difference, will you?

Q.:

A.: Please? I really want to know.

Q.:

A.: <u>Where are you, Kayo?</u>[5]

CHAPTER IV. *The Lesson Concluded*

Sid, it's taken me much thought to get a handle on your various absurdities, but at last I can say that I find your little statement about things being "fucked up" central to your personal confusion. That touching and revelatory remark is of the kind that I associate with somebody I came to love—reluctantly, against my own judgment. (I realize that I have yet to introduce Nod to you as much more than a cloud of dust. Well, dust he has become again, but enough of that!) People like you and Nod seem to carry in your minds some vague baggage about a celestial golden age, as if your "souls" (your word) once knew of a preexistent time that wasn't "fucked

[5]Further communication between us was delayed for almost a week. Never again did Kayo try to teach me a lesson by the Socratic method. Did my surprising facility with his terminology make him petulant or unsure of himself? Is it possible that his own grounding in philosophy is shaky, whatever his initial condescension toward me in this regard? Perhaps. We remember his failure in a foreign language at college. How very human our fabulous creature from outer space continues to be! I'm glad to say that in the following chapter Kayo brilliantly recoups his verbal loss here, however outrageous his position. My only regret is that I was not allowed to respond to his fierce volleys, for I'd come to enjoy the game.

up," one in which everybody had a good idea of who he was and what he stood for—and nobody had to worry about what he "ought to do," since everybody was lolling around naked and enjoying a communal feast of acorns or whatever. In other words, you hold to some fantasy or hallucination about the past that is your hope (however small) for the future and that makes you dissatisfied with the present.

I've got some news for you, Sid, and I'm giving it to you straight, and for your own good. People like you stare too much at the stars and planets. I bet you get up early to see the morning star on those days it's the evening star instead. The damned thing isn't even a star to begin with. I find that it says a great deal about people of your archaic ilk that you're most infatuated by the bright planet of your little solar system that is <u>completely obscured</u> by clouds, imparting to what you can't see "divine" attributes of love and beauty. If your mind is typical of those in your country, then the brainpans of your citizenry contain nothing but hot wisps and seething vapors.[1]

. . . So let us take for granted in this concluding portion of our discourse that idealism <u>is nothing but the projection of images into the phenomenal universe by a solipsistic magic lantern masquerading as an intelligence in harmony with the Sublime.</u> The subject is beneath our consideration, it's a dead issue, buried with Nod. Rid the primitive magic from your own dim lantern and you'll never be fucked up again; furthermore, you'll be well on your way toward that unconscious acceptance of radical and conservative time that marks the voters in our land.

The simplicity of each of these philosophical concepts

---

[1] Wrong, wrong, wrong! Kayo shows ignorance here even of the celestial objects I truly venerate. I have deleted most of his vigorous attack on me, for it goes on for pages, and the new rules of the match made me nothing but a sitting duck. What, I wonder, would Professor Duck himself have felt at this moment? Would he have believed that his noble effort at extraterrestrial communication was destined to end with vituperation of this sort? As for me, I would have clicked off my Rainbow for good had not that archaic expression "Me thinketh he protesteth too much" lisped its way through the "vapors" of my equally archaic mind. And so the sharper his attack, the greater my knowing smile!

makes them readily understandable. Radical time is composed of wars, famines, epidemics, global overpopulation, growing debts, decreasing standards of literacy, disappearing resources, increasing pollution, brutal crime, the despoiling of cities, the collapsing of bridges, the selling of addictive drugs in playgrounds, rape, incest, child molestation, pornography, censorship of the press and all other forms of repression (including torture), racist acts, corruption in business and government, massacres, terrorism, the meltdown of nuclear power plants, an ozone depletion that threatens to melt the polar icecaps, the deployment of ever-deadlier weapons, etc.—all of those local, national, international, and global events and developments (I've given but a hasty sketch!) that throw a mind like yours into either chaos or despair.

What gives us our dauntlessness and smiling courage? To answer that let me ask another question. In looking at a clock, Sid, which hand is the more important? The answer is obvious. Consider radical time the minute hand, ever whirling madly about. The movement of the hour hand is too deliberate to be caught by the casual eye. <u>But what if it doesn't move at all?</u> Before you dismiss that conservative philosophical conception of time as inapplicable to your planet, I want you to engage in a mental exercise that at first may strike you as cruel.

What I want you to do is to recollect, as best you can, all the pictures you've seen in your lifetime of your various presidents at play, during those often lengthy periods in which they indulge in their personal forms of relaxation while the advisers remain faithfully at the bilge pumps of the ship of state. You know the photographs and film clips I'm referring to! Your president is swimming in a pool or the ocean, splashing water on his wife or private secretary; he's playing some sentimental tune on the piano; he's racing after one of his kids in a game of touch football on the White House lawn; he's lobbing turf instead of a golf ball into the air; he's falling down one ski slope after another; he's remodeling an attic; he's chopping wood. Or perhaps his arms are gracefully upraised, fingers of each hand making the letter **V**, in a daily gymnastic or martial-art routine that ambiguously combines the traditional signals of surrender and victory.

Now, if your memory remains up to the task of our little exercise, think of what has occurred in your radical time over the expanse covered by the pictures (nearly half a century of your personal time, I would guess), comparing it with anything you can recollect that has been done to solve the most obvious dilemmas. That is to say, has a solution to any of the major problems of radical time been found? Are your minorities better off, safely out of their ghettos and at last enjoying productive lives? Are your cities now wholesome and vibrant centers? Have you found a practicable scheme for husbanding your resources and disposing of your wastes? Have you co-operated in any international proposal to control a population growth whose external pressures already make your borders leak? Is your world, thanks in part to your great nation, on the path to international understanding, the catastrophic weapons already dismantled in your land and elsewhere? Whatever the political party of any of your presidents, whatever his unique stance, nothing, you must agree, nothing has been done, nothing has truly changed.

Should this be a cause for alarm or satisfaction? Alarm for you, perhaps, victimized as you are by that old idealistic heresy that deludes you into thinking you must find a synthesis beyond party or ideology or reason itself, a solution (I put this bluntly) that lies out of any world. No wonder you can't tell a conservative from a radical, a Republican from a Democrat, or even know what time of day it is! A reasonable satisfaction for us, though, who know that solutions are as dangerous as they are impractical, and that ideologies are simply the two ways of determining time.

The notion of the eternal present is not among us the mystical notion it must be for you heretical idealists; it is nothing but a realistic acceptance of conservative time, an acknowledgment that the problems as well as the glories of the past are identical in kind with the present ones and with those yet to come. How fortunate we are in knowing that conservative time is static, thus preventing anything rude or genuinely new from happening! The same war is fought over and over, and the same enemy remains—his definition is that he is the enemy, and always he opposes our unchangeable beliefs. No problem is ever resolved, nor do we expect or want it to be. Now, I grant that there are apparent worsenings of any given problem, which have the merit of making us see it as the invincible "Gibraltar" it truly is; and certain deceptive ameliorations of it. But any theoretical solution of that problem implies for us a frightening dislocation, a willful yanking of that hour hand, our obvious stay against chaos. With us, radical and conservative times find their proper balance. For example, an old folk saying of yours, "The more things change, the more they remain the same," will gain for you a new philosophical-political dimension if you rephrase it in terms of our parts of time: "The more radical the time, the more conservative the time."

No doubt it is because of the primacy of the latter that both ways of telling time find their unconscious acceptance in the minds of a populace so healthy and happy that it pays less attention to the daily news of radical time than it does to the most predictable situation comedy. Even our president, who generally is an honest and happy guy himself, doesn't by and large take our philosophical conceptions of time or anything else into conscious account. Actually, it is the obligation of the presidential advisers, particularly those who serve behind the scenes, to be aware at every moment of our categories of personal and political time, particularly of the two parts of the latter, in order to keep the chief executive from some deplorable faux pas, such as his mistaking a gastric upset for a national malaise, an error that permits a wholly internal event—one not even in radical time, but in trivial personal time, for Allah's sake!—to undermine the authority of conservative time.

All that I've said above, my naïve little Sid, is preparation for my revelation to you of the most concealed political fact of my land, the secret that both proves the dominance of conservative over radical time and lies behind my rise to éminence grise.[2] In my lifetime, we've had the same president,

---

[2] In order to keep the reader from an unquestioning acceptance of Kayo's despicable and yet diabolically convincing argument, let me seize upon his sudden flurry of foreign terms of which éminence grise is the last. Doesn't it suggest the confused or divided nature of our essentially insecure storyteller, who, however much he approves of the egalitari-

chosen over and over again in the fairest and most open of elections that a democratic nation can devise. The electorate knows nothing about this, for he campaigns under different names and new face-lifts, and indeed is currently being dissuaded by his advisers from the surgical sex-change that would surely cost him the female vote. So long as he is saved from his small follies, he will continue as viable symbol of our people's greatest need—the preservation of the status quo, warts and all. Without him we would be lost, fogbound, bewildered. He is the politician of a thousand voices, a mortal gifted by Allah with stage presence and a golden tongue. His true name is and always has been Teddy, though only the inner sanctum is privy to this knowledge. It provides Teddy and close advisers like me much hilarity that every opposing candidate for our highest office, in desperately calling upon <u>Unitedians</u> to vote for the change that nobody wants, is subliminally supporting the permanent officeholder by mouthing his name in the central syllables of the one noun that defines us all.

Give a final look, Sid, at the mental pictures of your presidents caught in those intimate moments of relaxation that ought to reveal their individuality much better than an official portrait shared with the national flag. At some particular point in your concentration, don't their faces tend to blur toward a generic likeness, the only difference among them the variety of ages, with even that difference nearly removed by the skill of the presidential specialist in makeup? Don't you ultimately see a single, composite face? Only if you have not properly absorbed my lesson will you find the possibility I'm suggesting to be distasteful or unmannerly.

And with that, my dear Sid, I rest my case and your overwhelmed and sulkily acquiescent mind. Let us leave this philosophical disquisition—this digressive <u>supplement,</u> if you will—to return to a narrative still weaving the gossamer threads of a web for a beloved victim yet to be defined.

anism of his beloved <u>Papa,</u> apparently cannot throw off the hated influence of a princely butler? (<u>See</u> note 2 of the previous chapter.) The reader must decide whether or not I am grasping at straws here, whether or not my knowing smile has become somewhat forced.

CHAPTER V. A *Ceremonious Event*

I have already indicated the exceptional importance of Aznap-Cola to my country, so it will come as no surprise that for generations the chief executive of my family firm was on intimate terms with the chief executive of the nation. I don't know which of the wily Aznaps (surely his name someday will be in our history books!) managed to introduce a machine for dispensing our carbonated beverage into the presidential mansion by offering its head inhabitant a special slug—a golden oval—that would obediently drop into the "change return" box upon each release of a bottle of the then addictive liquid.

That little slug had an immediate effect on the fortunes of the company, for whatever is a favorite of our president is of course a favorite of our populace. In the old days we probably had a succession of genuinely different presidents, though I can't prove this to be true; in any event, each successful candidate received his own slug from the company, with lucrative consequences for the donor. For example, a new beachhead for our troops during any of our wars abroad meant a new beachhead for Aznap-Cola, and soon we had an international clientele. One persistent but never-substantiated rumor about the past complicity between the federal government and my family has it that the invasion of a sweltering little country far to our south had more to do with the estimated thirst of its inhabitants for Aznap-Cola than with its leftist leanings.

My father was as innocent as any other citizen of the fact that Teddy had been our president for decades. True, Papa's gallant egalitarianism impaired his inherited keenness of observation; nevertheless, it seems likely to me that his ignorance of Teddy's identity was chiefly a consequence of the skill of the president's plastic surgeon and of Teddy's own plasticity as actor on the world's greatest political stage. For

Papa had an almost immediate access to our White House, upon the election of a "new" president. You see, even before Papa's birth it had become a Unitedian tradition that within a week of the inaugural ceremonies the newly installed head of the nation would invite the head of Aznap International to the executive mansion for a dinner, following which the chairman of the board of the bottling firm (Papa's grandfather and then his father) would give him a newly minted golden oval, bearing on one side the profile of the new officeholder and on the other the Aznap-Cola trademark. This ceremony was broadcast first by radio and then by television, but only attracted a huge audience after Papa became the one to present the slug. (Everybody knows that television shots can be fudged; Papa, however, was at the president's side, ceremony after ceremony.) But why should I marvel that honest Papa couldn't see Teddy beneath the "Frank" and "John" when the same can be said for all the members of his little family? Being the sort of man he was, Papa, almost from the beginning, brought along Vladimir and Dilsey as well as Maman and me.

Whether or not Teddy ("Frank") was initially disconcerted by the number of guests Papa brought with him, I cannot say, for I was but two weeks old at the time. Good politician that he was, though, Teddy-Frank immediately saw that the inclusion of a butler, a cook, and a mother with her baby at the dinner and at the televised ceremony over the after-dinner coffee and mints during which folksy Papa handed him the shining oval would win him more affection with the populace than could any lengthy speech of his own. Soon the guest list included not only the country's first lady[1] but the president's chef and the various White House maids and other servants. The only person to object to the majority of these added guests as beneath his dignity was Vladimir. Papa and Teddy-John alike

[1] Does Teddy take on a new wife prior to each presidential campaign, with the old one "married" off to a rich sheik or foreign tycoon, or provided with some other handsome sinecure? Or does the first lady undergo with her husband a series of cosmetic changes? Though Kayo's response to these interesting questions was ambiguous (he said Teddy was "as faithful as the next man"), we later will gain at least a partial answer.

overruled him; and Papa had his way even over a reluctant Teddy-Bob on another matter. Rightfully concerned over the possible imposition of a second brand name upon an occasion that over the years had come to mark the election of a new president in a true democracy more satisfactorily than any showy inauguration possibly could, Papa was firm in resisting Teddy-Bob's wish that the meal be catered by the popular fried-chicken chain whose crisp wings and little drumsticks would normally be denied him by the culinary requirements of his high office.

When I was but twelve, I impressed Teddy-Tommy, a president of considerable modesty and charm, as somebody to listen to. Papa had barely given him the slug—indeed, the technicians were still removing their lights and cameras and the dirty dessert plates were still on the table—when a secretary wheeled in a television set. The chief of another state (the nation whose language was the one most favored by Vladimir) was scheduled to make what our DSP² had alerted Teddy-Tommy to as possibly a major provocation of his allies, which, of course, chiefly meant us, the strongest of the lot.

The nearly simultaneous translation of the major portion of the address into Unitedian was so loudly derided by Vladimir as pedestrian or inaccurate that neither Teddy-Tommy nor the rest of us could understand anything but the fact that the foreign leader was contemptuously abrogating some agreement or treaty made with us regarding proliferation of something or other. Diffident and genial though he was, Teddy-Tommy finally shouted at Vladimir, "Shut up!," a phrase that had been repressed within me for so many years that I began to giggle helplessly. I admit to having been in a state varying from heart-thumping hysteria to impudence from the instant the foreign president began to speak in that language whose intricacies Vladimir mercilessly had been attempting to drill into me for years. To this day, my heart thuds whenever I hear somebody speak in that nasal tongue; even a person with a stuffy nose makes me alert, ready to fight or run.

Vladimir looked from me to Maman. "Madame," he said

---

²Democratic Security Police, an undercover agency with agents both abroad and within the ASU.

coldly to her, "votre enfant est méchant—non, non, il est mauvais, un vrai diable."

"What kind of lingo is that, friend?" Teddy-Tommy asked. "In my house, we speak Unitedian."

Vladimir said, "I was suggesting to Mrs. Aznap that she control her child so that I—pardonnez-moi, you—could hear the rest of the speech."

"Clam up, kid," Teddy-Tommy said, not unkindly, to me; it was clear that he shared my dislike for Vladimir. "Let's all watch this." For the foreign president was engaged in what seemed a most peculiar activity for a television broadcast by a chief of state, especially one that was being viewed throughout the world. From an inside pocket of his immaculate suit coat, he extracted a silver cigarette case. He nodded imperiously to some off-camera presence; soon a hand brought a pair of scissors to the desk at which he was sitting. At once he began methodically to snip each of his cigarettes in half, explaining that since it had been determined that smoking was bad for the health, he was serving as an example for his countrymen and the rest of the people on the globe by publicly renouncing at this instant and forever his own deleterious habit.

"By Allah!" Teddy-Tommy cried in awe as the image of the other president began to fade while the sound track picked up his rousing national anthem; and our president took one last puff of his cigar, before obediently dousing the butt in his cup of cold coffee. "By Allah, you've got to hand it to that guy, bastard that he is! What immense pride! Who else in the Allah-damned world could have found such a foolproof way to make himself give up smoking?"

"Mr. President?" I asked. Lost in admiration as he was, he did not answer; so, with greater brashness, my heart still thumping briskly, I called him by his first name.

Apparently Teddy-Tommy responded more readily to nicknames than to official titles, for he gave me an affectionate smile. "I hope you follow that advice, my boy," he said.

"I shall, sir; and I hope the same for you, sir." (Thump, thump: my heart was the tail of a half-grown puppy uncertain whether to be gaily mischievous or scared enough to puke.)

"We all should be grateful to that son of a bitch."

"Actually, sir, I feel sorry for him." (Thump, thump, thump.)

"Sorry?" Teddy-Tommy looked at me in surprise. "I realize that a nicotine addiction is a mean one to break. He's bound to get nervous and unpredictable, maybe declare a small war or sign a pact with one of our mutual foes. Our spies have got to stay awake. Did you notice the jewel on the ring finger of the hand that brought the scissors? That little sapphire belongs to our most trusted DSP agent, I'm thankful to say. But it's obvious that old President Charley never will smoke again, whatever else he may do."

"And why not, sir?"

"What a ridiculous question! Don't you know anything about pride, son?"

"Could you make a public vow like his, sir? And then stick to it?" (Thump.)

"I don't have the pride. Pretty soon I'd be smoking in the bathroom, with the door locked and the window open. Sooner or later I'd be caught."

"Then maybe you're more your own man than his pride will ever permit him to be." (Thump, thump.)

"Say that again, my boy?"

"Why are some people prouder than others?"

"They consider themselves superior to the rest of us. They demand, and get, public respect."

"They require the homage of everybody else, to maintain their pride?"

"People who act proud and don't get respect are laughed at, of course. They're buffoons or madmen."

"Then, if you're a proud man and publicly announce you've given up smoking, you really are forced to kick the habit in order to maintain the admiration of others? If that's the case, who's really controlling your will?" (Thump, thump.)

Teddy-Tommy whistled. "So you're saying that proud old Charley is unconsciously acknowledging, by his public announcement, that he's really a puppet of his people?"

"Yes, sir; a really proud leader is a slave to the glorified image the public has of him, don't you think?" (Thump.)

"How old did you say you were, son?"

"Twelve." (Thump, thump, thump, thump, thump.)

Teddy-Tommy said indulgently, "I imagine a boy of your talents has a good bit of pride himself."

"My <u>Papa</u> has taught me that excessive pride is a sin against our Unitedian belief in equality, sir."

"Very well put, my boy."

"But if I dared to imagine that a child such as myself had somehow managed to win the respect of the president of the greatest country in the world—" (My heart had calmed; I was captain of my fate.)

"You certainly have won that respect, young fellow. Your precociousness astounds me."

"Then I have a proper reason to be proud, sir. I must do everything in my power to keep that respect, mustn't I?"

<u>Papa</u> winced at my remark; he detested cleverness almost as much as he did the arrogance of pride. Teddy-Tommy laughed in delight, though, and slapped me on the back. "You're a true politician, son," he said, and lit a new cigar with obvious pleasure. <u>Maman</u> gave me one of the adoring glances she normally reserved for Vladimir; as for Vladimir, he turned down Teddy-Tommy's proffered cigar for the more expensive brand he kept in his own coat pocket, expansively blew enough smoke in my direction to make me cough, and said fondly of me to Teddy-Tommy, "<u>Mon petit écolier.</u>"

Imagine Vladimir taking a reflected glory in the achievements of my young brain! I like to think that his general nastiness toward me was at least in part the result of envy.

"One thing you can say about me," Teddy-Tommy earnestly said, as all of us were lined up for a good-bye handshake with him, "is this: <u>I am a modest man,</u> and can break any public vow I might conceivably want to make. Though I never had a paper route when I was a kid, I'm the sort who <u>looks</u> as if he might have. I am humble before Allah and was endowed by Him with no more of the right stuff than He gave to everybody else who has benefited from the free-enterprise system. We all go to the same church, so to speak, and want the federal government out of our hair. And here's a second thing you can say about me, for I'm sure enough of my manhood to accept wisdom from the mouth of a child: I am ending at this instant the belly-up foreign policy that has let a certain pompous marionette push his country's sass up our country's ass." As Teddy-Tommy was escorting us to the steps of the mansion, I heard him whisper to <u>Papa,</u> "That boy of yours bears watching, pal."

CHAPTER VI. *"Whatever Flames upon*
the Night . . ."[1]

If, in the preceding chapter, I seem to have lingered unconscionably over the details of a small triumph of my juvenile years, I have done so not simply because its recollection (unlike that of most events of my childhood) <u>makes me feel good.</u> It turned out to be the beginning of that stochastic process that propelled me through the back rooms of political influence to Teddy's private study at a fateful moment in which, peering once again (for it wasn't the first time, I assure you!) through the gunsights of a family heirloom at a target daily become more beloved, I knew to my horror that <u>this</u> time my country's stability demanded that I squeeze the trigger. How am I to be blamed, then, if the blood on my hands is the consequence of what must be every child's dream—that of winning praise from the president of his land? And if that praise itself came for my staunch support of everything Unitedian against the pretensions of a foreign tongue?

Let me dwell on that last fragment of a sentence.

[1] ". . . Man's own resinous heart has fed." This heading, as well as all other chapter titles, apt or otherwise, is supplied not by our fiery author but by his humble drudge, who here cannily separates two of the most famous lines of Irish poetry to make absolutely sure he will not have to pay a copyright fee for the use of a couplet that doesn't even rhyme. Believe me, the salary of such a slighted professor as I is not so "fat" as a crude and envious welldriller might think! If my own country house bears some surprising resemblances to one elsewhere in the galaxy whose fate is the major subject of this chapter, the reader should bear in mind that I never have had the vast profits of a soft-drink empire to pay for my heating bills.

No doubt in my previous chapter you noticed, Sid, the curious affinity in personal attitudes between Charley, that foreign president, and our butler. I have already indicated that as soon as Charley began his televised speech in that tongue so beloved by Vladimir, my terrorized glands released all their juices, giving alertness to my mind as well as vigor to my heart. Is there something intrinsic about this language that grants the fluent user of it, whether it is his native language or not, a supreme arrogance, a maddening and sophisticated irony that cuts like a blade through an opponent's defenses, finding at once each and every logical weakness within his position, the verbal edges of the attacker's vorpal weapon honed in particular to destroy whatever is finest in that position? In short, is this language a much better tool of ignoble seduction and negation than it is of the generous love and affirmation at which the Unitedian tongue excels? With a snickersnack of foreign phrases Prince Vladimir laid low my beautiful <u>Maman,</u> with a snickersnee of others he ridiculed my <u>Papa</u>'s stammering egalitarian views. In wise retrospect, then, I can see that my entire career in politics (a profession in which the good acts are inevitably mixed with the reverse—i.e, necessary assassinations, etc.) stems from a childhood victory made in the name of all who speak Unitedian over the insidious poisons of a foreign tongue.[2]

After the betrayal, economic ruin, and death of my <u>Papa</u> forever ended my youth, I torched the house in which I had been engendered,[3] an act in perfect accordance with my eleventh and most consequential rule of conduct. I weakened only enough to save a few trifles, such as the portrait, a clumsy five feet by three, of my young <u>Papa</u> (commissioned by Aznap

[2] As Kayo himself makes apparent, this unexpected, irrational, and perhaps textually misplaced attack on a particular language is wholly the result of his hostility to Vladimir. Unfair as he is, I find myself smiling at his rhetorical questions and indulgently answering them in the affirmative.

[3] I am an enthusiastic supporter of Historic Corinth, a society dedicated to the preservation throughout our region of classical-revival dwellings like my own as well as old classroom buildings my university would like to raze. As such, I am appalled by this casual confession, however justified Kayo considers himself to be.

International at the time he became titular head and, until his ouster, brilliantly illuminated in the corporation headquarters lobby) in which, seated before the family hearth, his hand on the head of a handsome Irish setter (a dog belonging to the painter? The only canines we owned were mongrels who came begging at our door for shelter and food), he smiles radiantly through a haze of dark tones intended to impart to this oil painting the dignity of ancient masterpieces; a lovely little snapshot of Maman in a low-bodiced white gown (her wedding dress?); the baseball with which I had smacked Vladimir where it would hurt him the most; and (for I was sure that sooner or later it would produce a second deadly sting, this one most assuredly not self-inflicted) the weapon with which poor Papa had ended his unhappiness.

It was long after dark on an August evening that I arrived in my Rent-a-Wreck before that now abandoned house at the familiar country crossroads, the desire for arson already flaming within my vengeful chest. The one unsmashed headlight of that rusty vehicle whose rental cost had deprived me of my supper lit up the For Sale sign before I turned off the switch and furtively parked the car under the ungainly boughs of a jungle of lilac bushes that Papa always had hesitated to cut down because of the sanctuary it provided the sparrows. The late-summer cicadas sang as they do, regardless of the season of the year, in films that would impress the audience with darkness, solitude, suspense. I assumed the momentary flicker of light in the room above the woodshed to be a hallucination created by my own conflagrant intention. By Allah, I would deprive Vladimir at least of the money the ancestral homestead would bring him! In the despair of his final days, Papa had neglected not only to pay such bills as the one for the insurance premium on the house (abetted by the morning sunlight, my sharp eyes had read through the envelope stamped Final Warning that lay unopened on his desk) but to rewrite his marriage-day will, in which he had bequeathed everything to his starlet bride. If the first seemed too mundane for his grief, perhaps he procrastinated over the second from the wish not to let the pettiness of anger or revenge nullify his lifelong love and generosity of spirit. Never would he have guessed that Vladimir would escape with my spellbound Maman only days after his own hasty cremation, leaving me without sustaining funds or even the thoughtfulness of a forwarding address. If only my Maman had discovered the spunk of our latter-day emancipated women, at least in regard to her spineless adoration of a particular prince![4]

. . . The utilities in the house had been disconnected, and all of Maman's clothes and jewelry were gone, every stocking and golden bracelet; but the furniture remained, perhaps because those overstuffed and faded pieces had never been of value to anybody but Papa, who had inherited them from his own father. I knew their location so well that I stepped around the hassock and recliner in the dark, needing the momentary flare of a match only to find the objects I was removing. I had difficulty with the painting, for its ornate wooden frame was nearly too large for the backseat of the tiny car; finally, with some ripping of upholstery, I wedged it between the roof and drive-shaft hump, and then returned, by way of the woodshed (drear locale of Papa's suicide) for the gasoline can stored there. I had prepared for my conflagration by piling all of my once dreaded language books, those ordered for my use by Vladimir as well as those from my college career, on the kitchen floor, and was ready to douse them with the inflammatory fluid when I heard a creaking of the kitchen stairs. The stairways of an old house can hold for hours or days the memory of their most recent users, releasing at last, and in measured order, the pressure of footsteps, either in an upward or downward progression; in my fevered fancy, I thought perhaps I was hearing my Papa's stealthy movement downward, as, revolver in hand, he was on his way to his death.

"Stop!" I cried, seeing the flicker of an approaching candle flame; but the presence was not that of a ghostly Papa. Rather, it was that of a living woman, barefooted and wearing a long white gown. "Maman?" I asked in wonder, but it was actually Dilsey, clothed in one of my mother's cast-off gar-

[4]In a rambling discourse too full of expletives to be transcribed, Kayo details his sudden poverty. Evicted from the only house he ever had known, he had been sleeping on a bench in a nearby lakeside park. This reference to his mother carries the only criticism he will ever make of what we must recognize as her shocking, totally unacceptable, behavior.

ments—perhaps the very wedding dress or bedtime apparel pictured in that photograph I had just stashed with my other valuables in the car. I have never been anything but a reluctant reader of "great books," rapidly memorizing their plots via the summaries in the Cliffs Notes series to pass one required course or another; but the moment I recognized Dilsey, I knew that hers was the fate of all faithful servants in classic texts—to be forgotten by her negligent masters and mistresses, to be left to starve or freeze, in the vacant ancestral mansion.

"Oh, Dilsey," I whispered, hugging her tightly. "Forgive me! I would have burned you to death—"

"Wait," she said, and began her painfully arthritic climb back up the steps, to her room above the woodshed. When she returned, wearing her best dress and pearls (both of them also salvaged from the liberal piles of my <u>Maman</u>'s discarded attire), she was carrying a battered fiberboard suitcase (no doubt filled with more of the same as well as her toilet articles) and the one bit of Vladimir that he had purposefully left behind, his official butler's monkey suit worn only for our rare formal dinners. She tossed the uniform on top of the books, as a sign that she hated V. every bit as much as did I, and was my willing conspirator. At that instant, I swore to myself to care for her forever, however incongruent such a promise seemed to my rules of conduct. Had I not dissuaded her (surely her laborious movements would have doomed her to the flames), she would have lit the pyre herself, by tossing her candle at the drenched collection of books and clothing.

Conscience, my dear Sid, is nothing but the fear of being caught in a criminal act. As I escorted Dilsey to the car, listening to those mournful cicadas and to the distant howling of a hound, I thanked Allah with each slow-motion step of our old cook for the prescience of that doughty ancestor who had made this task so simple for me by moving to such a remote spot. To make sure my Rent-a-Wreck wouldn't let me down at an embarrassing moment, I started the engine before dashing back to throw a match at the waiting pile. What a satisfying swoosh! I didn't even care that my eyebrows got scorched. We were halfway to the nearest town (the home of a university almost as prestigious as that more easygoing one

I had just managed to be graduated from) before I heard the first siren.

It was lucky that Dilsey had just enough cash in her purse to pay for our motel room that night. I wouldn't have wanted the responsibility of making her snooze outdoors; and whatever would I have done with that painting of my Papa, enough to convict me of arson had a snoopy policeman found me cuddled up next to it on some park bench.

CHAPTER VII. A *Salacious Chapter*

For me, the next six months constituted the typical period of humiliation that is part of the young hero's learning process. At least, that's how the plot goes in any of those weighty Bildungsromane (a foreign term never employed by V. I found in a handy Cliffs Notes guide and used an impressive eight times in one of my more ambitious college essays) that undergraduates have to lug around in their book bags. Indeed, I don't know how I would have survived this period (for my recently completed education had prepared me for nothing but a life of ease as the titular head of Aznap International) had it not been for Dilsey—she whose well-being I had just sworn to protect. As I have already stressed, without my arrival as a kind of torch-bearing knight she no doubt would have died of starvation or sadness in that empty house. After all, she had been deserted by the two members of the family she most loved, Papa and me. And yet it turned out that she had salted away over the years from her little salary a considerable number (I'm still too embarrassed to say how many) of thousand-dollar government bonds, a patriotic but not very productive method of investing one's savings that even my Papa scorned.

At my suggestion, she cashed in all her bonds so that we might make the down payment on one of those large and run-down dwellings found everywhere in the Collegetown area of the nearby community. Decades previously, every one of these buildings had been divided up by plasterboard into apartments to be rented to wealthy students willing to pay through the nose for the privilege of living in a bohemian atmosphere. (Naturally enough, I am speaking here from the landlord's point of view.) Buying such a ratty warren was a clever move, indicative of my Aznapian entrepreneurial talents, for (as Papa had more than once informed me) a number of astute landlords in that university town had started with a mortgaged house on "Mediterranean" or "Baltic" Avenue and ended up owning a whole passel of railroads while going to jail only once or twice; and it had the immediately practical advantage of giving Dilsey and me a little apartment (however squalid) of our own.

If I had the inherited shrewdness, I lacked, alas, the necessary experience to deal with real-estate agents, plumbers, heating and roofing contractors (how I got taken on that little piece of property!), building inspectors, various exterminators who specialized in rodents or cockroaches or carpenter ants and termites. None of the human predators was a whit more ruthless than I was willing to be, but all were infinitely more practiced at extortion. Having been but recently graduated from their ranks, I didn't even possess the necessary know-how to get the better of students. Oh, those carefree members of a privileged class of society who simply won't acknowledge the necessity of turning off a light, closing a window against a wintry draft to save fuel or a pipe from bursting, and locking a door to prevent the theft of even the leakiest gas stove or the most worn-out sofa from their furnished rental units! And believe you me, when a landlord notices a young female tenant with lustrous, newly shampooed hair flowing sinuously over her shoulders and down her back, he doesn't see so much her beauty as the new wad of hairs now no doubt clogging another of his sinks![1]

[1]My readers are probably as astonished as I that a novel from outer space could descend so precipitously into a drain clogged with sticky globs of hair. As justification for my editorial decision to keep within this manuscript all such sordid minutiae from the most debased period of our author's life, let me say that it was from his experiences as a landlord verging on bankruptcy that Kayo, upon becoming a confidential adviser to the president, drew public attention to the need

. . . And I thank Allah for the growing suspicions that made me put off such a risky if ultimately remunerative enterprise, even though the precarious nature of our finances caused my dear, stiff-jointed Dilsey to take a job as a fraternity cook. After all, I was but a callow youth, and was hesitant about putting myself at the mercy of the underworld. You see, already I had made some initial contacts with two unidentified figures wearing fedoras and dark glasses, though as yet I had given them nothing but the vaguest allusions as to what I had in mind. Clearly, though, were I to proceed with my plans, I would require substantial assistance from the Mafia,[2] for the project was of sufficient magnitude to require the bribery or coercion of an entire police force.

In any event, I thought it wisest to be circumspect, especially after I began to have the uncanny feeling that I was being spied upon—though never (in quickly turning around while I was walking down the street, say) did I catch anybody tailing me. I mean, there were always people going in my direction, but nobody wearing a fedora or a trenchcoat or a uniform. Still, I considered very seriously the possibility that Vladimir might have hired an investigator to catch me in some criminal act, to spite me for depriving him of what had wrongfully become his. A little bit of paranoia, as I quite properly told myself, is an asset to anybody who would get ahead in our competitive world.

to conserve precious Unitedian resources. That is to say, he convinced a dubious Teddy personally to lower every thermostat in the nation's White House, place bricks in the tanks of all the presidential toilets and twenty-watt bulbs in every chandelier, etc. At the risk of appearing a prude, I do admit to having censored here Kayo's lengthy description of a proposal for transforming that albatross of a house into a veritable pleasure dome of delight for clients with desires both normal and bizarre. Kayo's scrupulous attention to detail no doubt would have added spice to this drab interval in our text, but God knows there will soon be spice enough without it.

[2]The first of a number of references to the "Mafia," a word whose indiscriminate use in our country is an unfortunate slur against a people whose impulsive generosity I have long admired. Kayo is certainly not prejudiced against Italians (if indeed his planet contains a boot for them), and so I assume that for him the word simply refers to any closely-knit group of mobsters; the reader can think of such groups as, say, French, if he or she so desires.

I soon had more definite reasons for my caution. There were, for example, telltale clicks and little beeps on the telephone while I was pleading with the plumber (whose last bill I had not yet paid) to do something about a third-floor toilet leak that was buckling a fussy second-floor tenant's ceiling. At night, I heard rustlings in the wastepaper basket, and on several occasions the subdued clang of the garbage-can lid just beyond the kitchen door. And yet I never caught sight of an intruder, however quickly I jumped out of bed, my hand on the butt of that family heirloom I now kept perpetually strapped by a shoulder holster to my skin. Conceivably those stealthy sounds could have meant busy rodents (had the exterminator once again not done the work he had charged me for?) within the house, raccoons without (for that town was Raccoonville every night), but no furry creature, whatever his form, would <u>steal</u> my balled-up scraps of paper or politely return the lid to a can. Who was trying to find out what I ate and what I wrote? I rebuked Dilsey for filching tidbits from the fraternity freezer, even though those delicacies were for me, and made sure my discarded scribbles contained nothing but the most elevated sentiments. Once I was even awakened by the flash of a camera at the window; a candid photographer had managed to raise the sash and push aside the curtains, presumably to catch on film whatever lewd scenes tired old Dilsey and I might be enacting in the darkness.

I realized that somebody considered me a pretty big fish on the day in the supermarket that an extraordinarily attractive young woman wearing tight jeans knocked the egg carton out of my basket with an "accidental" swing of her heavy shoulder bag, and as apology invited me to have a drink in the bar of the downtown hotel where she was staying, following which she welcomed me into her expensive penthouse suite. Of course I accepted her hospitality. Whether Vladimir, the Mafia, the Democratic Security Police, or a foreign government (part of that woman's beguilement was the touch of a possibly sinister accent) was behind this investigation, I felt I must behave as would any virile young man, especially one who would have been a fool not to realize how attractive his physique made him to those of the opposite sex. Though my paranoia was rampant, I didn't want to augment anybody's suspicions about me by an abnormal reluctance that might suggest I had something to hide (i.e., arson and plans for further illegal activity).

"What an interesting conversationalist you are!" she said, standing pensively at the window while shrugging off her denim jacket and shirt, though I'd been careful enough to speak of nothing but the superiority of neoprene faucet washers to the old cork and soft rubber kinds and other such bits of useful information that had come to me as a landlord. "And what a fascinating and dangerous man," she went on, watching me disrobe as she tugged at her own jeans to free them from her generous hips. She wore neither brassiere nor panties. What a ravishing body she had!

"Why do you say 'dangerous,' ma'am?" I asked warily, as we both approached the bed.

"What else should I say? Where did you get such a big gun?"

"An inheritance from my father, ma'am," I said, with admirable <u>sangfroid,</u> unloosening the shoulder holster I had forgotten about and dropping it with apparent casualness to a spot on the floor by my side of the bed where I could retrieve it instantly.[3]

She lay down next to me, gently biting my ear while stroking me where it was most gratifying; I returned her various kindnesses. "Poor boy," she whispered, her voice taking on a breathier and in every way more pronounced accent. "You must hate capitalistic system."

[3]Kayo and I hotly quarreled over the inclusion of this particular exchange, as well as over the entire bedroom scene. My resistance to the scurrilousness of this material gave him more than one opportunity to refer to me as "just another dumb Nod." At last I acquiesced in the use of a crude and clichéd innuendo not only at vain Kayo's insistence, but for the psychological insight into his steamy depths provided by the passage. Note that at this sexually heightened moment, he says that his "big gun" was inherited not from "my beloved <u>Papa</u>," which he would have said in reference to the actual steel-barreled revolver, but from "my <u>father</u>," as if he recognizes here a debt to a certain prince. Note too how easily he then falls into yet another phrase of the language he most despises. May I point out (with excusable pride) that such a rhetorical analysis as this is a good illustration of the kind of insight that old-fashioned critics like me have provided for decades?

"Why you say that?" No doubt it was the passion induced by her grasping and stroking that made me speak as ungrammatically as did she.

"What capitalistic pigs do to your father! Believe me, I know what greedy swines really keel that kind friend of proletariat! I know rage in your bosom, dear friend, and I offer luff and way to crash down evil system."

"You're a Communist spy! Well, let me tell you, Olga or whatever your name is . . . _Ouch,_" I cried, for she held firmly by her nails to the most sensitive part of my biological makeup when I tried to show my revulsion to her by a quickly aborted leap from the bed. Of course, her attempt to appear to be such a spy was so unconvincing—perhaps _amateurish_ is the word—that I knew at once she was a member of our own Democratic Security Police.[4] "Listen to me, Olga, I'm a patriotic Unitedian through and through, and not for all the love in the world would I—"

"Olga!" she repeated, with apparent pleasure; and then dropped all pretense at a foreign accent. "What an ugly name! Of course I'm no Communist spy, that was just the most de-

---

[4]The occasion of another argument between Kayo and your scribe, for I doubted that "Olga" could possibly be so inept as his dramatization made her out to be, if she were indeed an agent of an organization that would be the equivalent of our own well-schooled FBI or CIA. Kayo found this objection a further example of my "appealing naïveté." Actually, he said, he should have recognized "Olga" for what she was from the moment she clumsily knocked his egg carton to the floor, since his was a free and open society, and the tabloids (much to the detriment of an already imperiled national security) frequently exposed the more lurid exploits of the bumbling secret police. For my personal instruction (and no doubt because of his own conceited and arrogant nature!) he then had me take down, word for word from my computer screen, a directive he had written to all DSP agents, foreign and domestic. As perhaps his first missive upon assuming the powers of a presidential adviser, he obviously took pleasure in its diction and stern good sense. It required all agents to enroll in accredited college courses in Method Acting and in whatever language whose accents they would be mimicking. "The superiority provided by fluent command of one other tongue can advance an otherwise lackluster career," the directive encouraged or warned. It concluded by declaring that highly placed officials would thenceforth "be conducting unannounced 'spot checks,' particularly to determine the expertise of female agents at the crucial art of seduction."

grading fantasy I could imagine for myself, nothing but a joke. . . . Oh, but please keep calling me Olga, cruel master!" While managing to maintain her grip on me with one hand, she slithered her sensuous way over my belly to extract with the other the revolver from the shoulder holster on the carpet, cackling all the while with a ferocious or hysterical joy. Naturally I thought myself in the talons of an agent who had gone berserk, and would have ripped myself loose, whatever the consequences, had she not extended the weapon to me, butt first, while releasing her other hand as well. I left the bed, carefully keeping the revolver aimed at her.

"Now Olga must do everything you wish her to, however vile and unspeakable," she whispered, running her tongue across her upper lip. "Look in my suitcase for whatever you need to satisfy your cruel lust."

My examination of the contents of the suitcase explained at once the reason for her second, and momentarily more successful, ruse. As soon as I saw that collection of drugs, hashish pipes, leather corsets, bondage collars, whips, etc., I had the mental agility to realize two things: (1) the Mafia, secret agents as they themselves sometimes are for our government, had passed on to the DSP some malicious gossip about my personal proclivities, hearsay based only on some hints dropped to them about my proposed business; (2) the DSP (was I possibly being considered for a sensitive post?) was testing the validity of that information. Whatever respectable airs certain members of the underworld may put on because of the shady but eminently patriotic goals for which the government on occasion employs these nasty creatures, the fact of the matter is that the confidential reports of the Mafia are to be trusted no more than are the invoices submitted by our defense contractors.

Now, Sid, I have a perfectly understandable, and usually restrained, impulse toward violence, as you already know; and it really put me into a rage that anybody in our country would be naïve enough to confuse anything that I might want to do to earn a living with my personal moral character. But I realized I needed to emerge from this affair with a spotless reputation. I took a pair of fur-lined handcuffs from the suitcase. "Turn over, Olga," I said roughly, giving her a smart smack on

each of her lovely buttocks after she obeyed, and then imprisoned her arms behind her back with the cuffs.

"What are you going to do now, master?" she asked, her
words almost muffled by the pillow.

"I'm going to make two telephone calls," I said, my Aznapian shrewdness serving me well. "First, I'm calling the police, to tell them I've caught a perverted Communist spy; and
then I'm going to report your disgraceful behavior to the
watchdogs at the Feminist League."

As I had guessed, the handcuffs contained a hidden release mechanism; bounding from the bed, she held a razor
blade, previously concealed somewhere on her body, at my
throat before I had dialed the second digit. "I'm an agent of
the DSP acting upon orders from the highest source," she
snarled. "Put down that phone, buddy." Then she slapped my
own buttocks, but not without affection. "Congratulations,"
she said. "You've passed with a full bill of health the most
rigorous investigation our nation can provide."

And so it came about that on that very night (after a bit
of excusable dallying) I boarded an unmarked jet for our nation's capital, on an urgent mission so top-secret that I was
forbidden even to wake Dilsey, to tell her that I was leaving.
Faithful Dilsey, so mistreated by me! I remembered my vow
on the night of the fire, and promised myself that I would live
by it in the future. Let me say, Sid, that I've known but three
true friends—Dilsey, _Papa,_ and Nod. I never told _Papa_ how
much I loved him, and I murdered Nod, but I did keep my
vow to Dilsey, as you will discover (along with much else) in
the next chapter.

CHAPTER VIII. _Kayo as_ Éminence Grise

As I came to realize in ghost-writing Teddy's fictitious au-
tobiography (yes, fictitious, and necessarily so: how else could
I pin a single identity upon this splendidly polymorphous creation, this gorgeous chameleon with the innate ability to re-

flect whatever colors the fickle public most wanted to see?), the struggle to get to the top is of much greater dramatic interest than is the view from the cushy chair on the summit, however panoramic it may be.

I don't mind telling you, Sid, that I would like to linger over my many achievements as Teddy's most trusted adviser and confidant. Guess who, for example, won most of the poker games that Teddy played with his "kitchen cabinet," that secluded group of dedicated advisers whose names I have sworn never to reveal? It takes an extraordinary savoir-faire to play your cards properly while participating in (nay, leading) a discussion of what to do about a revolution in tiny Montenegro (or wherever), a piece of real estate that just happens to contain a rare mineral necessary for any civilized nation's advanced weaponry.

Alas, I understand your impatience for matters other than this! Have I not constantly piqued your curiosity about that bosom companion whom I ruthlessly shot down? Poor Nod, beloved by me: he was a sadly outdated outlaw of your "Robin Hood" sort, one as devoted to his huge and antique binoculars as I to that equally large gun that already has played such a crucial role in my narrative. Trust me to tell his story completely; for the present, while I finish as hastily as possible my necessary preparation for it, I say no more about him. (Except that those italicized words, which once constituted a favorite expression of his, now carry for me an almost unbearable pathos.)

As I briskly entered our White House on the dawn following my "affair" with the agent, I was met by a bearded gentleman with haggard eyes who put a finger to his lips before whisking me behind some coats in the hallway closet. "I've been up all night with him, waiting for you to come," this man whom I shall call "X" whispered to me. "Listen, do you remember where you were on the night of January 61, 5873?"

"Of course," I whispered back, for the date was inscribed in my memory as that of my childhood triumph. "I was in this very house, with my good Papa, my beautiful Maman, and our two family servants, the loyal Dilsey and the perfidious—"

"Shhh," "X" warned, for my voice had begun to rise with that last adjective. Asking, with much solemnity, "Do you recognize this?," he took a small object from his vest pocket. He lit his Zippo so that I could better see that object in the dark and camphoric closet, managing, while holding the lighter aloft, to scorch the sleeve of a presidential coat. (Whatever the speed with which I want to cover this ground, Sid, my concern with detail—which has served me in good stead both as writer and adviser even though you may consider it obsessive at this moment in which I hover at the edge of a revelation about that mysteriously gleaming thing—accounts for my references to the Zippo, camphor, etc. I forbear to say anything about the new stench of burnt wool, other than that my coughing caused "X" to hold his hand over my mouth until I recovered.)

"Why, yes," I said in astonishment. "That's Tommy's profile! It's the slug to the Aznap-Cola dispenser that <u>Papa</u> presented to him that night! How did you get it?"

"It's now yours. Guard it well," "X" said, with an emotion that made his voice tremble. "Here's mine," and he withdrew another slug from his pocket, one with the profile of the even earlier President Bob.

"I don't understand," I said—a true confession of a condition I grant you is almost as unusual for me as my admission of it; but ever since I had accompanied "Olga" to her penthouse suite, I seemed to have been existing in some childhood dream or pubescent fantasy. And, like "X" and the president, I had spent a sleepless night, in my case as the lone passenger on a jet airliner—a young man staring out the window at the twinkling lights that marked one city after another of our vast and enigmatic land, an impecunious young entrepreneur wondering innocently about the role he was to play in the Unitedian destiny.

It was only after the fraternal handshake with "X" that formally concluded my rite of membership into the "kitchen cabinet"—or, more accurately, the shadowy Order of the Oval Token, code-named OOT—that I learned the remarkable fact you already are privy to. I mean, that "Tommy," "Bob," and all the rest—including the present officeholder, the ebullient but possibly flaky "Oscar," known more familiarly to the populace as good old "Ozzie" or "Oz"—were various pseudonyms of the same man.

Almost a decade of my personal time (thanks to Allah and yours truly, conservative time hasn't budged a minute!) has elapsed since I gratefully received that slug in the coat closet, in a ceremony even more unostentatious than the one a decade before that—the ceremony in which Papa had entrusted the identical golden oval to the leader he knew only as "Tommy." No longer does that familiar red-and-white Aznap-Cola cooler hum away in its friendly fashion in the main corridor of our White House, for Aznap-Cola is a beverage of our revered past. Those slugs, then, have no utilitarian use whatsoever! It suggests something about the symbolic nature of a brand name like Aznap-Cola that those little slugs, collected one by one by our president over the years, continue to serve as powerful talismans for the tight little unit that unobtrusively runs our nation. I am not of your soupy kind, my sentimental Sid, but I do admit to a certain mistiness of the eyes, attributable only in part to the smelly atmosphere of that closet, when I discovered what it meant to be awarded that shining token!

What had caused my selection into this elite group? The Aznap name of course was a factor, but not in itself sufficient. As part of that closeted briefing, "X" worriedly told me of Teddy-Oz's present mental problem, one surely understandable in a leader of his talents. To put it simply, he was undergoing an identity crisis. The crux of the matter had less to do with his variety of disguises than with the fact that, no matter which one he donned, he seemed incapable of ever doing anything new and wonderful. In consequence, he had come so to question his own existence that he was constantly pinching himself or sticking pins in his arm.

"Now, of course," "X" continued, "the very stability of the land depends on the fact that he continue to do nothing that is either 'new' or 'wonderful.' Only once did he do something that you might at least call original, and all of us in the OOT held our collective breath, but it turned out not to be risky at all. Teddy—and now you, like the rest of us, are privileged to call him that, in privacy—has always had difficulty remembering names (his one political liability). And yet he has come to remember you fondly as Kayo, even though for some years, when he was recalling the night of January 6l, 5873, he would say to us, 'You know, <u>that Aznap kid,</u> what's his moniker?' I assume you remember what you told him that night?"

"Yes," I said, my heart once again beating with vigor in my memory of it. "It was about President Charles, and how pride made him a puppet."

"What you said gave Teddy an extraordinary sense of the free will he possessed for being a president of engaging modesty, as you may recall. Some months after that night, President Charles visited Teddy at the White House; nothing came of that visit except the customary polite animosity, and subsequently Charles went on to the single province of one of our neighboring nations—need I be more specific? As an OOT member, you will learn to be indirect—where the people speak, though with a barbarous accent, Charles' own language. Ultimately, nothing much came of that visit, either, though there is no doubt that Charles was encouraging those people to secede from the government that legally bound them (one that has the good sense to speak in our own fine Unitedian tongue!). He deliberately began to fan some rebellious sparks into the blaze of revolution, for he wanted that province a part of his own colonial domain. As I say, nothing came of that impertinent attempt, for Charles apologized, and no more was ever said. You wouldn't know that your advice to Teddy helped him quench <u>that</u> hot little linguistic fire."

"I had no idea." I was smiling with pleasure, eager to know.

"Teddy got Charles on the phone the moment that bastard returned home. 'Listen, fellow,' he told him, 'you either back down, or I'm calling a press conference to let the world know that while you were at the White House you surreptitiously <u>smoked a cigarette.</u>' A bold lie, Kayo, but it worked! And that's the reason that your name makes Teddy's countenance glow, and the reason that for some years he has been wistfully asking to have you at his elbow. 'Let Kayo grow up first' is what we advised him over and over. And now you have matured, and just in time, thank Allah!"

Well, that's the kernel of the nut, Sid. Having exposed it, I'll give in to your impatience by playing (to change metaphors) a quick game of <u>ducks and drakes,</u> skimming the stone of my life on the surface of the political waters of the next few years so vigorously that I leap completely over the happiness (the tears of joy, etc.) that my reunion with Teddy gave him. As I saw it, my task was a delicate one: to keep Teddy aware enough of who he was so that he would cease pricking his arm like a drug addict while discouraging in him the enthusiasm that might result in any "new" or "wonderful" act.

No doubt you are thinking that this is quite enough for one young man to be worried about, but let me tell you I had other anxieties as well. Remember, if you will, my vow to Dilsey. If I had saved her from one house, I had left her in another that the bank was about to take from her, whatever her valiant effort to pay the monthly mortgage with her pittance of a salary as a fraternity menial. When I apprised "X" of my responsibility to a faithful family servant, he sternly told me that as an OOT member, my past life <u>was a closed book.</u> While this view was wholly in accordance with my eleventh rule of conduct, I have already indicated some petty violations of it, such as my spiriting away of <u>Papa</u>'s portrait, which I had hung in our dingy living room, where I devoutly hoped its radiance would give poor Dilsey some cheer. Would that portrait (the question haunted me) be tossed out with Dilsey and the garbage when the mortgage was foreclosed?

With some distaste, for he disliked any compromise with the rules, "X" told me that an account could be set up for me under an assumed name in a foreign bank, with sums for Dilsey drawn upon it. How much money, he wanted to know, was I willing to put into it? Not until that moment did I learn that OOT members selflessly devote themselves to their country. Except for me, they were all independently wealthy; from their hidden positions of political influence, of course, they were able to see to it that certain corporations whose well-being was of particular concern to them were not forgotten when contracts were being sought, etc. That is to say, OOT members received fringe benefits that I couldn't take advantage of but not the salary I so desperately needed!

A letter added to my misery, one that had been still in my pocket, unopened, at the time "Olga" spilled my carton of eggs on the supermarket floor. Written (with numerous misspellings) by <u>Maman</u>'s aunt Mirabelle from the southern hamlet in which Emmamae had been born, it was a plea for funds from me for various indigent relatives. From that letter, I learned of another instance of dear Papa's benevolence; for years, with never a word of complaint to anybody, he had been supporting a previously undernourished clan of skinny sharecroppers from whose ranks my Maman had been plucked because of her sylphic beauty.

Now, I suppose I could have employed "Olga" or somebody of her ilk as a bloodhound, to sniff out the trail that led to Vladimir, the holder of all the remaining Aznap cash, in order to forward that letter to him; but you now know as well as do I what he would have done with it. One can take a bitter and righteous pleasure in assuming a responsibility that belongs to another; but beyond that, Sid, I really wanted to take over a role assumed so unbegrudgingly by my Papa. Apart from his native shrewdness (you can argue about how effectively he used it), his only legacy to me was a good heart, and I wasn't about to reject that. And I could imagine Maman's smile (on her deathbed or whenever) upon finally learning that not Vladimir but her own son for decades had been the anonymous benefactor of her clan!

Be that as it may, I saw that all of my responsibilities (to Teddy, Dilsey, and now Mirabelle) might be met with a single, clever move. That is to say, conceivably I could make Teddy his old, optimistic self by getting him occupied with some harmless enterprise that would be to the economic advantage of Dilsey and the others, and in some small way to the nation itself. What I had in mind was a federally sponsored corporation that would manufacture items of benefit to the citizenry, particularly to those who lived on farms or country estates. (One's inventiveness, after all, is circumscribed by the nature of one's own experiences. I had already exhausted whatever inventiveness I had gained from my limited experience as landlord in an urban environment.)

Teddy himself had been born on an isolated ranch in one of our largest states, and liked to talk about the goodness of the rural delivery mail carriers, who, in addition to their assigned duties, let ranchers know if their cattle were on the road and sometimes delivered medicine, whiskey, and other necessary supplies. I suggested that he could do a favor to all our deserving rural mailmen as well as to their clientele by insisting upon uniform and resilient posts for the roadside mailboxes, which so often are knocked down by snowplows or careless drivers. The flexible pipes once used for cow stanchions, I told him, were far superior to any of the fancier and far more expensive posts of oak or wrought iron currently on the market; since they no longer could be purchased, why couldn't the government set up a little factory to manufacture them, and then insist on their use by all patrons?[1] I could assure him of a responsible manager and a hardworking labor force, all of them faithful and level-headed Unitedians.

Or, if this idea didn't attract Teddy's interest (it didn't), how about the development of dredges—suction motors with long hoses, equipment portable enough to be transported in the bed of a pickup—to be used to vacuum up seaweed and muck from farm ponds, to prevent them from reverting to nasty little swamps that breed mosquitoes? The material dredged up would be high in nutrients, perfect for truck gardeners to spread on their fields, if not to package as a breakfast cereal full of vitamins and fiber. A bored or unimaginative Teddy put his thumbs down on this appealing concept, too, as if he cared not the slightest for increasing our food supply while pleasing our water-loving native birds (especially swallows and herons) and renewing recreational facilities for swimmers and fishermen.

The only project for which he displayed the slightest concern had the welfare of both city and rural dwellers in mind. It involved the manufacture of sturdy aluminum boxes with a hinged sawtooth lid to hold plastic wrap. Like other Unitedi-

---

[1] Urban readers probably need some clarification about this proposal. I think what Kayo has in mind are flexible hollow pipes with a couple of graceful bends that enable them to extend handily enough to the shoulder of the road, when used as posts for mailboxes. I took one from my own cow barn, employing it for this purpose to thwart the destructive tendencies more of a neighboring farmer who caroused every Saturday night at the psychic's tavern than of any misanthropic snowplow operator. In misjudging his steering around the corner at my crossroads, my neighbor regularly inflicted serious damage both to his pickup and every new wooden post I laboriously installed. After I made the change to the stanchion pipe, he damaged nothing, though sometimes I still am awakened by a gay little clatter as the easily reattachable mailbox pops off its bracket to bound harmlessly over the grass.

ans, Teddy had known the exasperation and humiliating sense of helplessness created within all would-be users of that sticky roll upon the inevitable collapse of its flimsy cardboard container.[2]

But no, not even for such a <u>universally needed</u> venture as this last one would he permit the federal government to enter the sphere reserved for moneymaking by the private sector. You can imagine my indignation, Sid, when "X" and others of the OOT handed these as well as other ideas of mine over to the corporations with which they were connected, and these corporations began to make handsome profits from them!

Sometimes it takes the failure of a succession of ingenious ideas before one comes up with the simple solution that should have been thought up in the beginning. Teddy, as I have said, was born and raised on a ranch; and in nearly every one of his various disguises, a love for horses (mules, in one sorry dissemblance) has been a constant. John bought a ranch, Bob spent vacations on another, the more sophisticated Frank jumped fences in the pursuit of foxes, etc. Too, there exists in our land the tradition that <u>a born leader belongs on horseback.</u> Add to that heady mixture an appeal to patriotism and a request that Teddy himself lead the opening-day parade mounted on his favorite steed, and of course you end up with a theme park like the <u>Kayo Corral!</u> I snitched that bit of land-use area from the waiting grasp of one of "X" 's corporations at the last moment, I can tell you!

Teddy was so gratified by the proposal that he readily agreed to make Dilsey, Mirabelle, and the others of the latter's clan <u>Civil Servants</u>—which meant tenure and pensions and precious little "accountability"—so long as a niche could be found for his cousin Freddy, who had a drinking problem. And so, with a little flourish of his pen, Teddy signed the document that helped to make him content with himself, or

---

[2] Naturally enough, I abhor the deceitful and criminal facets of Kayo's nature; but my intuited belief in the unity that underlies everything within our universe is certainly strengthened by the knowledge that another intelligent being, one many light-years away, could come up with some of the same answers as have I to a few of life's lesser problems.

himselves, and took care not only of Cousin Freddy but of my faithful Dilsey and that small troop of barely literate sharecroppers whose well-being my own expansive heart would not distinguish from my own.

CHAPTER IX. A Jealous Teddy

In musing over what I reported in my last chapter, it occurs to me that you may have gotten the idea that Teddy was, and is, a wimp, except for his victory over President Charles. Nothing can be farther from the facts. While it is true enough that the general disposition of the public, as well as the watchful eyes of his advisers, kept him from accomplishing anything new or wonderful, he was vigorously involved in everything that remained unchanged, like wars and military preparedness.

When he was Frank, he became immensely popular for his verbal assault on monolithic communism, an attack that unified the Assorted States by abetting their respective economies with defense projects, and that innocently led to an unofficial war in support of one of our "friends," that half of a country whose amiably corrupt leaders were trying to resist takeover by the other half, which was led by a well-known patriot and declared Communist. This divided land was so tiny and remote that we were confused as to how to pronounce its name; we ended up calling it Domino, for in Teddy's view that was what it was, a piece of plastic standing on end. As he explained in one of those marvelously persuasive television addresses, using a map and other visual aids, everything spread out on a White House conference table and filmed from an overhead camera, "Here you have monolithic communism," and he placed an open-jawed dragon at the border of Domino, "and here," he went on, pointing to Domino itself and a curving row of other pieces of plastic, "all of the other as yet uncommitted countries of this strategic region. Now, if Domino falls"—and Teddy deftly flicked that piece of plastic with a finger, causing all the rest to topple, the last one right into the mouth of the waiting dragon—"you see what inevitably will happen."

Of course, I was still a child when I viewed this performance on television, but like adult Unitedians I remembered it as a controlled laboratory demonstration of the most convincing sort. Unfortunately, that war was so nasty and prolonged that Teddy's popularity (though he remained as golden-tongued as ever) began to diminish, and, at the advice of his alarmed advisers, he abdicated—that is to say, he got himself reelected as Bob, who had a mandate from the public to end our involvement, something he was finally able to do by declaring that we "had met all our objectives." Actually, he had taken his cue from one of our senior legislators (a man of enough wisdom to be unsuccessfully courted for membership in the OOT), who years earlier had suggested we declare that we had <u>won</u> the war and so could send our troops home. At the time, it seemed such a bitter joke to the public that the advisers, however much the idea appealed to them, had to persuade Teddy to wait before implementing it in the subtler way that he did.

Veteran advisers in any organization dearly love to talk about "the old days" to a neophyte in their midst, and so I heard a great deal about Domino. That particular engagement (it had so exhausted Teddy that it might have had something to do with his flakiness as Oz) had been resolvable by words because it had been occasioned by nothing more than words to begin with. The culprits were <u>monolithic communism</u> and <u>Domino,</u> a lethal mix. "Q" said we should have downplayed the enemy patriot's professed communism, seeing it for what it was, an attempt to get weapons from one of the ASU's most implacable foes, while playing up that patriot's statement (one made early in the conflict) that he desired to use the founding documents of our own democracy as the basis of his new constitution—bold lie though that declaration might have been. Whether true or false, "Q" continued, the enemy leader all along had despised and feared <u>the dragon,</u> which itself felt the same way about <u>the bear:</u> and this was something that he, "Q," had known from the start.

"Hindsight, hindsight," jeered "R," who apparently had

been the most vociferous supporter of the belief that bears and dragons were the same fearsome animal. And hindsight though it undoubtedly also was, every one of those senior OOT members now cursed himself for not advising Teddy at some early point to change the name of the game from <u>dominoes</u> to, say, <u>backgammon</u>—any game, that is, with pieces that can't be balanced on their ends. All of them looked approvingly at me, I'm pleased to tell you, Sid, when I said that since you can't trust any foreigner to be what he says he is, no matter what label he sews on his combat fatigues, why hadn't we called that hotheaded patriot who started the whole mess a <u>Fascist</u> instead of a <u>Communist,</u> thus rendering him harmless, language-wise, to our stated foreign policy and acceptable to Teddy and the voters?

Jaunty as Teddy outwardly seemed, that unfortunate Domino affair, as I have hinted, had aged him, giving him periods of moodiness that even the popular success of something like the Kayo Corral couldn't overcome. It seems to me that in most of his disguises he meant well (this is true of the majority of Unitedians), but that by the time he became Oz he was neurotically dissatisfied by his inability to achieve something <u>new and wonderful</u> for which posterity would remember him, or them. After all, he'd been in office a good long time!

One day Teddy asked me, "What are we going to do about Nod?" That was the first time I'd heard the name mentioned, so of course I thought it to be another of those volatile little Dominolike countries that are off the face of civilized maps. "Nod is a person, Nod is an outlaw," he said irritably. "A madman, a mystic, a damned <u>idealist,</u> for Allah's sake. . . . Oh, forget it, just forget it," he said angrily, as if I had been the one to bring up the name, and then turned his attention to some subversive activities the OOT was proposing as a means of undermining a shaky democracy in our authorized sphere of influence whose recently elected president had been showing some alarming leftist leanings.

I've already revealed to you some remarkable secrets about politics in the Assorted States United, Sid, and in this chapter I have stressed more than I have anywhere else in my text the crucial role that language plays in the decisions we make. We

Unitedians are remarkably optimistic, knowing that when we stumble because of diction our hands may fall on a linguistic nugget of gold—precisely what happened from our Domino misadventure. From that mishap, we learned the impropriety of speaking of <u>monolithic communism,</u> and learned as well that a <u>dragon</u> can be a playful and politically useful creature—in short, a dragon can be a "friend" in the way no bear is likely ever to be.

Teddy may have changed his language, replacing <u>monolithic communism</u> with the phrase <u>the Communist menace,</u> words that refer only to bears and send indignant shivers up and down the collective back of all Unitedians, but here's a secret shared by every member of the powerful Order of the Oval Token since Domino: <u>communism, as an ideology, is as dead as our national bird.</u>[1] Speaking for myself, I can't imagine a country anywhere in our world that would voluntarily put itself into the septic claws of a totalitarian regime like the one that not only your Vladimirs want to escape from! Who in his right mind would opt for censorship, brutal repression, mind-altering drugs or the quick-freeze of exile for the most noble-minded of dissidents, a bureaucracy that gets the cars and color televisions? Who would want to join a populace so depressed that, to prevent mass intoxication, vodka is rationed to them, drop by drop?

Now, what may surprise you—my final shocker—is that such staunch exponents of conservative time as the OOT would actively search for ways to breathe life into an ideology in rigor mortis; but consider what would happen to our <u>unity of purpose</u> and patriotism, not to mention our prosperity, without such an ideological opponent. What would be the fate of his advisers as well as of Teddy himself? Perhaps you can begin to understand, then, the calculations underlying a foreign policy for lands in our sphere of influence that supports despots and the unjust distribution of wealth, and that destabilizes whatever economy these poor lands have by keeping the value of our own money so high their governments can't even meet the interest payments on their debts to us—doing all this, mind you, while showing horror at any genuine

[1]The forgetful reader may wish to consult chapter 1, note 3.

attempt to control population growth on the part of these "developing" countries as an undemocratic and <u>antilife</u> solution. We do take a deliberate risk, I admit, in forcing every one of these nations to perceive communism as a still-tenable, if desperate, ideological possibility, but our sense of "balance" and stability makes the risk worth taking, of course. It strikes me as curious that nobody outside of the OOT, so far as I know, has discovered this most reasonable explanation of a foreign policy that so works to the disadvantage of its apparent intent (i.e., to smack down the well-known "menace"), but there you have it, crystal-clear.

Enough of such matters, which may both weary you and strain your credulity—that is, if you're at all like our stubborn Teddy, whose thoughts during my early years as an OOT member moodily strayed from <u>the Communist menace</u> to nothing more substantial than the obscure Nod, and then back. "Have you done anything about him?" he sharply asked me one afternoon, while we were having crackers and beer.

"Who?"

"Nod, of course."

"What would you like me to do, Teddy?"

He evaded the question. "That—that <u>do-gooder,</u>" he exploded. "He may be a Communist, for all we know. What does he do but make simple folk unhappy with things as they are? Pie in the sky, a goody-goody world of brother-and-sisterhood, that's what he's after."

"What's he against?"

"The same old clichés of malcontents! He's against ghettos and acid rain and nuclear weapons—even <u>war itself.</u> Do you know what I think?" Teddy paused, giving me a wary look. "I think that oddball thinks <u>he</u> can make things <u>new and wonderful.</u>" And then, as if this fact made Nod my personal responsibility, "He's from your part of the country, you ought to know."

"Why not appoint him to a blue-ribbon commission to study at length one of the issues he raises?"

"Oh, come on, Kayo, that's how we handle somebody who already has visibility! Naw, I wouldn't want to give an unknown troublemaker all that publicity. Let a sleeping dog die, is my philosophy."

"Die?"

"Whatever put *that* ugly thought into your head, my sweet boy?"

To think that kindly Teddy was becoming so jealous of some crazy peasant that he wanted him dead! This was a matter for the gravest deliberation by the OOT, and I resolved at once to call the members into one of our closed sessions—which, of course, means, since the body is secret to begin with, that Teddy himself had to be denied admission. To prepare myself for that session, I called for everything about the peasant Nod that our DSP files contained. In other words, my dear Sid, your curiosity (or at least some of it) is about to be met with some most interesting details.

CHAPTER X. *The Nod File*

The file I received was thicker than my own narrative promises to be, and consisted of information obtained by interviews, the study of old newspapers for any reference to Nod or his family members, and whatever interesting data (they were minimal) that disguised DSP agents had stumbled upon, or over. Photocopies of the handwritten reports of the latter were included, and one of them I judged as probably the work of the fetching but maladroit "Olga." All of this material had already been sent to Teddy, the contents of the file being summarized for him by our DSP chief, P. Eureka! Electrolux[1]— he whose sweeping investigations into various dark and unsavory corners of Unitedian life had led to the rumor that he had a light bulb in his ever-buzzing head. As you will soon find out, Sid, PEE apparently had collected the dirt on Teddy's various identities. Here we have an explanation of the

---

[1] According to Kayo (who perhaps shouldn't be trusted), the exclamation point after "Eureka" was added by a proud young PEE (Kayo's shorthand for the absurd name), then a "private eye," following his discovery of evidence substantial enough to permit him to extort handsome sums from his own wealthy client.

otherwise puzzling fact that this disreputable detective has been in charge of our undercover work almost as long as Teddy has been president—a tenure achieved in his case without a single alteration (alas, for <u>any</u> change would have been an improvement) of name or image.[2]

You might be interested in knowing, Sid, that the tool of the <u>summary,</u> whether provided by PEE or the OOT, is a significant means of influencing our preoccupied president, since it contains the only words he is likely to scan on any given issue. I present <u>in toto</u> the summary of the Nod file that PEE (so fawning to his superiors, so arrogant to his hired help) prepared for Teddy:

Dear "Oz,"[3]
Here's the dope you wanted on that little spick. Let me say at the start that the accurate and efficient work displayed by my agents in tracking down this obscure peasant, Nod (actual name, Michael or Miguel Quexana, sometimes spelled Quixada or Quesada), gives the lie to the self-serving attack made on them by the greenhorn member of your private staff. You may personally have signed that "directive," but I know its actual author. "Oz," I deeply resent your permitting him to go over my head in sending his smug orders to my agents. Who in hell does he think he is, making my trained employees take acting and language classes as if our dangerous but essential work was like some play put on by college kids? Here's another example of that confusion over authority

[2]Is Kayo as jealous of PEE as Teddy is of Nod and (judging from the contents of his summarizing letter) PEE himself is of Teddy and Kayo? Or does our hero actually sense a moral superiority to the DSP chief? Vituperation often proceeds from a mixture of motives, I suppose.

[3]As Kayo pointed out to me, the quotation marks around the nickname can be interpreted to mean one of two things: either (1) the obsequious PEE wants Teddy to realize that he's not certain he should be on such familiar terms with the highest official in the government, or (2) the crafty PEE wants Teddy to know that he's aware of the counterfeit nature of that name. "A typical stratagem by that conniving _____," Kayo said. I delete a scatological noun presented without quotation marks.

that has made me beg you again and again to elect me to your "secret" advisory body—whose "concealed" name, by the way, as well as the identity of every one of its members, is known to me.

As for the spick, that prying idiot has obtained the genealogies of practically everybody of influence and power in the government. You are correct in believing that he has spread malicious reports about your ancestors—though you have nothing to worry about on this score. He traces your "Baum" family line[4] back to Attila the Hun and declares you to be the third cousin of President Charles of Gaul. One of his occult symbols (dismiss his allegations, "Oz," as the work of a real nut) is the diamond shape, and in staring at it he declares that everybody is descended from frogs, kikes, spicks, wops, sharecropping niggers, white trash, etc. (For his version of your "genealogy," as well as those of your recent "predecessors," see appendix.)

As for the genealogy of said Subject himself, my agents have found it impossible to discover his nonspick ancestors, though in cases like this you can be 99.44% sure of some nigger or wop impurities. What I'm saying is that he was born out of wedlock to unknown parents, one or both of whom dumped him on the "doorstep" of his unmarried great-aunt, one Miss Habersham or Havisham (in either case, a WASP name, maybe an alias), who has lived all her life—obviously from perverse inclination, since ours is a free and prosperous country—in a cave on top of Mount Sinos in a wild region of our Lake District (see appendix for map). She is ninety years old (a rough estimate) and ekes out a living from her herd of goats, the pittance she receives as caretaker of a chapel, and possibly from potions she makes from herbs and bark

[4]So "Oz" is a "Baum," another bizarre linkage (see chapter 1, note 6) between Kayo's text and writers of my own Finger Lakes region! L. Frank Baum, the author of The Wonderful World of Oz and other titles too numerous to mention, was born in the peaceful town of Chittenango, N.Y., whose downtown sidewalks are paved with yellow bricks. Will there someday be at least a historical marker at my crossroads to identify my farmhouse as that of the scribe of the present work?

for the gullible peasants of that remote region, who consider her a <u>witch.</u> (Her vicious billy goats kept my agents from interviewing her.)

Miss H. and her goats having long ago had the good sense (or so the neighbors gossip) to butt him out of their cave, Subject is presently roaming about that general region. One of the half-dozen female agents staked out in the countryside, cleverly disguised as tattered shepherdesses in search of their lost flocks (this whole operation, "Oz," has put our budget out of whack: I trust the costs [see itemized expenditures in table "B"] will come from your discretionary funds), actually made contact on three occasions with said elusive Subject, but only in a visual and verbal—i.e., not physically intimate—sense. (Probable reason for lack of luck here: the spick is a portly little fellow of advanced years.) From her report (see section 2) you will note that he travels about on an equally elderly horse (some funny-looking binoculars hanging by a strap from his <u>not overclean</u> neck), and has a second pack animal loaded down with what seem to be chiefly books, perhaps taken from his office at the time he was fired from his post as a professor of literature at the "prestigious" nearby university. (Were you to add me to the membership of the elite OOT, "Oz," we might have some profitable discussions about what we ought to do about universities that hire such fruitcakes, as well as about the federal welfare that permits unsuitable peasants not only <u>to grow up</u> but to secure for themselves the "education" they then inflict upon the young.)

According to the chairperson (how I detest the "fair sex" legislation you refused to veto that makes me use that term!), dean, and provost whom my agents interviewed, said Subject was terminated for being a general nuisance and for not keeping up with the research in his field. Apparently in his later years he wore disreputable clothes (jeans and cowboy boots, for example) and began to use <u>classroom time</u> either for sermons about the stars or harangues against the "new research" and administrators in general.

I have included (see attached exhibit "A") a copy of

one of these works of "new research" that allegedly drove Subject to madness, since it may include a clue to all of his harebrained attacks on your policies. Our best cryptographer can't break the code: handle with care, it may be subversive stuff, even though Subject abhorred it. Indeed, material like this apparently continues to make Subject paranoid enough to believe there are enchanters at large in the world, including (believe it or not!) me as well as you. He is convinced that these enchanters deliberately are attempting to prevent him from ever again seeing anything sacred or universally true. (For his allegations against you and the new research, see sections 3, 4, 5, 6, 7, 8, and parts of 10 and 14, as well as enclosed cassette of a speech beginning, "Beware! A dark and sticky molasses now is spreading thickly, o'er our green and generous land," made before a handful of students from a tree stump at the entrance to the Student Union.)

Yes, much as you surmised, "Oz," said Subject over and over again has pronounced you a phony wizard, one incapable of ever achieving anything either new or wonderful; but what do you have to fear—at least from him? (I believe you will sleep peacefully from the moment you have the good sense to elect me to the OOT.) Forget your spick-nigger-wop! He already has "fallen off the ladder," as his female chairperson cheerfully said. This cracked Humpty Dumpty and self-proclaimed outlaw no doubt raves as he roams the wilderness, but whose ear would be receptive to his mad messages? It is true enough that one of our "shepherdesses" got a slap in the face from a gap-toothed peasant bitch (a Polack?) simply for trying to find out if it was true that said Subject had stolen one of the bitch's chickens—but can you truly be serious in thinking this kind of loyalty to a thieving bonehead is the beginning of a rebellion against your rule?

Except for the last resort, the DSP is helpless to do anything to silence this mixed-breed degenerate who so offends you. He's not violated the law (except perhaps in the matter of the missing chicken). What good would it do for the DSP to invent scandalous rumors about him if nobody cares and his actual behavior is the real scandal?

My long experience as your DSP chief lets me know that those in the public eye are the ones I can nail, not the mangy mongrels who piss low on the totem pole. How about dealing me in, at the next poker session?

Your fellow public servant,
P. EUREKA!

P.S. Tell that mangy Aznap I'm countermanding "your" so-called "directive."

"Well, boys," I said at the closed session of the OOT, after reading this summary aloud, "this smells like a kettle of ripe fish! An enchanted peasant, an insanely jealous Teddy, and a mutinous and blackmailing P. Eureka!! Do you suppose we can ever put a tight lid on all of that?"

Prologue to Part Two

Beguiled by Kayo's story, anxiously awaiting the shrewd solution or solutions he obviously will be proposing for the triple-headed problem that the Order of the Oval Token must solve to maintain the fixity of conservative time so necessary for the well-being and national purpose of all Unitedians, the reader may be upset by the arbitrary break in the narrative at this point. No doubt he or she is asking, "Did Kayo himself make this peculiar separation of his manuscript into two parts?"

My answer: "No, the decision is mine alone!"

I hear a chorus of baffled or enraged voices: "Why? Or why here? Kayo hasn't even reached the suspenseful moment in his own life with which he artfully began his narrative, the 'narrative hook' at the Kayo Corral that concludes with his own apparent death."

Each member of that chorus will probably find further justification for outrage in my frank admission that the break angered Kayo himself. We can tell that he has found it difficult to face up to the horror of his murder of Nod, even though his compulsive need to confess to that act of ultimate betrayal must be accounted as the prime psychological reason for his decision to respond to Professor Duck's extraterrestrial entreaties. (Recall, if you will, Kayo's first brief message, snared by me.) How he has teased us with "what is yet to come," while standing before the mirror, boasting of his good looks and accomplishments! No doubt such an ego buildup has been necessary for him. And now, having finally broken through his mental block with a cunning stratagem (I refer to his use of a surrogate, the narrow-minded and duplicitous DSP chief, to introduce the basic facts about his beloved Nod), how eager he is to purge himself, to talk, talk, talk! My readers will remember how patiently I had to coax him into communication with me, and how, at a later moment, I feared that in his petulance he would sever all contact; but at last, aha!, the reverse is true.

For the moment, then, let him remain no more than what my computer manual calls a "flashing cursor" [sic], a transparent oblong running nakedly up and down and across my screen, his frantic obscenities transformed into little beep, beeps that can't harm the most sensitive and old-fashioned of sensibilities! Meanwhile, I will explain to all concerned the reasons I simply had to take a break.

As my reader knows, I am a beleaguered senior professor. In transcribing PEE's summary of the Nod file, I made no self-conscious notations regarding certain suspicious similarities between ex-Professor Nod and me. (I'm glad to say our dwellings have little in common. Haven't I already shown my delighted surprise at the resemblance between my house and the handsome one that Kayo inexcusably burned down? However messy it gets, it is unfair to describe my Greek revival farmhouse as a "cave.") But the reader can guess how wary I became, as I transcribed other details of PEE's summary that conceivably might apply to me, if only through hints and insinuations. I was not overly bothered by any oblique aspersions cast upon my intelligence or attire or to casual references to assorted goats, horses, and even a witch, for these could have been sly embellishments to the text made by my playful Kayo. What did cause me to sniff a possible rat were the apparent allusions to the "new research" that had led me, only moments before I intercepted the words for Professor Duck on a historic night, to search so desperately into the heavens for a transcendent sign.

I am no more paranoid than Kayo, but the thought occurred to me that the poststructuralists themselves, whose theories about words provide them with a principled refusal to honor the integrity of any text, might well have been tampering with the narrative. My reasoning was twofold. First, I found it wildly improbable that such a peculiar or exotic philosophical infection as that at the core of the "new research" could have extended into the remoter regions of our expanding universe. (Alas, as the reader will discover to his alarm in part two, it has so spread, and may indeed have something to do—though this is mere speculation on my part—with those terrifying "black holes.") Second, I was keenly aware that the skepticism of all poststructuralists—especially of the Derrideans, with the "radical chic" of their cultural alienation—can turn them into cruel jokesters at the innocent thud of anybody else's dropped cliché. It struck me as a horrifying possibility that Kayo's entire manuscript was an elaborate hoax, one played upon me to make my personal idealism, my belief that life and texts alike possess spiritual meaning, look foolish.

I am not of your humble sort that accepts ridicule or a practical joke with a self-deprecatory grin. I may not get as violent as Kayo, but I certainly can feel anger, especially when it may be justified! The first thing I did was to cut the telephone-line communication between my Rainbow and the central university computer, and to look for any wires or peculiar transmission devices that didn't belong on my console. (Had that white-uniformed repairman been a deconstructionist?) Then I took advantage of the break to read everything I could readily find about the "new research," for, as the reader will remember, I had quickly reacted to it with righteous indignation, but perhaps without the full knowledge that cautious people require before making heartfelt indictments.

My intuitive responses come right out of my psyche, not my "gut," and are always correct; my first reaction was on target. And in carefully reviewing Kayo's story up to this point, and comparing it with what I had learned from my painful study of this recondite material, I could find nothing in the narrative capable of being construed as a subtle support of the "new research." I affirm this view, however much some of the characters (Teddy, in particular) would seem to favor or to illustrate the single adage to bear the deconstructionists' seal of approval as an acceptable "universal truth"—namely, <u>Qui nescit dissimulare nescit regnare</u> (He who does not know how to dissimulate does not know how to rule).

Now I turn to another matter that also gave me pause. In speaking of Nod's actual name or names as well as of his "enchantment," PEE makes the first clear references to the enchanted Spanish knight of that Earthly text that is mirrored, in however distorted a form, on Kayo's planet and within his own story. Readers of the present work whose lives have been enriched by Cervantes' masterpiece will recall that the prologue to <u>his</u> second part begins with a well-deserved obloquy of the author of a counterfeit <u>Don Quixote,</u> a writer of lesser talent who thought to make some cash from the popularity of the first part of the genuine article by cranking out a second part before the authentic author (or his authorized scribe) had his ready for the expectant public. (Cervantes' scribe, the ever-resourceful Cid Hamete Benengeli, gives the impudent imitator his comeuppance by having a minor character from the fraudulent work enter the true second part to confess that he and his fellows are nothing but phonies.) Never will I cease to be amazed by the seeming "coincidences" that bind lives, both past and present, on our planet (and, as Kayo's story so nobly implies, elsewhere in the universe) into one unity! By the time that <u>Kayo: The Authentic and Annotated Autobiographical Novel from Outer Space</u> is on the stands, the public's curiosity in extraterrestrial contact may already have been satiated by the appearance of, and attendant well-orchestrated publicity for, a book about such matters by that younger and perhaps more famous colleague of Professor Duck. I refer, of course, to Professor Carl Billions, prolific writer, television personality, activist for good causes, and sometime astronomer. Do you know that in the final "Note" to his book he acknowledges the help received from (among others whom I have met) <u>Professor Duck himself?</u>

I hasten to say that I'm not impugning Professor Billions in any way; it is clear that his <u>blockbuster</u> will lend further credence to his famous name. While it is possible that he had heard rumors of my project (it is hard to keep secrets within my university), I am willing to believe his statement, found in that same "Note," that he got the idea for his work as far back as 1980—that is to say, long before Kayo and I began our collaboration. (Why, though, does he insist on publishing this "fact"?) I can only hope that readers will make a judicious comparison of his text with mine, with reference to what each promises and delivers. How much extraterrestrial "contact" does Professor Billions actually present to us? I've given his book a hasty reading during this break, and can tell you the answer, if you don't already know: precious little!

I'll tell you where Professor Billions goes wrong. He spends so much time trying to demonstrate the ingenious equations and equipment a scientist would need to dream up in order to capture a message, to decrypt it, and finally to build a kind of space chariot according to its specifications, that he doesn't have sufficient space left for much more than a brief frolic by his Argonauts (Auriganauts?) on what seems a typical Caribbean beach, though we are to believe (perhaps) that this sunny stretch of sand lies at the very center of the galaxy. Like Kayo in trying to help Dilsey and Teddy as well as Mirabelle and her clan, Professor Billions invents complicated solutions for his problems—instead of discovering (as did I) that a little home computer is perfectly adequate for receiving an extraordinarily informative narrative across the immensity of space, and that any cosmetics mirror will serve as a handy decoding device.

Let me admit that he's one-up on me by having a beautiful and intelligent <u>woman</u> as his protagonist. (For icing on his cake, he has another female serve as president of our country.) But does he ever show the slightest insight into the degree to which life elsewhere reflects our own? No. Does he know anything about how they measure time elsewhere? No. Does he know that so-called alien intelligences read versions, however garbled, of <u>Don Quixote</u> and other texts—no doubt including his own, for which he will get no royalties? Again, no. Is he aware of the frightening pervasiveness of poststructuralist thought throughout the universe? Of course not; and the reason for all his ignorance can be found in the admission that Professor Billions finally is forced to make, one that undermines our very confidence in his entire enterprise. That is to say, he confesses (however indirectly) that he <u>made everything up.</u> Need I say more?.

PART TWO

CHAPTER I. *Kayo the Problem-Solver*

"Nobody has ever <u>blackmailed</u> his way into our group," "R" said, following my reading of PEE's summary. He looked from member to member of our little assemblage. "To the best of my knowledge, that is." He paused. "However, that might explain how some of us were appointed." He gave "Q" a lengthy and suspicious stare. "At least I know that <u>my</u> election was aboveboard."

"Q" 's sky-blue eyes widened and he half raised an arm in protest, the closest approximation to hostility or resentment his "body language" was capable of. He was the single environmentalist and "dove" in our group, chosen to give the balance of an opposing view. It was a role, like any other; and, though outvoted on every issue, he accepted his inevitable defeats with sweetness. "It wasn't I who got us into the Domino box," that aristocratically long-nosed honeysucker reminded "R" in his ever-agreeable voice.

"Gentlemen, gentlemen," the bearded "X," always the moderator, admonished. "We are a dedicated, unified, and (with certain exceptions, made at Teddy's own insistence)"—here he looked at me with obvious approval, for already I had become recognized as everybody's fecund "idea" man—"a self-perpetuating group. Yes, not a soul ever has managed to use a threat to bully his way into our midst, and nobody ever must be permitted to."

"But what other options do we have?" "Q" asked reasonably. "If Electrolux does possess the secret of Teddy's identity—"

"Which one of us has been loose-mouthed?" "R" asked angrily. "Was it you, Kayo? You're the newest member! Were you boasting to a girl friend who just might have been a DSP stool?"

"Come off it," I said. "I'm an Aznap."

"Maybe you are and maybe you're not," "R" said.

I flushed. "What do you mean by that?"

"Maybe Electrolux has bagged some stuff on you as well as on Teddy to use whenever he needs another dirty pile for his vaulting ambitions. Doesn't his summary hint that you're a mangy mongrel? Who knows what he's picked up about all of us, for that matter? In my opinion, this is a case that requires the last resort."

Oh, Sid, I had the answers to all the problems raised by PEE's summary, and it was perverse of me to let them wrangle for half an hour! But how they went on, much to my amusement! I mean, wondering how to employ the last resort against the DSP chief, since the DSP itself was and is the agency we traditionally employ to rid ourselves of pesky individuals at home or abroad. "R," our hawkiest hawk (one particularly nasty rumor has it that though his lungs are not diseased he can cough up blood at will), suggested that we hire the Mafia. That remedy reminded "Q" and others of numerous blunders made under joint OOT-DSP authorization by such unsavory "hit men"—for example, the notorious "poison pen" caper some years previously that had intensified rather than eliminated the bellicosity of the despot of a petty but nearby Communist state. Anyway, as "X" remarked, what was the point of replacing one blackmailer with a grandfather and his whole blackmailing family? "All right, Kayo," "X" then said, having finally noticed that I had been silent, a smug smile on my face, during all the furor, "what's the obvious solution to this mess?"

"Well," I answered, "let's handle the easiest part of it first—I mean Teddy's unease, the psychological state that has provoked his seemingly unwarranted jealousy of an obscure peasant. For some time, his heart and possibly his mind have been the battleground for two contradictory desires, both of which may mean more to him than does life itself. You tell us"—and here I nodded encouragingly at "R"—"what you think the more important of these desires to be."

"Though the fickle public may be forgetting, every sensible person <u>ought</u> to know the correct answer," "R" gruffly responded. "It's to maintain the integrity of conservative time—to keep everything from the chaos of change."

"Do you agree with that, 'Q'?" I asked. "Do you feel this is the more important of Teddy's warring desires?"

"Well, no, not really," "Q" said, with an embarrassed glance at "R." "What I've really admired about Teddy, especially in recent years—I mean, what wins my complete loyalty—is his desire to do something <u>new and wonderful.</u>"

"What we see from these two competing responses within our own microcosm," I lectured eloquently to the attentive group (when the golden-voiced Teddy finally has to quit, it would be hard to imagine a more fitting successor than I), "suggests that this Nod fellow just may be on to something, with his speech about molasses and the like. Things have gone on unchanged for a long time now, as we know they should and indeed must; but habit can make Teddy and the public alike forget how good they have it. I suppose from childhood on most people would like something <u>new and wonderful</u> to happen, at least now and then. What one quixotic revolutionary proclaims in his madness today, a whole people may proclaim as the truth tomorrow. So what I propose is a two-pronged attack, one to buttress <u>things as they are</u> and the other to give Teddy and the public that piece of candy so favored by 'Q.' To do both at once will, of course, release Teddy from his jealous mind-set, and Nod can return to obscurity."

Well may you ask, Sid, how one goes about making people value anew what they've complacently lived with for decades; the problem, though, is less difficult than it seems. I spoke first of the recently instituted but already highly popular Kayo Corral, and how that theme park—a tribute to the grand myth of our past, upon which our patriotism still depends—had at least temporarily mollified Teddy and brought more revenues than expected into our needy federal purse. And then I made to the OOT the proposal that was to win (as did the other prong of my attack) Teddy's enthusiastic approval, and ultimately the plaudits of every television anchorman in the land. Sometimes at night, Sid, I feel a rankling in my gullet (perhaps a human failing, one shared even by you!) that my contributions to my country must of necessity be presented to the public at large as the contributions of some-body else; but never mind.

As Teddy gradually put my first proposal into operation, piece by piece over the years, it worked like magic! What I suggested was that we turn representative examples of "things as they are" into model theme parks. That is to say, we should put fences around everything that malcontents like this Nod conceivably might complain about; then we should charge admission at the various gates, and have guided tours of ghettos, disposal dumps with their leaky fluids, wilderness areas with their dead lakes and leafless trees, depressed farming regions, brothel districts, conservative-time think tanks, and so on (as some fresh challenge to the status quo arose), ad infinitum. If you think that the people who got stared at—those in the ghettos or on the farms, for example—resented the intrusion, you need to think again! It was the first time that anybody outside had paid them any attention, you see; and since they split among themselves a percentage of the gate, Teddy got nothing but rousing applause for finding a way to help them that not only rigorously eschewed federal welfare but gave the "downtrodden" pride in what they were. "Q" was the first member of the OOT to be won over completely, for he was worried that the church he and only a few others faithfully attended was "losing its sense of mission" and saw its salvation as one of the theme parks. How eagerly the public paid the steep ticket price, for guiltless peeks into a series of bordellos, say—or for a guided and completely safe tour through a picturesquely ravished ghetto, where one could watch drunken brawls, wars between competing adolescent street gangs, the theft and disassembly into parts of shiny new cars, and see somebody get his "fix"! Naturally enough, all of these events soon became expertly staged by the participants to give them greater drama than you would ever find in the simple exigencies of life itself. With considerable pleasure I tell you that this easily-arrived-at solution made us one nation in a way we never had been before.

My second proposal was harmonious with the first, since it too involved a kind of "fence," though in this case the whole country became the patriotic "theme park." I suggested—hold on to your own little hard hat, Sid!—an immense bell jar or protective "dome" for our nation, one impregnable against any nuclear missile that <u>the Bear</u> might toss at it. Given your wildest imaginings, can you think of anything newer or more wonderful than that? I mean, no more plans for moving whole populations about in the six minutes' time we'd have during a red alert, no more silly nightmares for our children, everybody's home a room in the same safe castle! Your most inventive Disney never dreamed up such a fantastic park, the theme, of course, being the <u>absolute security</u> that modern know-how and state-of-the-art technology can give us!

Until he saw that pint-sized foreign agents bearing bombs in suitcases might still wiggle under that dome along with other illegal immigrants, and that there were lots of other ways for one nation to do in another if it put its mind to it (noxious germs and gases, poisons in the watersheds, etc.), "R" grumbled at the "radical" nature of a proposal that might do away with war itself. After a time it dawned on him that, as a spin-off to the proposal, certain corporations he was fond of might be engaged in the development of exotic military hardware. Actually, the more he <u>thought</u> about it, the more enthusiastic a supporter of it he became! "R" even seconded "X"'s suggestion that "Q" be the one to brief Teddy on it (I didn't mind: Teddy would know the originating brain) and to "get the nation moving" toward its implementation. "Q"'s own gratitude was contagious; soon we were all our happy little family again—happier, alas, than my childhood family ever had been. How I wished my dear Papa—always a generous dispenser of those gleaming Aznap-Cola slugs, never honored with one himself—could have joined me at that instant, so that we could have had a "dad and son team" aboard the OOT!

Indeed, the group became so ecstatic over this two-pronged way to go that it forgot entirely (until I reminded my giddy colleagues) that our most serious problem—the black-mailing Electrolux—remained. The key to this particular dilemma, I said, possibly lay in the DSP chief's own words. I held his letter aloft, tapping it significantly. We already knew, I went on, that Electrolux was a bigot of the most despicable sort; but it seemed to me that this letter contained a greater number of racial and ethnic slurs than we normally would have expected, even from him. And how did we account for what clearly was his sudden obsession with genealogies? I reminded my auditors of that perhaps unguarded moment in his letter in which Electrolux had called Nod a "prying idiot" in possession of "the genealogies of practically everybody of influence and power"—a category to which the DSP chief would feel that he himself belonged, and quite near to the top. He had included a number of Nod's genealogical tables in the appendix, while omitting the one for his own family. One could say, of course, that the Electrolux family line was irrelevant to the matter at hand. And yet could we not infer, from our own familiarity with the boastful nature of the chief detective, that had it contained any illustrious progenitors (even so dubious a one as Attila the Hun) the Electrolux table would have been given? A reasonable hypothesis would be that he was ashamed of what Nod had uncovered about his ancestors—and that his insistence on the dubious validity of Nod's genealogical research was a consequence of his own perhaps hysterical desire to deny what he knew to be true.

I told my rapt audience that my conjectures would never have taken this direction had not I always wondered what the P. in P. Eureka! Electrolux stood for. In this summary to Teddy, the initial of the signature seemed scrawled with such haste or guilt to be almost illegible. Had he, I wondered, ever revealed to any one of them what his first name actually was?

"Never," whispered "X," and the rest nodded their solemn concurrence.

"Well, then, I'm sure we're on to something big here," I exclaimed. I pointed out that no man alive disregards the first name his parents gave him at birth (often one that honors a father or a grandfather) unless he is ashamed of it; in the case in question, the first name had to be especially humiliating or repugnant for its recipient to find <u>Eureka</u> (either with or without the exclamation mark) a preferable choice. Were we to discover <u>nothing more than that name,</u> we probably could blackmail that rascally blackmailer into lifelong silence. Since it was likely that Nod's genealogical table of the Electrolux family included this name among its other secrets, and since that peasant was lurking about in the wilderness of a region of our country that I (having spent my formative years within it) knew better than most, I would seek him out and secure at whatever cost all the information I could. (I didn't add that I also was intensely curious to find out what Nod knew about my own parentage!)

Would I be chasing a "will-o'-the-wisp," as "R"—still opting for his <u>final solution</u>—contemptuously referred to my quest? Of course, having approved my other proposals, especially the last, "R" (out of regard for me) had to agree to this one, too, however lily-livered he felt it to be. "May Allah go with you," "Q" said, and the group piously bowed its respective heads in a prayer for my success.

Sid, my joy in the shrewdness of everything I said on this day makes me here bypass all the vicissitudes of my pursuit of Nod to reach the moment I first caught sight of him before his flickering campfire. I propel you so violently forward in my story because at the instant I saw Nod I also saw somebody else engaged in an action that proved how correct I had been in deducing that Nod indeed possessed a dire secret about PEE. As I burst through a thicket to greet Nod, I saw "Olga," now a grimy and bedraggled shepherdess, step out from behind a similar bush, her eye at a telescopic sight, her finger on the trigger of a rifle aimed at Nod's upside-down[1] heart.

---

[1] The next chapter explains this curious adjective.

No further proof was needed not only that Nod possessed that secret, but that the yellow PEE would do everything in the power of his clandestine agency to keep it from my grasp.

"Stop!" I screamed,[2] the word lost in the crack made as the bullet began its journey toward a target it obviously couldn't miss, since the cross hairs of the magnified eyepiece that "Olga" was squinting through were but twenty feet from her intended victim. As I say, I am precipitate in my telling of this event, and so will withhold what actually happened until the following chapter. But how singular that an obscure peasant should be central to the thoughts of our president, his entire body of advisers, and the head of the powerful Democratic Security Police! And that I, who now would save Nod, in the end was destined (oh, my sad, old refrain) to kill him!

CHAPTER II. A *Secret Revealed and* *a Memorable Embrace*

"Stop!" I screamed, but too late, since (as I've already reported) the bullet was speeding toward its target. Although he never realized it, Nod even more than I had reason to be grateful for four lucky contingencies: (1) "Olga" 's lack of expertise as a sharpshooter (thank Allah I'd not sent the DSP agents to a school for marksmen: had "Olga" taken but one lesson before PEE countermanded my directive she still might have drilled Nod); (2) Nod's own clumsiness at his athletic exercises; (3) a hot coal that had popped out of the campfire; and (4) the presence of a skunk.[1] In my hurry to include this

[2] The very cry that Kayo made in his own darkened house, while attempting to prevent what he took to be the apparition of his father from killing himself all over again. Kayo, I would say from these two examples, has good impulses, and in my personal opinion has the most compelling of reasons for the murder that so haunts him. But (even more than Kayo himself at this moment) I am in advance of our story.

[1] Kayo had some worries about the inclusion of the skunk, and I agreed

attempt at assassination in the previous chapter, I neglected to mention that Nod had stripped off his trousers and underwear for greater freedom of motion, and, clothed only in his shirt, was practicing somersaults and headstands near the warmth of his fire, with a number of chipmunks, a pair of raccoons, and (yes) that single skunk as his audience. Just as the rifle cracked, he lost his balance on his head, and so tumbled upon his back, one fat buttock landing by chance on the displaced coal.

In her desperate squinting through the telescopic sight, "Olga" could not have seen me, unless she was walleyed; nor could she have heard my cry, which (as I've also reported) was one with the explosion. Nod's tumble and consequent cries of pain and outrage must have convinced her that she had accomplished her mission, unseen, and she vanished back into the dark, the haste of her retreat probably unaffected by the sudden new fragrance in the air. (That skunk was closer to "Olga" than were the chipmunks or for that matter the pair of raccoons. And yet—however much it contributed to the <u>ambiance</u> of the moment—I seriously doubt that the skunk sprayed her. Even if it did, "Olga" was as responsible an agent as her ability and experiences permitted her to be. Would she, then, have permitted an effusion, no matter how pungent, to distract her?) At first, I too believed the bullet had struck, and ran to offer what succor I could, waiting only for the odor to disperse. (Actually, it seemed to leave almost as quickly as did "Olga.") Nod had rebounded with such vigor from the offending coal that he was staggering about on his feet before I reached him.

"I don't believe we've met," he said, rubbing his rump

with him that four lucky circumstances <u>did</u> stretch my belief. "You are thinking of my opus as a work of fiction," Kayo responded. "Recollect, my dear Sid, that since life frequently contains what is implausible in mere fiction, the use here of a fourth circumstance by a writer as talented and as careful of detail as I not only is proof enough of the authenticity of this event, but is an artistic means of gaining in advance the reader's assent to further adventures that belong <u>more to life as we know it</u> than to the imaginative fluff of a dreamer." Still, the way in which he downplays in the following pages the obviously crucial role played by a "real-life" skunk suggests the unresolved doubts of a person who is at once consummate artificer and truth teller.

with one hand while examining his binoculars for damage with the other (for he had not removed their strap from his neck while exercising). "Would you like a cup of java?" he asked cordially, waving the binoculars in the direction of the pot steaming on the coals. "You're a bit late for dinner, you know."

"Shhhhhh," I warned at length, for his voice was so hearty I feared it might carry to "Olga" 's ears; I could still hear the sound of her constant coughing (a kind of retching) and of thickets crackling before her blind rush, followed by a faint obscenity as she apparently collided with a rock or tree in the dark. "Olga" was obviously not one of your cold-blooded and disciplined assassins, who make sure of their success by pumping shot after shot into their downed and writhing victims. (As a general principle, I would say that Unitedians— who by and large go to Sunday school as kiddies, at least on religious holidays; are chiefly instructed by our public education system in the virtues of the tolerance mandated by the very nature of our democratic society; and visit their white-haired grandmothers in the nursing homes, to celebrate the old folks' birthdays—don't relish shooting people in ambush, even when it's required, as part of their job. Moral squeamishness, then, far more than the happenstance of a skunk in the vicinity, accounts for the fact that "Olga" never ascertained whether or not her single shot had inflicted a mortal injury. Isn't her retching the clinching proof of my point?)

Nod gave me a puzzled look. If you can believe it, Sid, that <u>old fart</u> (I use the term affectionately, and indeed often called him O.F. right up to the end) didn't even know he had been shot at! It was my first insight into how oblivious he could be to the dangers about him, or for that matter to anything that might violate his innocent belief in human kinship. On this occasion, he took my warning to lower his voice to be a prudish hiss of rebuke for his state of undress. "Oh, I say," he said in alarm, an odd but old-fashioned expression that meant (as I was to discover) he had nothing to say, being struck wordless except for the phrase, even as his famous <u>I say no more</u> usually meant only a pause for breath by that verbal geyser. He made what was both an apologetic curtsy and an attempt to reach his underwear and trousers, a half-bow that brought his attention back to his dangling binoculars and caused him momentarily to forget he wanted to clothe his nether parts.

"Here," he said, getting the strap tangled in his grizzled and unkempt beard before handing the binoculars to me. The puzzled expression had never left his face; he kept staring at me with doubt and yet with what seemed a wistful hope or expectancy—as if he were looking at me for some hidden sign of familiarity, as one might gaze upon a stranger who once had been a close childhood friend, or upon a companion returned after decades of travel in foreign lands. Odd as it may sound, I wondered myself if at some time in the past (an earlier existence, perhaps? But I don't believe in such foolishness!) our paths had been joined in some journey or adventure. I'm not one of your "queers," Sid, and believe you me if you could have seen those hairy and bony legs, those ancient private parts (shriveled by the cold, I should add) that now and then were revealed beneath his long and dirty denim shirt, the potbelly the shirt covered but could not conceal—if you could have seen all this, you would know that the tenderness I felt for him (yes, from the first instant, while he was trying to balance himself on his head, and was so vulnerable both to gravity and that seemingly merciless rifle) had not a tittle or jot to do with sexual juices. He was old enough to be, if not my grandfather, a father far older than most, for Allah's sake! Besides all that, his breath was garlicky, and I detest the smell of garlic at least as much as Vladimir always has. Of the binoculars, Nod said gently, "Meg gave them to me when she sent me out of the cave. They're for looking at the stars."

"Meg?"

"My great-aunt."

"Miss Habersham?"

"You know her? Everybody does, I suppose. It's Havisham, but she wouldn't care. We don't put much stock in names, Meg and I don't."

"But you obviously care about genealogies."

"Oh, no, not at all, except in the most general sort of way, for what they reveal about all of us."

"I understand you stare at a diamond shape that tells you something about genealogies."

105

"Oh, I found the <u>diamond shape</u> described in a book. Some books fight those of the enchanters, you know." His face became cherubic (not hard for one whose cheeks are chubby and rosy to begin with) at my mention of that shape. Joyfully he pranced off to find a stick with which to draw a diamond in the dirt before the fire. The upper tip of the diamond—or second base[2]—represents any living person at the present moment, he said; the diamond spreads out to include the ever-growing number of our ancestors. But since the population of the world has been rapidly increasing for centuries, whatever the downturns it has experienced because of plagues and wars, the number of our ancestors as we proceed backward in time obviously can't continue to grow in a geometrical progression, two becoming four, four becoming eight, eight becoming sixteen, etc. The diamond, then, soon reaches its widest—the distance between first base and third—and begins to diminish toward home plate. In other words, what we get is an increasing tangle of roots (in the ground between the pitcher's mound and that home base, say) connecting each and every person alive. Inbreeding, if you like, and no doubt accompanied by what we now think of as incest. Given such a fact, there is no such thing as "race," only the species to which we all belong. Indeed, go back all the way back, to home plate and beyond, and you'll hear the Umpire's first and miraculous words, the "play ball!" that brought every living creature, including the chipmunks, raccoons, and skunks, out of their dugouts!

"Of course," Nod said, "this is a manner of speaking: the Logos (if two words can be said to be one) more likely was a spark, something closer to the neoplatonists' view of things."

"Then the <u>diamond shape</u> isn't an occult symbol, after all?" I mused. I can't tell you the reason for my vague disappointment, Sid, for I'm not superstitious, or a believer in the uncanny. But still, the past from which we came is such a mystery! "I heard from P. Eureka! Electrolux that it <u>was</u> occult, and yet that from looking at it you knew—"

---

[2] A baseball fan myself (and once a pretty good catcher of fly balls, for one always delegated to right field!), I was delighted to know the cosmic extent of the game's appeal. Perhaps someday, if all goes well, we will have a <u>Universal Series.</u>

"No, the shape is logical, mathematical, and wholly scientific, as you can now see. I don't mind using rational tools when they help. . . ." He gave me a grin too mischievous to be completely cherubic. "Do you know what the initial P. stands for?"

"I don't, not at all, and that's what you've got to tell me, to protect your life! Let the secret be known to others, and it won't do Electrolux the slightest good to try to seal your lips!"

"Of course, you don't find secrets like that in the diamond shape," Nod said, somewhat smugly, ignoring my clear hint about PEE; oh, how irritating he could be! And note, Sid, how he refers in his next sentence to the obvious fact of his firing: "Before I left my university post," he went on, "I was what you might call a computer freak. I mean, I could tap that little computer the administration so obligingly put into my office right through the mainframe and into any other computer I desired. There is a religious denomination headquartered in a western desert that has a marvelous computer, one programmed to give the genealogies of practically every Unitedian and for that matter many other prominent world citizens. The information within this computer is available to anybody who comes by with a genealogical question, and one would think that the chief spy of our land would know of its existence, but apparently he doesn't. Now, anybody who recognizes the validity of the diamond shape is bound either to be amused or appalled by the pretensions or bigotry of any member of our species, and I'm afraid I took some time from my own research (which, by the way, was scoffed at by the literary faction assuming power in my department) to investigate the backgrounds of the most narrow-minded and bigoted people in control of the nation."

"Bypass all the crap, for Allah's sake!" I said, in nervous anticipation. "Just tell me what the P. stands for."

"I almost got caught more than once, prying my way into that religious computer," Nod said thoughtfully. "Allah apparently was on my side as well as theirs, I'm glad to say. You very well may be asking (though I see you're not) why I didn't approach the church elders directly for the information, since they gladly would have given it to me gratis, without my resorting to such an illegal procedure. I'll tell you why I didn't, whatever it says about a streak of malice in one who whole-heartedly believes not only in the kinship of all living creatures but in the underlying and always hidden oneness of the phenomenal creation. I hope I don't disappoint you with this confession."

"You don't need to <u>come clean!</u> All I want to know—"

"In due time, my impatient friend." Nod patted me on the back, and once again gave me that quizzical or inquiring look, as if he were trying to see <u>who I really was;</u> but it was already clear to me, Sid, that he didn't know, for the truth of my parentage was not to be found in floppy or hard disks any more than it was to be found on a baseball diamond. That is to say, I knew that I was, for all legal purposes, an <u>Aznap,</u> that being the name recorded on my birth certificate; and no genealogical computer, no matter how smart or holy, would say anything different.

"I didn't want to approach the elders directly," Nod said (giving me the kind of sly wink you would expect from a criminal so unrepentant that he is boasting of his life of crime), "because they automatically <u>bless</u> the name of anybody whose genealogical record is being asked for, whether he or she belongs to their church or not: their belief may be somewhat different from that of most Unitedians, but they are just as tolerant as other pious citizens. I didn't want to be the cause of a blessing for P. Eureka! Electrolux! So you can see the extent of my personal malice toward him."

"And the <u>P.</u> stands for what?"

Nod gave a little giggle. "<u>Pinocchio!</u>" he exclaimed.

"A wop name?"

"Precisely, but more than that is contained within that name."

"I don't follow."

"What facial characteristic do you associate with 'Pinocchio?' "

I whistled. "The long nose, of course. Do you mean to say—"

"Yes, indeed! He was born with an unusually noble proboscis to a family obviously proud of its heritage."

"So, according to his own disgusting terminology, he's a wop kike."

108

"One who at some undetermined time underwent, no doubt to the anguish of his parents, what is called 'a nose job.'"

"And so that cute little nose he's so proud of is his living lie! Oh, my Allah, Nod, what you've revealed has not only saved your life but maybe that of your very country! You'll have the eternal gratitude of our president and everybody close to him, I assure you." And I was so happy, Sid, I whacked him both on the chest and back, and then did a little dance around him, whirling his binoculars in wild circles by its strap. He looked at his binoculars apprehensively, but only said, "Now, don't you have something to show me?"

"Something like what?"

"Like the binoculars. Something you value very much."

What an odd fellow he was! To humor him, and, of course, out of gratitude, I loosened a button on my shirt to extract the revolver from the shoulder holster that (as you know) I always wear next to my skin. "Be careful, it's loaded," I said.

He wanted to respect what I valued, I could tell, but he balanced it in the palm of his hand as if it were a black widow spider grown to monstrous size in some biotech laboratory. "Why do you like it so much?" he asked.

"A gun's a handy thing to have, these days," I said. "You never know when you might need it. Listen, you don't even realize that somebody just tried to take your life! Somebody was just staring straight at you through a telescopic sight, right over there," and I pointed. "She missed, but let me tell you if you hadn't told me what you just did, she would have come back, sooner or later. If you're always alert and carry a loaded gun, you'll never have to worry again about the return of unsuccessful assassins. Always get a bastard before a bastard gets you, that's one of my mottoes. At any moment anybody's life may be in terrible jeopardy. You see, Nod—"

"I've looked at it enough," Nod said, returning my revolver. "Hide it, put it away," he said mildly. "The animals won't come back until you do." Can you believe it, Sid, that dumb O.F. hadn't the slightest interest in the practical advice I was giving him! When I tried to give him back his binoculars, he told me to amuse myself with them while he retired to the woods to put on his clothes. Here he'd been standing before

me in nothing but his shirt, not only telling me about diamonds and genealogies and the secret of Electrolux's initial
but coaxing me into his little game of show-and-tell, and now
in his modesty had to hide behind some tree to zip up his
pants! I guess he also had to "relieve himself," as the euphe-
mism goes, but was too embarrassed even to admit that! What
a goofball, is all I could think, as he waddled away, dragging
his pants behind him.

I heard his piss hitting the dead leaves, and then the soft
nickering of his horses as they responded to his presence.
After he finished talking to them, whispering to each of them
by name (one was Tammy, the other Smoky),[3] the silence became, as another odd saying has it, "noticeably palpable,"
and I suppose a logical impossibility like that is the reason
that people of your silly temperament respond to <u>absolutely
nothing</u> as if you were in the presence of something profound.

Have you ever been alone before a dying campfire in a
dark and silent woods, Sid? You know what a poor opinion I
have of your inveterate stargazing, but at that moment I <u>had</u>
to be doing something (I'm not one of your passive types),
and so I focused the binoculars on what sensitive "poets" like
you tiresomely call <u>the celestial vault.</u> What you can see up
there <u>is,</u> I admit, fascinating, for a moment or two, if you don't
let it get to your head. I mean, a blur turns out to be dozens
of stars or maybe a gassy nebula. You can see blue jewels,
and red ones; and sometimes a planet is enclosed within a
ring and sometimes has moons—not one, like ours, but maybe
three or four. Who knows, maybe without even knowing it I
saw the little sun that keeps you cozy. I don't suppose those
bulky old binoculars that Meg had given Nod were the best
even when they were new, and the lenses were smudged (Nod
wasn't the tidiest person I've met), but still in looking through
them I got the feeling that I was spying through a pair of

[3]From here on, I resolutely refuse to call attention to any more of the
quirky similarities by which Kayo (prankishly or not) would yoke his
faithful amanuensis to a character in his story. My own quite well
known modesty makes any implied relationship between yours truly
and a recently introduced but major figure nothing but a personal
embarrassment. Furthermore, I don't consider myself an <u>old fart.</u>

tunnels into something that went on for a pretty long distance, if you know what I mean. And then, when I felt a little something or other touch, or maybe even nibble at, my ankle, I really let out a gasp! It was one of those nervy little chipmunks. They'd come back, one by one, looking for more of the handouts with which Nod had spoiled them, I suppose—a perfect example of the reason that Teddy decries public welfare; and behind them were the pair of raccoons, their solemn eyes glittering either with the firelight or maybe the stars. The skunk was still off somewhere, probably recharging its glands at the nearest skunk cabbage or whatever those creatures use for a service station. But it was a human voice I needed to hear (I'm willing to admit this), even if it was just my own, calling out the name of another. "Nod, you fruitcake," I cried. (PEE's own description, which showed that he and his agents at least could hit upon an occasional truth.) "Damn it all, where are you?"

"Kayo?" he asked tentatively. He had been standing at the edge of that clearing for I don't know how long, staring at me with all the hunger of the furry little animals!

"Yes?" I responded. It was so reassuring to hear my own name come back, almost like an echo, that it didn't occur to me for a time that he shouldn't have known it.

"Kayo!" he cried, rushing toward me, his arms wide. "It is you, then! You've come back, just as you promised! I never believed you would, because of the enchanters. Oh, fool that I am, to have trusted neither long nor enough! Did you find her? Did you give her the message? And what did she say?" He hugged me so tightly that for a moment I was almost as confused and nutty as he; that is to say, Sid, I thought that Nod was my own Papa, a figure as small and portly as he, and how good it felt to be in my beloved Papa's arms! There we were, locked in an embrace, chipmunks and raccoons at our feet, the glowing embers of the fire one with the eyes of those varmints and with the multitude of stars above us.

I've never had a feeling quite like this before, Sid, not even on the day that my Papa tightly hugged me on receiving the news that the stock market had taken off. I was still elated by what Nod had told me about PEE, but my feeling was chiefly based on no more than a mutual confusion of identities—which suggests a general truth: i.e., you can best love somebody else before you know who he really is. It didn't take long for Nod's garlicky breath and (I might add) his distinct <u>body odor</u> to bring me back to less ethereal ground. Consider this sentimental moment a sop I throw at you, for being such a good little scribe,[4] and savor it to your heart's desire between this chapter and the next, which will glide over some essential and interesting terrain at nearly the speed with which I put ground between myself and Nod's campfire soon after I had become disentangled from his arms.

CHAPTER III. *The Authentic Adventures of Kayo Aznap*

I found it a strange experience to be mistaken for somebody else <u>bearing my own name,</u> a "Kayo" who apparently had been off delivering a message to a beloved mistress and now was being fervently welcomed back for the reply he supposedly had in his possession.

Anybody would want to extricate himself as effortlessly as possible from a situation as socially awkward as that. Given his naïveté, I'm sure that Nod would have accepted anything I made up as answers to his questions. But what was the point of lying to a sweet and already deluded guy, one fat and small enough to remind me of my dear <u>Papa?</u> Why go to the bother? After all, I already had obtained from Nod himself

[4]I was—and remain—grateful to Kayo for this perhaps gratuitous piece of "sop." However, knowing far more than did he about the insidious nature of the "new research" saturating the universe, I wanted at this juncture to call out to him, <u>Beware!</u> These days, you have to be extremely careful as to how you phrase your epiphanies, insights into cosmic unity, etc., for somebody is ever at the ready to prove you've simply been deluded by the conventions of language. By and large, Kayo is a pretty smart dog, but it seems to me that ever since he first caught sight of Nod his words have lost some of their old bite.

the dope that mattered to <u>me</u>. When he turned to a saddle-bag for some crackers to quiet the chittering chipmunks (he wanted to listen solemnly and without distraction to whatever good news I had brought), I naturally enough took advantage of the diversion to slip away—and with much better grace than had "Olga."

Mark it down as but another oddity of <u>real life</u> that Nod had considered me to be Kayo, bearer of good tidings, and that, upon my return to the White House, <u>I became precisely such a courier</u> to Teddy and my fellow advisers. For now the weight of PEE's knowledge about Teddy's identity was perfectly balanced (another example of my guardianship of conservative time) by the weight of our knowledge about his name and his forebears. And so he was prevented from ever again trying to muscle his way into the Order of the Oval Token as part of a mad and egoistic scheme to grasp for himself the absolute control of the Assorted States. And now that PEE's secret had been revealed to us (and Teddy certainly let him know that it had!), Nod was safe, at least from the likes of <u>him</u>. (A retrospective tragic irony lies within my present awareness that I was Nod's protector against both PEE and—as you soon will discover—the kindly but unpredictable Teddy.)

As for PEE, let's drop him gingerly from the text, regarding him as no more than a snakelike cleaning attachment, one hissing up through the slit of its mouth only its own poisonous waste. (To put it in less fanciful terms, he busied himself in the futile effort to gain back his blackmailing power by attempting to convince Teddy and the members of the OOT that he had completely lost the foul prejudice within which he had so entrapped himself. He wanted to fool us and perhaps himself into thinking that his first name—although he still refused to come out of the closet with it—was anything but a source of personal humiliation; and so, thenceforward, PEE's public utterances made frequent, if half-choked and confused, references to the brotherhood of womankind and the sisterhood of mankind, whatever [he couldn't help from adding] the crucial differences of sex, religion, nationality, and racial variations in nasal cartilage and skin color. Let the credit for this beneficent, if hypocritical, change be given to Nod, for what he found in his radiant <u>diamond shape</u> as well as in the memory banks of a distant computer.)[1]

The years immediately following were happy and fruitful ones for Teddy and his advisers as well as for the nation as a whole. The separate theme parks were quickly established, creating little islands in a pacific socioeconomic sea, while research on the vast but invisible dome—that theme park to enclose all theme parks—briskly went forward. This research invigorated the military hardware business even more than had the development and deployment of our largest nuclear shell-game missiles—the famous SGMs. (I don't want to engage in patriotic boasting, Sid, but I think you should know that there are <u>literally thousands</u> of these SGMs in our country, some real and others paste-ups, constantly whooshing by on rails everywhere. Believe me, they make our motorists look twice at every grade crossing!)

That dome, as I have perhaps implied, would be Teddy's great contribution, the proof of his now frequently reiterated promise to the public to offer, as Oz, the <u>new and wonderful</u> gift that everybody had wanted from the beginning of civilization, which (as all Unitedians know) got both its start and first technological boost from the immediate and clear-cut division of the world into good and evil tribes. In one of his vibrant televised interviews with reporters (we in the OOT were always apprehensive during these ordeals, but had nothing to worry about on this occasion), Teddy said that, upon completion of <u>The Dome,</u> the SGMs and their trackbeds could be converted by private enterprise into a new passenger and freight-train system (the old one was an embarrassment to us) that would certainly show up the technology of a certain pipsqueak nation, however much it had taken over the world market for cameras and toy cars by illegal dumping.

Occupied as I was with important details (primarily economic ramifications of the work on <u>The Dome</u>), I never wholly dismissed Nod from my thoughts. Allah knows why that piddling peon could continue to attract anybody's attention, Ted-

---

[1] We know that Kayo long ago picked up from his dear <u>Papa</u> a belief in egalitarianism. Still, the moral uplift of this passage strikes me as an entirely new tone.

dy's or mine! Still, I continued to remember that sentimental moment beneath the stars. Who was the Kayo that Nod had mistaken me for? I could have dismissed the whole affair, embrace and all, as the consequence of a common enough confusion (at some time or another, who hasn't been mistaken for another person?) that had been compounded by the equally mundane coincidence of a like name. My name, after all, is a familiar term of address for any number of young males, for Kayo was a character in a comic strip avidly read every day by the previous two generations both in my nation and abroad, and, being syndicated by Universal Features, Inc., perhaps even beyond our planet.

And yet that meeting with Nod had struck a greater resonance within my memory than any comic strip could explain. While joyfully engaged in the embrace, I'd had the strange feeling of living within the pages of a book, as a character somehow possessing a fuller and more gratifying emotional life than I actually did.[2] As I chewed upon the worrisome bone of a certain Kayo bearing a message for a certain Nod, something struck a bell. But of course! What I'm about to reveal to you, Sid, is an extreme example of the kind of coincidence that can happen only in a real-life situation, however much it depends in part on fiction. You probably don't remember (look back if you don't believe me) that in speaking of my formative years I mentioned that I had been named for a distant Aznap forebear who wrote a famous book, The Authentic Adventures of Kayo Aznap. What an imagination my earlier namesake possessed, in recounting those fantasies he considered true! Now, there is a foolish subordinate character within those adventures who is called—you've guessed it!—Nod, and he's somebody my namesake is always carrying messages for.

Something you should clearly be able to recall (since it

[2] Great books can create such an illusion, no doubt because the author has touched upon the deeper identity shared by us all. Oddly enough, this passing remark by Kayo made me realize—with a shock in which regret was mixed—that I am Sid only within this imaginative fabric woven by a fabulist from another realm. The reader must bear in mind (as, alas, must I) that not only "Sid" but "Kayo Aznap" and "Nod"— and for that matter all the other names within our narrative—are inventions of an anonymous author, who uses them in the pursuit of both personal and cosmic truths.

is contained in the final chapter of part one) is the fact that Nod's actual name, before he lost his professorial wits over something called the "new research," was Quexana or Quixada or Queseda. (By the way, these various discrepancies suggest his radical uncertainty from the start as to who he was.) In meditating upon this whole curious affair, it struck me that this nuthead had taken mental refuge from the "new research" within what to him must have seemed the far more comforting confines of that famous Aznapian epic (a deduction that, as you will discover, turned out to be as true as others I have made). The astonishing extent to which he transformed his identity into that of a fictional character is attested to by the fact that so long as I live I will revere him not as Professor Michael or Miguel Quexana, etc. (or even as "Mike"), but only as my befuddled compatriot, Nod.

I don't know how faithfully your version of the story reflects ours, but I suspect yours to be an inferior and hopelessly garbled product, since you call yours <u>Don Quixote,</u> thus giving emphasis to the engaging, but less significant, of the pair of characters. That's not to say that our version (an early and perhaps primitive example of our creative genius) is not without its faults—at least, so far as I can tell from the Cliffs Notes, the reliable source of all my information about literary matters. In any event, to avoid any misconceptions on your part over a book of some consequence to my own story, let me clue you in to what really takes place within this classic plot.

According to the Cliffs Notes guide, then, the dumb peasant Nod is so addled by all the western novels of pioneer days he's read that he thinks himself an actual present-day <u>cowboy,</u> and somehow persuades the aristocratic <u>Sir Kayo</u> (in some editions of this extraordinarily popular work, <u>Kayo, Lord Aznap</u> and in others <u>Prince Kayo</u>), a man of former wealth but still of the perspicacity that originally brought him to our democratic shores, to accompany him on his journeys. The narrative, of course, shows the influence of our strong egalitarian heritage, the point being that Nod and Kayo are true buddies beneath the skin. It's a given before the story ever starts that this ersatz cowboy Nod once caught a glimpse of a prostitute in the plush casino of the fabulous Gold Nugget hotel, the biggest and most profitable gambling hostelry in a new resort town so incandescent at night that it illuminates half of the western desert in which it is so improbably situated.[3] Dope that he is, what Nod sees in his mind is not a prostitute but that typical heroine of the legends of the Old West—one of your curvaceous blond-haired tomboys wearing a short skirt and cute cartridge belt, somebody who, when the occasion demands, can be a pretty damned good gunslinger herself, and indeed goes about to your county fairs and roundups to win one blue ribbon after another for her incredible marksmanship. Still, beneath her gorgeous bosom lies the compassionate heart that is the true gold of the West. The name that poor Nod invents for this narcissistic image, this reflection of his own pathetically yearning soul, is <u>Diana,</u> and it comes straight out of our mythology.

Now, the actual woman who is the source of this fantasy possesses the common and unmythical name of <u>Jean.</u> Before becoming a hooker, she worked her way up by her bootstraps to get an advanced degree in science. There is no doubt in anybody's mind that Jean would have ended up as a brilliant, pioneering female scientist[4] were it not for the crooked card sharks in the Gold Nugget casino. You see, they tricked her vacationing daddy so badly that he owes them almost half a million dollars. When one of them says to another, "Shuffle the deck and pass the cards," you'd better keep your eyes open, I can tell you! As the Cliffs Notes guide so judiciously comments, their perverted principles prevent these card sharks

---

[3] Kayo told me that the resort town continues to prosper in all of its brilliance. At the time of its conception as the mecca of his nation (for thus does capitalism enshrine gambling, its <u>élan vital,</u> whatever the planet on which that economic system flourishes), the federal government built nearby, at public expense, a mammoth dam for hydroelectric power, much of its juice intended to lighten the gambling hearts and wallets of the citizens, while weighting down the purses and foreign bank accounts of certain influential Mafiosi. (In response to Kayo's call for energy conservation, Teddy might have put dim bulbs in all the White House chandeliers, but he steadfastly refused to dim the glory of the West.) All of this background material no doubt adds to the phantasmagoria to be found within <u>The Authentic Adventures of Kayo Aznap.</u>

[4] And a galactic forerunner of Professor Billions's recent heroine?

from accepting the integrity of any given hand, and woe to anybody who plays the game thinking he can win with native truthfulness and generous feelings of human fellowship! And so Jean, to keep her father from jail (even though you and I know who belongs there), has been forced by these ruthless gamblers into a lucrative life of shame from which they garner 98 percent of the take.

You may be interested in knowing, Sid, that these card sharks, their brows typically hooded by caps with dark green bills of translucent celluloid, their eyes hidden behind thick spectacles, are very much part of the shrouded Unitedian prehistory. The Cliffs Notes guide tells us they may trace back to some lost urtext. Perhaps they once were trickster shamans, perhaps embodiments of the Demiurge, belonging to the mythos of an entirely separate culture. In any event, the word book is always connected with them—they <u>win the book, make book, know every trick in the book, bring to book,</u> etc.

What I almost forgot to mention, Sid, is the real irony of the story. Though Jean is obviously much brighter than Nod, she immediately fell in love with him at first glance herself, and if that clod hadn't been galloping over the desert so enamored by his fantasy that to honor Diana he falls through one mirage after another—trying to capture outlaws, tame wild horses, stop herds of stampeding cattle, etc.—she would have had the chance to tell him so. (Prince Kayo is always running back and forth, humoring Nod by trying to deliver messages to his wholly imaginary beloved—Kayo's adventures as messenger constitute the essence of the book, but I reluctantly forgo them here.) As it stands, though, Nod is so oblivious of this flesh-and-blood Jean that just the mention of his name causes her to stamp her foot on the nearest termite, even though her heart is every bit as compassionate as Diana's, if not more so.

The whole story, you see, is a case of hopeless love, both physical and spiritual. On his deathbed, Nod finally realizes he's not a cowboy but an incipient financier who could have made a fortune on the stock market, and so have rescued Jean, whom too late he knows he loves, from her fate; and she ends up in prison, having picked off those gamblers, one by one, as they came out the swinging doors of the Gold Nugget casino. Saddened, Prince Kayo goes back to his native island, to sit on his throne and ponder (as any wise and kindly and impoverished ruler inevitably must) the brevity and bittersweet nature of life. I really can't tell you why The Authentic Adventures of Kayo Aznap has enamored generations of readers, making them laugh even as they weep; superior though it obviously is to your Don Quixote, to me it sounds similar to any other of the plot outlines of our "great books" in the Cliffs Notes series. Once I leafed through the actual novel, looking for scenes with the card sharks, for to dream up characters like that strikes me as a truly worthwhile imaginative act, but I never could find the right pages in that formidable tome.

I imagine that's all the fiction you're willing to take, Sid, so in the next chapter I'll stick to nothing but real-life situations.[5]

---

[5] In the previous chapter, I swore I would stop pointing out similarities, whether accidental or fiendishly planned by him, between Kayo's text and my personal life. In this chapter, though, he simply is passing time by making a further condensation of a Cliffs Notes summary of a venerable work of fiction written by some great-granddaddy Aznap. Whether or not this clear difference between Kayo's true text and a fictional one frees me from my promise (in my opinion, it does), I simply must intrude here to defend the honor of my wife, also named Jean, who is not, and never has been, a prostitute—nor ever will be, not even (I wager) from a generous motive of the sort that has ensnared the fictional Jean. Both Jeans are brilliant women, both are educated in the sciences, and that's the end of the matter. It would take a conniving poststructuralist with a twisted Freudian bent to see in the fictional Nod's twice-fictional Diana the Diana of my own stimulating sexual fantasies during otherwise wholly faithful moments of intimacy in the past, or to see in the fictional Jean's anger at the obliviousness to her of the fictional Nod any of my Jean's bafflement at the extent to which I have necessarily ignored—nay, almost forgotten—my husbandly duties during this period in which I have been engrossed in my transcription of a text of ever-increasing complexity, so far as reality and imagination are concerned. The whole matter of truth vs. fiction is a vexing one; but how much better to try valiantly to distinguish between the two than to avoid a throbbing headache by a crude denial of the possibility of any truth! Are you still with me, reader(s)?

CHAPTER IV. *Idaho Potatoes and Cuban Cigars*

"Did you know about this?" Teddy asked me one day with unusual sternness, thrusting a newspaper under my nose. The paper was the morning daily put out by students of the university in my native Lake District. On the front page was a large photograph of Nod's horses, chewing some tulips in front of the university's administration building. Having apparently just dismounted from one of the horses, Nod was attempting to boost an attractive and obviously quite reluctant woman wearing a white dress into the saddle of the other horse, while campus patrolmen and a battery of reporters, photographers, and television cameramen, as well as a scattering of neatly clothed students holding placards, looked upon this unexpected intrusion with obvious alarm.

Although Teddy no longer employed the DSP to gather intelligence on Nod, he had commenced to subscribe to all the Lake District papers—in addition to the student tabloid, the afternoon daily owned by a corporate chain that put photographs of dogs on the front page and gave a capsule listing of national and international disturbances and cataclysmic events between the sports pages and the classified section (the kind of paper, that is, that wholeheartedly supports conservative time), the weeklies with the still-prickly, pale-pinkish complexion that betrayed their distant origins in the underground, and even the various shopping and entertainment guides that occasionally used news stories as fillers.

"Come on, Teddy, why should I know about it?" I asked crossly, putting on my reading glasses (an indication, Sid, that time is still rapidly passing in my account: five or six years had elapsed since my single and brief meeting with Nod, and since the day that Teddy, with one splendid gesture, had convinced corporate leaders and their research scientists of the viability of <u>The Dome</u>—that gesture being the generous dispersal of funds borrowed from a consortium of foreign investors eager for our high interest rates.)[1]

Three of Teddy's recent characteristics had commenced to irritate me: (1) his increasingly agonized absorption in whatever Nod, that nittering nabob of negativism (nice guy that otherwise he might be), was saying or doing; (2) the high-handed manner in which Teddy always made it clear that, so far as he was concerned, Nod was nobody's responsibility but my own; and (3) (note how neatly I always compartmentalize my thoughts), the way he began to whistle a tune you would recognize as "Home on the Range" whenever the chores of his office really began to get to him. And sometimes at a meeting of the OOT he would suddenly sing out, apropros of nothing at all, "Oh, give me a home, Where the buffalo roam." He had been born (as you know) on a ranch, and ever since the day he had led the parade of horsemen during the festivities that had opened the Kayo Corral he had been full of nostalgia for his childhood romps through the sagebrush on his pony.

Naturally enough, in looking at the photograph, I thought that Nod's two horses and the derring-do he was displaying had aroused Teddy's usually dormant spite and envy; but when I pointed out to him that the fat and swaybacked nature of this pair of animals made them not even worth the annual cost of their worming medicine, he simply snapped, "Forget the photograph! Read the article. Read what that arrogant _____[2] says not only about our Zemblan policy, but about administrators in general and presidents in particular."

Being a speed reader, I scanned the article (which was

[1] It takes supreme confidence in one's authority as writer (a power the poststructuralists would wrest from all authors) to leap over time as casually as Kayo does here. One of my favorite sentences by a superb French novelist of a more spacious and romantic epoch is, as translated into English, "Seven years passed in this manner." Of course, we must remember that Kayo is referring to "personal time," a less consequential kind of chronological measurement for him than for us.

[2] Expletive deleted; as a throwback to one of Teddy's earlier presidential identities, this particular obscenity (so Kayo informed me) hints at the depth of his present frustration and self-doubt.

long enough to be continued on several inside pages) in the time it took Teddy to whistle his way only twice through "Home on the Range." The woman whom Nod had been unable to convince to jump to the saddle (in order to escape the law) was a famous novelist who taught at the university, and she had joined the students to protest the continuing investment of university funds in Zembla, a land in which the native Zemblans were denied certain amenities, including the right to vote, because of the difference in skin color that separated them from the ruling class. (Teddy and the OOT, of course, supported the democratic right of all Unitedians to invest their hard-earned money wherever they damned well pleased—this was our Zemblan foreign policy.)

I can't tell you anything about the merit of this famous novelist's works, because—a telling point?—they're not mentioned in the Cliffs Notes guides; but it's clear enough she was using her reputation to embarrass the university authorities as part of a well-orchestrated publicity stunt. I mean, all the news media obviously had been alerted in advance that she would illegally remain in the administration building after the closing hour in order to get herself arrested, which is the reason that the reporters and photographers outnumbered the student protesters and patrolmen. (Here, incidentally, is a prime example of how the media help make the news they "objectively" report.) If even Nod had heard about it from his campfire, you can bet there was nobody in the whole region who hadn't been informed. She had prepared a clever statement to read while the flashbulbs were popping and the video cameras were focused on her, something about the fact that investing money in Zemblan industries that paid lip service to equitable hiring practices was like buying sheets with a clear conscience from a company that declared itself an Equal Opportunity Employer even though its major stockholder and customer was the Ku Klux Klan.

Well, you can see how furious she must have been at Nod, for trying to interfere with her calculated subversive act! That bungler was on our side this time, Sid, so it was obvious that Teddy's whistling wasn't brought about by Nod's attempt (valorous though unsuccessful) to rescue a prize-winning lady novelist, but rather by the interview he afterward gave to the student reporter. (The police had to let him go, because they couldn't charge him with anything more than damage to a couple of tulip blossoms, which, as offenses go, is below that of stealing a chicken. He hadn't even been fined for his cathedral trespass of the previous year, which I'll tell you about shortly. Other than for his involvement with me, you can say that Nod really led a charmed life.)

I doubt if the reporter (or anybody other than Teddy) could have taken with seriousness anything that Nod said. College papers have a tradition of printing lies for the fun of it in a special issue, and most readers of the Nod interview probably saw in it but another example of the inventive irresponsibility by which budding journalists train themselves for the profession. After all, who could believe that Nod once had really been a senior professor at that university? That he had adopted a new identity to defend the sacred uniqueness of the individual from the encroachments of enchanters who included proponents of the "new research" as well as administrators in the university and the federal government alike?

That windbag had a good enough memory to recall major phrases from the same address that the university president had made throughout the nation (he was in demand as a speaker, apparently having a supply of good jokes as well as a fluid delivery) at commencements, annual meetings of corporation stockholders, testimonial banquets for outstanding entrepreneurs, and on other solemn occasions reported by the press, in which he had good-naturedly attacked our materialistic excesses—in particular, the "notorious" yuppiness of our youth. He had called upon those of the generation yet to assume corporate power to prove they were not self-centered, so concerned with personal advantage and possessions that they forgot compassion and the true meaning of life, which is to be found in the richness of our humanistic culture and in our vigilant concern with the needs of others; for the "good news" that we Unitedians bear to the rest of the world is the worth of every human soul. "And yet you will note," Nod told the reporter, "that as soon as these young people or producers of our humanistic culture attempt to follow such precepts, this champion of selfless virtue, no doubt egged on by his like-minded troop of vice-presidents (most of whom ought to

123

be managers of drive-in branches of small-town banks), wants them put in jail."

Nod continued in this scurrilous vein, connecting the "hypocrisy" of the university's chief officer with that of Teddy himself, who (so rumor had it) listened to his own little cadre of anonymous bank managers. "Beware!" Nod warned the reporter. "A dark and sticky molasses now is spreading thickly, o'er our green and generous land," and I didn't have to read further, for from here on all he did was to quote verbatim his own tree-stump speech linking administrators to the "new research," the harangue that I had listened to years before on the cassette. According to the reporter, Nod's last words, made as he was trotting away on one horse, the other following docilely behind, were, "Where are you, Kayo, in this dark hour of our need?"—words that made my heart take a guilty leap. When I looked up at Teddy, my eyes, much to my chagrin, were moist.

"The first thing I want to know," Teddy said with coldness, "is why he would want you with him."

"Be reasonable, Teddy," I said. "I saved his life, after all. And I left before giving him the message."

"What message?"

"The one from Diana."

"Who's Diana?" he asked suspiciously.

"Oh, she's just a figment," I replied, an answer that seemed to satisfy him, for he turned to the next thing he wanted to know: "Now, what's this 'new research'? What does it have to do with me and this other guy, that other golden-voiced skipper who runs such a tight ship? And what's all this about creeping molasses?"

It was obvious that Teddy had not read the book about the "new research" in the Nod file any more than he had listened to the cassette containing Nod's obsessive rantings. I had given the book a quick once-over, enough to sympathize with the DSP cryptographer who hadn't been able to break the code, but a line defining man (in other words, somebody not only like Teddy but like me or my dead but still beloved Papa, and maybe even like Nod and you, Sid) had caught my eye: it said that a "man" is the juncture of a series of interpersonal systems (language "signs" and so on) which operate through him, a definition that maybe you can read in two ways at once, only one of which permits him any will in the matter. I suppose a zany like Nod would interpret it simply to mean that all of us are stuck like amoebas in a cultural molasses that we're constantly ingesting. Nod was clearly paranoid in his attitude toward administrators as well as toward scholars of the "new research," believing they had jointly ganged up on him to get him fired; but some of the things he later confessed to me make me think that he hated presidents and other administrators as much as he did because their words and actions gave him the fearsome suspicion that the "new research" might, after all, be right.

Now, I admit my own knowledge of Nod was limited to a discussion with him about the diamond shape, his love of the stars and a mythical Diana, and the embrace we shared—as well as, of course, his charity to raccoons, etc. But it was painfully apparent to me that he was much like you, Sid—I mean, that he was an idealist, believing despite the evidence of his senses in the spiritual oneness of everything within the universe. (Reread my careful lesson to you, my dear and innocent scribe, and cease forever your fucked-up ways. If you don't, I'm warning you, you'll end up as mad and lonely as Nod himself, waiting for the bullet from his only buddy—a fate I wouldn't wish upon the most distant friend.)[3]

"Nod probably hates the 'new research,' " I told Teddy, "because it denies the possibility of anything new and wonderful ever happening."

"That's the first good thing I've heard about him," Teddy said approvingly. "He must appreciate my efforts—and believe me when I say the difficulties are enormous—to protect all Unitedians with The Dome."

"I'm not sure about that," I said. Teddy could have used a concise summary, or a briefing, of the contents of that interview with Nod; clearly he had become so perturbed that he had completely missed Nod's remark that The Dome and

[3]The reader will note the clear affection for Nod as well as me that is contained within this warning about "innocence" and "idealism." I smile at Kayo's anxiety that I (perhaps the sanest and most stable scholar in my university) might become as "mad" and "lonely" as one whose growing influence on Kayo himself already is apparent.

the "new research" were the same bottle of molasses, both being the consequence of a disbelief in divinity. That is to say, Teddy's espousal of an invisible protective shield for our nation was proof enough that he—like the proponents of the "new research," with their view of language as a series of signs in a hermetically sealed cultural text—felt that our Deity no longer was sufficient. "All I can say for sure," I said evasively, "is that Nod has serious doubts about the spiritual integrity of all administrators."

"Well, I'll be Allah-damned," Teddy cried, drumming his fingers on his glass-topped conference desk. "Who was it, Kayo, who saved that whole Allah-damned franchise of churches and cathedrals of which 'Q' is a card-and-tithe-paying member from bankruptcy, and this despite the fact that this particular religious corporation constantly criticizes our policies toward our neighbors to the south?"

"You did, Teddy," I said soothingly, letting him take all the credit. "Whatever the outcries about the need to separate church and state, you had the bravery to make theme parks of every one of their cathedrals."

"And who was the atheist who broke through the gate without paying admission to stand on the sacred altar in order to abuse the priest?"

"None other than Nod himself," I said. Teddy was referring to a typical quixotism by Nod that briefly had won him some regional attention. A charwoman of deep piety who was about to lose her little home to the bank made a daily series of prayers at the cathedral; to the devout, the faithful repetition of these prayers before a holy image can lead on the ninth day to a divine intervention that will ease the misfortune of the supplicant. On the ninth day that the charwoman came for her prayer, she found on the base of the image an envelope containing ten one-thousand-dollar bills, exactly the sum she had been praying for. Upon hearing that a charwoman had found the money there, the head of the cathedral, a bishop or an archbishop maybe, at once declared the money had been left as a gift to the church by a wealthy parishioner; he accused the woman of theft, and attempted to have her tried in court as a criminal.

It may strike you as odd, Sid, that the parishioner would

leave ten thousand dollars in negotiable currency precisely where the charwoman was praying for that manna. Had he wanted to give such a donation to the church, why hadn't he written a check—either presenting it in person (and getting profuse vocal thanks, with a personal blessing to boot) or at least sending it by registered mail? And yet one would have to be as simple as the charwoman to believe that she was right and the priest wrong. No, you have to accept the priest's version, as another of those astounding coincidences (like that odoriferous skunk) you find only in real life. Please accept this little story in good faith, for it truly happened, in a cathedral in my own Lake District.

Such a situation would seem invented (but that itself suggests divine intervention!) for the likes of Nod, who came at a brisk trot to the cathedral during services, tethered his horse to the theme-park fence, and burst past the cashier at the gate precisely as Teddy said—that is, without paying his entrance fee!—and strode to the altar, where he cried forth his conviction that the enchanters had entered the very citadels of worship, turning priests into bank clerks and administrators; for clearly they lacked the faith to believe in the miracles they themselves preached as the gospel truth. Anything that was <u>new and wonderful</u> was as unlikely to proceed from their hypocritical offices, he disdainfully added, as from the office of the president of the country. Nod was hurled down the cathedral steps by a couple of burly spiritual bouncers; no charges were filed against this sacrilegious interloper, since the church already had enough of a legal embarrassment in its suit against the destitute charwoman.

Silently, our heads bowed, Teddy and I contemplated the holy service that Nod had so rudely disrupted with his wild cries about pagan enchanters. Teddy sighed and said, "Every day he upsets me more. In my opinion, atheistic Communists like that peasant agitator can undermine the very spiritual foundations of our nation."

"Oh, come on, Teddy," I said affectionately. "You and I both know he's still a relatively obscure peon."

"One bad peon can make a basket case of all the sound ones."

Presidential advisers have to be lay psychotherapists. "Just relax, for goodness' sake!" I implored him. "Why don't you tell me what's <u>truly</u> bothering you, Teddy boy?"

He gave me a sad smile. Then he fumbled under the desk for the button that shut off the tape of our conversation, which from long experience I recognized as my cue to go to the door to lock it, first making sure that no DSP agent was snooping at the keyhole.

Teddy said, "For five years, eleven months, and thirteen days the best minds in our land have been engaged in the research for my <u>new and wonderful</u> gift of absolute security and peace for our nation. So far, we have exhausted the lending ability of six consortia of investors. The one happy note here is that—because of the high rate of interest we're paying—the first two consortia have sufficiently replenished their means to make new overtures to us, which means we can continue with our research forever."

"Will it take that long to construct the strategic defense initiative?"

Teddy ignored my question to whistle the opening bars of the "Home on the Range" refrain. "My major scientific spokesperson at the Think Tank tells me that we have surmounted one unsurmountable obstacle after another. Meanwhile, the wily enemy (not having the credit rating that would enable him to build a <u>Dome</u> of his own) has used his more limited resources to devise one technological means after another to defeat each of our achievements. Our foe now possesses so many ingenious quills aimed in our direction that my scientific spokesperson (who <u>does</u> manage to keep his sense of humor) thinks we should change the name of the animal from <u>Bear</u> to <u>Porcupine.</u> Early this morning, he woke me with the happy news that yes, <u>The Dome</u> at last can theoretically protect us from every missile that the enemy has in his arsenal."

"Why aren't you overjoyed, then?"

"The truth of the matter is that all of these missiles are of the old-fashioned lumpy variety, the so-called <u>Idaho potatoes</u> that our invisible net can catch and then bounce back at the assailant, whatever the size, number, and sophistication of the warheads or the trickiness of the decoys; but we have irrefutable proof that the foe is hard at work on slender and cylindrical weapons, code-named <u>Cuban cigars,</u> that will slip through the tiniest mesh we now know how to devise. And, quite beyond this not inconsiderable factor, the head mathematician on the project has calculated that, according to certain new theories regarding physical <u>chaos,</u> even a <u>Dome</u> made invincible to those deadly cigars will fail. You are to breathe not a word of this, not even to the other members of the OOT, but at present the outlook is bleak indeed."

"But not hopeless, I trust?"

"Nothing is ever <u>hopeless,</u> Kayo! But, as you know, I had wanted to crown my reign with this achievement for our people, and then, having accomplished the <u>new and wonderful</u> thing that the naysayer Nod said I couldn't, to retire at long last from office, as my Miranda—"

"Do you mean Alice?"

"—as my Alice has been begging me to do. To go back to the ranch where I was born, happy with myself and with my Alice, content with my little niche in history. . . . But for the sake of the ASU, I've decided to serve another four years, or however long it takes to iron out these new wrinkles in <u>The Dome.</u> I've been dawdling here all this day, trying to find a new identity the people will like, but my heart isn't genuinely into the task. What do you think of 'Michael,' which possibly derives (according to the dictionary) from 'who is like God or Allah'? To the people I could be the unassuming 'Mickey' or 'Mike.' "

I was incautious enough to remind Teddy that Nod's legal first name was Michael. Had he perhaps unconsciously been thinking (of course, I didn't add this!) that Nod's view, however crazy, of the <u>new and wonderful</u> was superior to his own? The mere mention that Nod had been Michael long before Teddy had been Oz or even Frank channeled all of Teddy's wrath against everybody—the <u>Bear,</u> the consortia of investors, the research scientists and corporate executives who had sworn to the viability of <u>The Dome,</u> and, yes, <u>me,</u> who had given him the basic concept, however much he declared it his own—to a murderous rage against a single and relatively helpless critter, that fat little porcupine whose quills could easily be plucked. (Of course, you remember, Sid, Teddy's long-ago slip of the tongue, "Let a sleeping dog <u>die.</u>")

I'd never before seen the glint of malice in his eyes that I saw there at this instant. "Listen, Aznap," he said curtly to me. "Nod is nobody's problem but yours, and I'm telling you that if you want to remain in the OOT and not be exiled like Miranda to a desert island populated with wealthy oil sheiks so loyal to me they would shish kebab the heart of anybody who betrayed my secrets—why, then, you'll silence that bastard for good. Why are you <u>here,</u> Kayo, 'in this dark hour of our need?' [In such a vicious manner did the kindly Teddy mimic Nod's sorrowful rebuke of me!] He obviously wants you to take care of him, and so do I."

And with that, he summarily dismissed me from the room. If you were I, Sid, and faced with a dilemma like this, what kind of solution could you possibly find?

CHAPTER V. A *Seer Become a Sawyer*

And so once again I found myself behind a bush at the campfire, but this time there was no "Olga" whose attempt at assassination I would desperately try to thwart. This time it was I who had drawn forth a weapon—the family heirloom, old and heavy enough to be a blunderbuss, that I kept in the comforting shoulder holster next to my skin, as I've told you many times; and it was only I, by the same token, who could conceivably prevent my successful use of it, the skunk and all of the other contingencies being absent.

The practical side of my nature told me to pull the trigger as many times as it took—<u>bam, bam, bam</u>—to end the career of this preposterous vagabond. Upon reading in a Lake District newspaper of the discovery by, say, two deer hunters of the moldering remains of the body in the forest (for, of course, it wouldn't be politic or even mannerly of me ever to speak to him of my accomplishment), Teddy would give me a friendly wink, a shy smile of gratitude, and threaten me no more with exile to a desert island.

Another side of my nature—more cautionary, perhaps

more inclined toward some hazy sense of human mutuality, something that no doubt had its source in my dear <u>Papa</u>'s staunch egalitarianism—advised me to rely on wit and subterfuge rather than on a hasty and irrevocable act. This side remembered Nod's splendid account of the <u>diamond shape,</u> including the Umpire's first words, the "play ball!" that sent us scurrying to our primordial positions in the game of life.

Actually, these two sides of my nature had been fighting each other in both stages of my journey, first by commercial transport and then by foot from the nearest hick-town airport (how many miles of highways and byways I walked, delaying the moment of decision by forgoing even a Rent-a-Wreck to take me as far as the trailhead!). Once in the woods, I felt out of place in my three-piece business suit (a bulge just beneath the left armpit) and natty gray fedora. I left the trails to hide behind trees or thickets in the green glades at the first distant cries of youthful backpackers innocently reveling in the sight of gurgling brooks and leaping deer or the taste of wild raspberries—for I didn't want anybody to be able to describe me, just in case I opted for murder. As I walked, I rehearsed in the smallest and most cunning detail my strategy for silencing Nod in a way that might be risky but would not rely on the <u>last resort.</u> Unless I told them otherwise, all the actors in my scheme (the television crew, Dilsey, Mirabelle and her clan, et al.) would be prepared for the striking of the thirty-first hour on the sixth day of the fifth lunar month of our year 5891—in other words, on the day immediately following, at 1:00 P.M. your time. As the bell on the church steeple tolled its final note, Nod and I would ride out for the duel that would result in my "death"—and I prayed that the quotation marks would still be neutralizing that word, after Nod pulled the trigger of a revolver that <u>had to be loaded.</u>

At the moment before I stepped into the clearing, I still hadn't decided which course of action to follow, even though the butt of the revolver was not only clenched in my fist, but my finger was on the trigger, and the muzzle raised. Dusk had just dropped her somber gown over the sylvan landscape.[1] I

---

[1]How do we explain figurative language like this, from our Kayo? Perhaps one who is bewildered by a conflict within the psyche finds a certain solace in poetic thinking, however clichéd.

heaɪd a loud but intermittent buzz, which I assumed to be the snoring of Nod beside his campfire; I could make out a dark shape before the flames. I suppose the physical fact of the deadly weapon in my hand, and the thought that if anything in my strategy went awry Nod might kill me with it, made my scheme to save his life while frightening him into abject wordlessness seem dubious and irrational in the very precision of its calculations. How much better to shoot him while he slept! He would die without opening his eyes, and thus spare me the eternity of nightmares that inevitably would result from his initial happiness at seeing me, followed by the look of saddened betrayal the instant before the bullet struck.

But just as I burst from my bush—muttering savagely to myself, Let the sleeping dog die! to keep up my resolve—Nod tumbled out of the heavens. (There was this one contingency, after all.) That is to say, the shape by the campfire had been made by his bulky saddlebags; Nod himself had been up a tree, sawing a limb, and now came crashing down, accompanied by a giant, leafy branch and his woodsman's saw. Oh, how quickly my murderous impulse vanished! How impulsively I rushed to his assistance, to return him to the life that had been astonished from his body! I straddled his fat stomach, I massaged his heart and pushed and pummeled his ribs (a good thing for him they hadn't been broken by the fall!), I even put my mouth to his own garlicky-smelling mouth, forcing the air from my lungs into his until I became dizzy from the exertion and maybe the smell and almost swooned away.

"Dead, forever dead," I moaned, falling off that inert mass, never even thinking how lucky I was that he had done to himself what I had dreaded to accomplish; and, of course, he chose that moment to sit up, and to look at me with a radiant smile while gingerly feeling his body for bruises. "So you did come back, Kayo," he said, as if I'd been gone for a week instead of six years.

"Oh, Nod, what a stupid-ass thing to be doing!" I cried, my love and grief instantly turned into righteous anger by the fact that the cause of these deep feelings within me had survived the violent drop, cushioned by his fat. "Nobody but an absolute idiot would saw off the branch he was sitting upon!"

"There, there," he said, patting me on the knee as if I

were the unreasonable child. "For the past week, I've been reading the theoretical works of the most pernicious of my enchanters—"

"The trickster shamans?" I asked, forgetting in my eagerness that he had added some enchanters to those contained in The Authentic Adventures. "The ones you'd better watch out for when they shuffle the deck and pass the cards?" In the final analysis, Sid, I'm no more heartless than "Olga"; having lost the opportunity for an easy murder (what's the difference between a sleeping and an otherwise unconscious dog?), I now was glad to rely wholly on that dangerous and difficult stratagem designed to save his life by convincing him that he was a murderer. If you take an innocent idealist—try this hypothesis for size upon yourself, Sid!—and conclusively demonstrate to him that he's a killer, I very seriously doubt that ever again will he be a troublemaker, somebody accusing others of hypocrisy while proclaiming his own screwball version of the new and wonderful to be better than anybody else's.

"Listen to me, Nod," I went on, believing that in his simplicity he was living only within the pages of that old Aznapian text. "If you want to defeat the gamblers from the casino, you can. They're on tour, at a western town nearby, taking enormous bets that the Desperado will defeat the Good Avenger tomorrow in the staged duel, the shoot-out that the Good Avenger is always supposed to win. You see, the devious gamblers have bribed the weak-willed actors who customarily perform the roles! To encourage high bets, these cruel enchanters are even willing to wager the generous-spirited and brilliant Jean—she who looks so much like Diana that the two are indistinguishable, the same pea in the pod—by gambling the pile of her daddy's IOU notes that holds her in vile duress to its owner. Diana has vowed to drug the pair of bad actors, if you and I will only come. To prevent a miscarriage of justice and morality, and to release Jean from her disagreeable servitude, Diana implores you to be the Good Avenger who rightfully, and in accordance with the script, fells me, the Desperado. That's the message I'm bringing to you from the one whose every request you are sworn to obey."

Nod gave me a pitying look. "Times change, Kayo," he said. "The enchanters take on a new shape with each new age, and adapt their theories and practices to it. If you're going to fight them, you have to <u>keep up with the times.</u> That's why I've been reading their books (which some say have already driven me to madness) more closely than ever I did before. I can tell you, Kayo, that, given the contemporary spiritual climate of our land, these books are dangerous indeed."

"The enchanters aren't gamblers or trickster shamans anymore?"

"They're always in a new guise," he said, still treating me like a child by enunciating his words deliberately. "Let us say that they always pretend to take risks in the games they play, such as <u>sawing off the limb they're sitting on.</u> But actually, whether they're card sharks or scholars, they have two sets of rules, one for you and one for them; and they are a particular threat to an idealist of my former caliber, one who believes at once in the truth of the <u>diamond shape</u> (that is, in the kinship, the biological link that binds all of us as brothers and sisters in a single human race) and in the singularity—the sacred uniqueness—of each and every one of us. For most of my life, I have found confirmation of these views, which at first glance may seem contradictory, in our great works of literature. No doubt, Kayo, you have deduced from these"—and he pointed toward his opened saddlebags, overflowing as they were with books tattered by use or misuse—"that I am, and always have been, a voracious reader and a <u>man of letters."</u>

"I know that you once were a senior professor at a prestigious university," I said.

"Ah, so my reputation has already spread far and wide," he said, pleased. "And I'm glad you referred to the university from which I was hounded by administrators and scholars of the new research as a <u>prestigious</u> one, since that adjective carries a supplementary, if archaic, meaning, to wit: 'of or characterized by legerdemain or deception.'" His sigh was so loud and so unexpected that for a moment I feared a rib actually had ruptured his lungs, the air escaping like that from a tire after the nail has been removed. "Here I must hastily admit that such accidental or hidden meanings of words are a particular delight to the ones I have called the most pernicious of the new enchanters, those who proclaim themselves to be <u>deconstructionists</u>; were it not for them, I never would think in such terms. Still, why shouldn't I use their own tricks on those prestigious scholars (and how outrageously, language-wise, they strut, glorying in their new fame!) who find opposed meanings in everything anybody says or writes? As a man of letters who always believed in the universality of great literature—for example, The Authentic Adventures of Kayo Aznap—I found this view quite unacceptable during my professorial career. Or, if it were true in certain ways, I knew it also to be quite false. Do you understand anything that I'm saying, Kayo?"

"You seem to be saying two opposed things at once."

"Et tu, Kayo?" he asked sadly. "And yet I know—for the old story doesn't lie—how willingly you, my bosom companion, one so close to me that my own identity is incomplete without you—I know how willingly you (who are the body to my soul) would join the ranks of the enchanters to advance your own cause and to defeat my own. Simpleton that you are, what do you know about the dark and powerful forces you have allied yourself with?"

How could I have been expected to understand blather like that! Either he was completely mad or there were events in, and meanings to, The Authentic Adventures of Kayo Aznap that the Cliffs Notes guide ignored. Do you recall, Sid, my obviously bizarre feeling, at the time of my memorable embrace with Nod, that my emotions were so strong that I thought I might be living within the pages of a book? My present queasiness came from my suspicion that I had put myself, willy-nilly, within a book I didn't understand, whatever my knowledge of the plot synopsis. What depressed me most was the possibility that I had missed something in the text that, combined with changing times (had something escaped my watchful eye over conservative time?), made worthless my strategy for saving Nod's life. If that was the case, I would be forced (whatever the nausea now deep in my stomach at the very idea of it) to use the last resort. "Listen, Nod," I said cautiously, "don't you care anymore that I've actually talked with Diana, and am bringing back to you the message that I thought you so desperately wanted to hear?"

Once again, he gave the profound sigh that only a windbag of prodigious capacity can make. "Six years ago, Kayo," he said, "I offered you a cup of java from the same pot that's boiling on the fire, but you escaped without accepting that simple offer of hospitality. Now, if you would sit on one end of the hefty limb that I've just provided for the two of us, I'll sit on the other; and while we drink some brew which I think is strong enough to keep you awake and alert to my meanings, I will narrate to you the salient and engrossing details of my life in a way that will answer everything you want to know, including the reason I just sawed off the very branch that provides us with the amenity of a fireplace sofa."

And so I agreed to listen, knowing that while he talked his personal time was ticking away like a bomb that his own words would either defuse or cause to explode.

CHAPTER VI. Nod's Story (Part One)

"For a number of quite understandable reasons," Nod began, "it was a simple matter for me to become a character in a book. The first is that my early years with my great-aunt, Meg, who was and still is a witch, gifted with extraordinary psychic powers, had the richness and sense of fantasy that one associates with the world of imagination; and a second is that after our humble meal of gruel and goat's milk she would read story after story to me—on starry nights before a campfire like this one, but built before the mouth of the cave that was our home. Let me add that the cave was and remains quite comfortable, and is just over the crest of the hill from a chapel for which Meg has been the caretaker for many decades. While I'm engaged in this parenthesis, I might as well say, too, that I consider this home the very center of our galaxy. No doubt there are those who would put that center elsewhere, such as on the white and sparkling sands of a tropical beach; but to me such a theory is as frivolous as the Cuba libre that no doubt produced it. Without hyperbole, I say that the cave and the chapel, no more than twenty miles from where we now sit and chat, are located in a scene of unsurpassed natural beauty—remote, and yet in touch (via the mailbox and newspaper tube) with all the news of our world, thus enabling Meg to hurl maledictions upon all who deserve them for their publicized actions.

"But to return to those stories that Meg read to me in my infancy and childhood. It is likely that our prehistoric ancestors also listened to stories by a fire at the mouth of their caves, and no doubt they too felt themselves transported out of their bodies by the voices of their storytellers, and by the mystery of the dark beyond the fire as well as that of the glitter above, those little campfires in the heavens that must have seemed so many mirrors of their own. . . . Perhaps, Kayo, you have heard the nursery rhyme about Wynken, Blynken, and Nod and the wooden shoe that sailed the skies?"

"Dilsey and I used to recite it together," I said. "Just before I would fall asleep. And, unless I dreamed it, sometimes my dear Papa (though I cannot be sure he was my actual father) would join in."

"So your parentage, too, is unknown!" Nod exclaimed, tenderly. "Ah, Kayo, here is another simple psychological explanation of the reason that some of us can so readily see ourselves as characters in a text dreamed up by another. And, as the old saying has it (though I wouldn't impugn either your mother or mine, whoever she may be, with such an expression), no child can be absolutely certain of his or her parentage, since only the mother knows for sure who the father is, and sometimes even she may be in doubt. But I was speaking of Wynken, Blynken, and Nod. When Meg recited that rhyme to me, I insisted in construing the first two as stars (though in that silly poem stars are fish, Wynken and Blynken a child's eyes, and the wooden shoe that serves as a starship only a crib: but when everything is fancy, maybe it all amounts to the same); and I believed that the third referred to me, the sleepy one. That is to say, long before I ever heard about The Authentic Adventures of Kayo Aznap, I knew myself as Nod, and as one with a special relationship to the firmament. I don't claim anything unique about this, for I imagine I was no different from any other child who hears that rhyme. The stories she later told me, a growing boy, simply solidified that relationship.

"I know how difficult it is for a shrewdly practical man of your sort, Kayo, to put yourself in the shoes (by the way, mine as a child were sewed by Meg out of soft goatskin, though in summer I went barefoot) of another, a drowsy boy sipping warm goat's milk from a crude wooden cup while listening to a witch whom he adored tell story after story, often about characters based on figures she saw in the night sky—a goat with the tail of a fish, a hunter with a jeweled belt and sword, the huntress Diana, whose countenance was the great moon itself, etc. No, a man of practicality, one so caught up in the daily business of the world that he doesn't recognize that ceaseless, treadmill activity for the madness that it is, couldn't be expected to feel how miraculous all that would seem to a little boy. To listen to those stories while the chipmunks, the raccoons, and the skunks quietly came out of the underbrush to sit nearby, as if they too were listening—"

"Of course I can sense all that," I said, stung that he would consider me so insensitive and oblivious; for, though Nod's campfire had not been built before the mouth of a witch's cave, and the witch herself was elsewhere, the present setting was otherwise a pretty fair facsimile of the scene of Nod's remembrance, including as it did, as if on cue, the reappearance of similar furry little beggars. I should say, Sid, as a parenthesis of my own, that although Nod and I were both sitting on that oak limb—big enough in circumference to be a log—that had tumbled down with him, none of its branches or foliage (well, of course not!) had as yet been removed; and so it was as if both he and I were in separate leafy bowers, little cavelike niches that hid each of us from the other. Through the leaves above I could see the stars, and before me was both the fire and a skunk, perhaps the very one that had released its aroma six years ago. It looked at me with what I took to be beady-eyed suspicion, which made me realize that if in one hand I held a cup of coffee, in the other I still held my revolver. Gingerly, I put the heirloom away in my holster, and would you believe it, Sid, that animal actually lifted a paw, as if we had come to an understanding! I consolidated this transaction between minds by tossing it a bad-breath mint from a cylindrical little package in my pocket intended as a gift for Nod himself. Do you know that cute little creature actually licked it!

"Storytelling, probably the first of the arts," Nod continued (can you imagine that he would have stopped?), "was born in response to the wonder we feel before the vast unknown, the wonder that makes any living creature, however small, seem to us a miracle of its own—which, of course, it is. From such awe (the emotion of the soul that links everything within the universe), science and philosophy and poetry were eventually born, too, as anybody who has gone to college knows. Perhaps politics and religion, sister institutions that they are, came into being as society's method of channeling (dare I say manipulating?) for its own ends that impulse or desire within the individual to sacralize the universe beyond his or her limited perception and personal body.

"As a veteran man of letters, as a former senior professor who was granted tenure in the days before his university became prestigious, I have given much thought, idle and otherwise, to matters like these, and to their relationship to the literature I seem always to have admired, that library of texts we call universal, and whose most valued member is none other than The Authentic Adventures of Kayo Aznap."

"I'm glad you still feel that way," I said, almost yawning those words. To tell you the truth, Sid, I was beginning to get drowsy, a condition that in me is always intensified by hunger. As a bachelor, I typically eat my meals in restaurants, and usually (as was the case on this day) bypass breakfast, for the sight of others munching hot cakes and sausages, both liberally soaked with syrup, returns me, however much I concentrate on my eleventh and most crucial rule (I assume you remember it), to my dear Papa's Sunday breakfasts, to the tinkle of that little crystal bell and his shy call, "Well, the crêpes are ready, folks." Nostalgia, that painful thrill in the belly, not only prevents proper digestion, but makes the dish presently before me so unappetizing I fear the ingestion of it will make me throw up. On the plane, I had rejected (for a double Scotch) the little tray of thawed food that masqueraded as luncheon fare, not because of nostalgia but because the conflict then within me was too intense to make palatable a minced patty of undeterminable origin or even the complimentary package of nuts from Macedonia or wherever. And consider the effects upon my poor body of my vigorous hike, maybe thirty miles, along highways, through the forests, up and down the hills—a journey to a host talking nonstop (unlike any plane on the regional airline I'd taken), and whose hospitality consisted of a single cup of bitter coffee!

"At the risk of dogmatism, something my students and colleagues often accused me of," Nod declaimed (in what no doubt was his old lecturing voice) from the security of his own little bower, "I say that the only true impulse of creativity, in science or the arts, is a holy or sacred one, the quest for unity. My enchanters find such a quest a delusion, as to my sorrow I realize. Still, great authors have always known (within their souls, if not their conscious minds) not only the truth contained within the <u>diamond shape</u> but that the dust from which their bodies was constituted is one with the atoms of the most distant stars. Or so it always seemed to me, Kayo."

"Hmmm."

"Great authors recognize the arbitrary nature of all of our social distinctions, of the classifications and barriers we set up to divide person from person, race from race (put that word in quotation marks), and nation from nation. And yet, as you know, society with all of its distinctions, classifications, barriers, wars among nations, and conflicts among humans is their very text! The power of such a peerless work as <u>The Authentic Adventures of Kayo Aznap</u> comes from its cosmic slant, of course."

"Of course."

"Has it ever struck you as odd that in that book in which you and I (and for that matter, most of humanity, since <u>The Authentic Adventures</u> for generations was considered the most universal text of all) find ourselves, the heavens go unmentioned—at least until you get to the very end?"

"Not really."

"And yet the story takes place, or most of it does, outdoors, in that vast desert with mountains on the distant horizon, a region in which (despite the glare from that city for gambling) the stars should be unusually bright, because of the rarefied atmosphere."

"Hmmm."

"Perhaps, as I suggested in an unpublished paper, the author suffered from myopia, for as even a cursory reading of his quite lengthy, two-volume text shows, very little of the phenomenal world is described with precision or clarity. No wonder, then, that he depends less upon what he actually sees (he was so blind he misread the geographical details on his map of the region he had chosen for his characters' adventures—if indeed he consulted that map, a matter still hotly disputed) than on the dreamings of his great but childlike soul to gain the cosmic effect. In a word (or two), he depends upon magical caves (and caves indeed are figures of the universe), upon mirages of oases or islands, upon fantastic haciendas existing deep beneath yet another desert mirage of a dark and forbidding pool, etc.

"Because of the extraordinary length of each of the volumes, Meg chose to read them to me inside our own cave, during the long winter nights. Perhaps The Authentic Adventures was the formative text of my life because the setting for that reading was so harmonious with the spirit of the text itself. Our bedroom, you see, was the grotto behind the parlor and kitchen—that is to say, behind the grotto that opened on the hillside to the wintry world. This inner grotto had shiny little stalactites on the ceiling (Meg had broken off and smoothed down their companions, the stalagmites on the floor: a good mnemonic device for distinguishing between the two is to recall that stalactites hold tightly to the ceiling) as well as little diamonds of mica that reflected the flame of the candle that she read to me by. We had a goatskin at the entrance to this inner grotto, to protect it from the blasts that managed to leak through the goatskin at the entrance to the outer grotto; and on the floor a soft carpet of sheepskins (Meg kept a few sheep among her goats, for this very purpose as well as to make those marvelous cheeses that I always thought of as a superb product of her alchemy, but which actually were produced by the careful aging of a proper mixture of the milk of both types of animal), and I had further sheepskins for my blanket. . . . I say, are you awake, Kayo?"

"Hmmm."

"To get the effect of the crucially important way The Authentic Adventures of Kayo Aznap worked upon my developing soul, you have to imagine, if you can, that you are a small boy embedded—oh, so warmly, so comfortably!—between layers of sheepskin, listening to the melodiously hypnotic voice of a good witch (for she is kind, and cares for your every want) as she reads—now wait a moment, while I find it . . . [Here my bower swayed ever so gently as Nod bounded to his feet, apparently running to his saddlebags for his copy of The Authentic Adventures; the bower swayed again as he dropped heavily onto his end of the log, and I heard the whisper of pages being hurriedly turned] . . . as she reads the following:

"For, tell me, could there be anything more delightful than to see displayed here and now before our eyes, as we might say, a great pool of pitch, boiling hot, and swimming and writhing about in it a great number of serpents, snakes, and lizards, and many other sorts of savage and frightful creatures; and then to hear issuing from the middle of that pool a most dismal voice crying: 'You, Cowboy, whoever you may be, that gaze on this dreadful pool, if you would reach the treasure hidden beneath these black waters, show the valor of your dauntless heart and plunge into the middle of its dark, burning liquor; for if you do not do so, you will not be worthy to see the mighty marvels hidden within the seven haciendas of the seven cattle barons who dwell beneath this gloomy water.' No sooner has the cowboy heard this dreadful voice than he abandons all thought for himself, and without reflecting on the peril to which he is exposing himself, or even easing himself of the weight of his heavy chaps and boots, he commends himself to Allah and his lady Diana, dives into the middle of the boiling pool; and then unexpectedly, and when he least knows where he is going, he finds himself amidst flowery meadows, incomparably finer even than the Elysian fields. There the sky seems to him more transparent and the sun to shine with a new brightness. Before his eyes opens a pleasant grove of green and leafy trees, whose verdure charms his vision, while his ears are ravished by the sweet, untaught song of innumerable little bright-colored birds which flit about the interlacing branches. Here he discovers a small stream, whose fresh waters glide like liquid crystal over delicate sand and little white stones, which resemble sifted gold and purest pearl. There he spies a fountain made of mottled jasper and smooth marble; here another, roughly fashioned, where tiny mussel shells, mingled with the twisted yellow and white houses of the snails . . .''

Here I fell asleep; and I fear that in re-creating this passage for you (and for that matter, all the events of this day), I am again in danger of doz . . .[1]

CHAPTER VII. *Kayo's Dreaming*

Sid, I've never slept so soundly (beguiled in my sleep by a succession of delightful images spiced with a few pleasurably fearsome ones) or for so long (for several days passed, at least as one measures time while asleep), even though Nod, upon my wakening, declared I had been asleep for no more

[1]As is apparent, Kayo did doze off again—and I confess to a blissful somnolence of my own, followed by a slumber filled with the most delightful images. If, reader, you are following this story in your warm bed on a winter's night, the present moment would be an appropriate one in which to lay aside this book (if you can bear to do so, knowing that joys and terror still lie ahead), turn off the light, and let the images and characters of <u>Kayo: The Authentic and Annotated Autobiographical Novel from Outer Space,</u> as well as those of the novel contained within it, <u>The Authentic Adventures of Kayo Aznap,</u> join in your dreaming with whatever they will.

If, stimulated by the story, you persist in wakefulness, attentive to the remainder of this footnote and the continuation of Nod's story, your eyes perceive here my grateful acknowledgment to J. M. Cohen, translator of <u>Don Quixote</u> in my own much battered Penguin copy. For in my own growing drowsiness, I lost contact with Kayo, causing me to crib much of the above passage from Cohen's translation, since in the majority of details it seems faithfully to mirror the description that Meg read to Nod, who read it to Kayo, who sent it across the cosmos to me.

than half an hour. But since I probably had been sleeping hours before he discovered I wasn't attending to his words (at least consciously: some of them apparently entered my dreams), I certainly slept far longer than he knew. When one leans back against a handy branch in a leafy bower, one sleeps like a child in a cradle.

Now, Sid, as practically all the Cliffs Notes guides say in their succinct notes about symbols, caves and deep pools are never caves and pools per se, but are metaphors for the womb—a pretty sweeping generalization, but something that may strike you as likely enough, at least in regard to Nod's own description of the carpeted inner grotto in which Meg read him a book so extraordinarily long that it is no wonder that her reading of it became the key formative event in his life. Indeed, Nod may have been one of the few people ever to hear, word for word, both parts of The Authentic Adventures; the Cliffs Notes guide remarks that the first part is so full of artistically unwarranted digressions, sometimes tales within tales, that only the rare reader enters the second part.

While it seems certain to me that Nod himself considered his cave to be a cave per se, one which in no way represented his nostalgic yearning to return to the womb of his as yet unknown mother,[1] yet it was for him, as he had so recently informed me, the very center of everything, which I guess is the way a good many of us Unitedians consider our childhood homes. And maybe because of something he said while I slept, in my dreams that cave I'd never seen was the womb of the starry universe itself, the home from which my preexistent soul had come, and to which it would return.[2] In my shrewd and conscious state an idea like that is so much tommyrot (Teddy, as Tommy, was almost capable of such stuff); but Allah knows all the perverse notions you're vulnerable to in your sleep. In any event, the witch Meg, dressed in black, beckoned me into her cave, warning me to step around the

---

[1] What a tantalizing phrase! [The underlining here is mine.] As a canny writer, Kayo withholds the identity of Nod's parents as well as that of his own father for a climactic moment; I would be a faithless scribe, were I to give away such secrets in advance.

[2] A grand and quite Wordsworthian notion, if I'm any judge!

fire on which chicken, treated with pungent sauces, was bubbling in a pot, and led me into an inner grotto both tiny and immense (as size can be in our dreams: ask any of your <u>Alices</u>!).

"Here time is, and here time is not," the witch said, "but do not confuse it with your <u>conservative</u> time or with any politics or philosophy born of language alone." In a deep and clearly masculine voice, she added, <u>"I say no more."</u> But after that warning, followed by a dreary sigh, she spoke again: "Here soul becomes body, and body becomes soul. Here you become Nod and Nod becomes you, as is written in the book no <u>gambler</u> can read." In her hand was a divining rod that served at her bidding as a kind of torch. With it, she illuminated a book on the floor—one as big as a basic dictionary and family compendium of knowledge, the kind of tome that includes appendices of the first names of people of both sexes, giving their etymologies; tables of weights and measures; the noble laws of our land, all of them based on the precept that every one of us is equal; flags and monetary units of all the civilized countries; the various signs of the zodiac; perpetual calendars that include phases of the moon; rules for card games; and so on. Nay, bigger than that: bind into that volume another, one that contains every one of those innumerable Cliffs Notes guides, if you can imagine a book so diverse and unwieldy as that. "In this magical book," Meg the witch said, in a dronelike incantation, "lie myriads of organic units or imaginary entities or whatever you wish to call them. Though built with words in their infinite permutations and arrangements, words whose meanings constantly change, they are of the sacred universe as well as the profane world, for they are born of the knowledge of the secrets of my cave, and indeed may be said to be individual little caves that ingeniously mirror mine." Following this bit of riddling nonsensicality, she said again, in a pontifical voice that seemed one with Nod's, <u>"I say no more."</u>

Then she pointed her divining rod at a constellation of stars in the ceiling, transforming them at once into a hunter with biceps and torso like those of a professional weight lifter. Bare to the chest, he wore your ordinary pair of faded blue jeans, their legs tucked into a comfortable pair of old cowboy boots, and around his waist a magnificent belt studded with precious gems. Would you believe it, Sid, there was a hole in his chest, big enough to show the throbbing of his generously bleeding heart, but he was rubbing that wound as if he cherished it more than anything else in the universe. "And here is she who killed him," said Meg the witch (another indication of her nonsensicality, for as anybody could tell he was far from dead), pointing her rod at one of the brightest objects in the ceiling. Right up there—close enough so that I could almost, but not quite, touch her—was the most beautiful cowgirl, wearing a short skirt, white boots of the sort your cheerleaders wear (with those little tassels, I mean), a cute cartridge belt draped rakishly about her waist; but what fiery jewels she had for eyes! If you can imagine her in a kitchen, you can also imagine her frying a chicken with those eyes alone. . . .

I want you to realize, Sid, that in telling you all this, I know that none of it is real, that everything I was seeing was influenced by the Cliffs Notes guide to The Authentic Adventures as well as by my acquaintance with a nuthead raised by a witch, that Old Fart who kept gassing on about the story of his life, some of his words obviously entering my unconscious mind. Allah knows how much of his life history (maybe the most valuable part of it) I'll never find out, having slept right through it. Even when I was dreaming, I knew what I was dreaming wasn't true to any fact of the world as we see it, because everything was all so imprecise, except maybe for the cowboy hunter and the cowgirl and maybe a raccoon and skunk or two that wandered across the starry ceiling. Everything else was absolutely devoid of all those sharp details that my conscious mind prizes so highly, and uses to its advantage time and time again.

At one awesome point Meg the witch lit up the whole cave with her divining rod, turning the floor into a deep pool that I dived into in order to keep from drowning, which doesn't make sense, but shows the hallucinatory power of the passage that put me to sleep. I dived right down to that hacienda, where I was served a magnificent chicken dinner with biscuits and honey (and as much beer as I could drink) by a lovely troop of maidens. None of them said a disrespectful word about my voracious appetite, or even giggled afterward about my lack of proper manners, as I leisurely cleaned between my teeth with the dental floss my dentist—my actual dentist, that is—says I must use, or my gums will rot, much to the detriment of my remaining molars, not to say incisors.

Here's the real disappointment of my dreams: the chicken and biscuits were all taste, having no substance. Such a meal could never satisfy anybody's hunger; and so I dived into a pool beneath this pool, and then a pool beneath that one, going farther and farther down or back in time or history, but always accompanied by the very same group of silent but beautiful maidens, who (I forgot this detail when I first mentioned them) unclothed and washed me before serving that food that made me hungrier each time I ate it. The very deepest pool of all was not your conventional pastoral pool, not the kind you would expect to find at a hacienda or even in the woodlands near the campfire where I was dreaming this fantastical matter. Rather, it was a kind of briny marsh, surrounded by fronds of a shape unfamiliar to me; the sky was forbidding and dark, intermittently lit by great thunderbolts. . . . Are you laughing at me, Sid?[3]

---

[3]Though Kayo was too embarrassed to wait for an answer, I'll say here that, no, I was not laughing at him in the slightest—for this entire account of his dreams (as the length of this footnote may indicate) is of extraordinary interest not only to me but to all who care about more than mere logic and reason. Let me at once point out (like the scholar who interpreted a kindred mental experience of Don Quixote's) two curious but crucial characteristics to be found in Kayo's dreaming. First (as is true of all the crucial visions described by our unparalleled Cervantes), the sublime is interfused with the mundane and ridiculous, proof enough that so long as we live (and "we," of course, here must include the inhabitants of planets other than our own), our souls cannot wholly separate themselves from our bodily senses. Second (a corollary of the first), the entire downward journey of what I take to be Kayo's soul probably led him into what vulgar minds call a <u>wet dream</u> and the rest of us refer to as a <u>nocturnal emission.</u>

Why do I find this hypothesis a likely one? As a bachelor, Kayo no doubt found an outlet in dreams alone for what the more fortunate of us find in a beloved partner of the opposite sex. And yet dreams play a part in the loveliest and most satisfactory physical coupling. In my own still-passionate (I'm glad to say) lovemaking, not only do I see my own dazzling Diana before the sexual climax, but typically, at the moment of climax and briefly afterward, a briny pool

Soon after perceiving this deepest pool of all, I began to rise from my subterranean depths, pursuing an overpowering aroma of <u>real</u> chicken; and, upon opening my eyes, what did I perceive but that greedy Nod, sitting by the campfire, munching upon a chicken leg. He had cooked a chicken, and eaten more than half of it, without even bothering to wake me up!

CHAPTER VIII. *Nod's Story (Part Two)*

"So you're awake at last!" Nod cried in delight, as I lunged toward him to grasp a piece of chicken from the flimsy aluminum pie plate (a discard from some frozen-food TV dinner?) he held in his hand. "I may have talked on for a minute or two before you fell asleep. Did you hear about my first awareness that there were enchanters of the postmodernist ilk in the world, certain <u>goblinlike</u> writers who preceded by

> similar to Kayo's, and likewise illuminated by lightning. So far as such mysteries are concerned, Jung is to my mind a far better guide than Freud. All that I personally can say with any certainty is that there is a part of us that existed prior to its birth within our present shape, and that it carries us back <u>at least as far as</u> our primitive, physical beginnings.
>
> Visions flow from the soul, instinctive responses from the body; perhaps both are encoded in our genes, but how little does the present, skeptical generation of students care for such matters! My most successful pedagogical demonstration as a teacher of bored and practical-minded undergraduates came when I suddenly sprang upon the seminar table, where I crouched and growled menacingly at them. The sudden flow of adrenaline that made their hearts pump, their bodies ready to fight or flee, was convincing proof to this young group of sophisticated doubters, most of them conceived in overheated apartment houses, that through their daddies and mommies they were connected to the entire human past. In a travesty of justice, the very success of this teaching device (one of my students fainted) became the first excuse the administrators needed to question my general competency.

decades the pernicious deconstructionists? Perhaps you fell asleep earlier, while I was mentioning the coolness of the cave in summer, its warmth in winter? I'll repeat some of that, and if you've already heard it, just raise your hand. . . . My, you <u>are</u> hungry, aren't you, Kayo?" he marveled, watching me wolf down the meat on the only decent piece left; and he handed me the pie plate as if he were the most generous person in the world, even though it now contained nothing but the wings and the neck.

I don't know why a crazy dream about a witch in a cave that was the womb of the starry universe and about a series of ever-deeper pools would give me a <u>moral</u> sense, Sid, but all at once I remembered something in the DSP file about Nod, and I almost choked on that chicken neck. "Where did you get this particular fowl, delicious as it is?" I asked suspiciously.

"Sonya Monosovich."

"A gap-toothed peasant bitch, probably a Polack?"

"I wouldn't call her that, not at all: no, a lovely woman, Meg's nearest neighbor, who also knows about the healing power of herbs; and who, when Meg dies, may indeed be the next occupant of the cave, for Meg has willed it to her, since Meg knows that <u>my destiny lies elsewhere.</u> On many a winter evening, Sonya came to the cave, to play the most transporting of melodies—haunting, gypsylike airs—on her ancient violin. Literature is not the only form of art in touch with the stars, Kayo. Without stretching the truth, I can say that Sonya's playing is in tune with the music of the spheres."

"You didn't steal this chicken from her?"

"Oh, what a mendacious mind you must have, to think I would steal what Sonya so freely gives! Her chicken is nourishment to my body, her melodies to my soul; if there was anything of hers I would steal if I could, it would be her musical talent. Not being bound to language, music (some say) is a higher form of art than that to be found even in such a glorious accomplishment as <u>The Authentic Adventures.</u> On the other hand, in the sounds of notes and words alike one can sometimes hear the sacred stillness lying behind the liquid dripping that marks the passing of time in the most subterranean grotto, in its deepest pool."[1] He went on to discuss the marvelous acoustics of the cave, which made it a delight for Sonya to play there, summer as well as winter, despite a modicum of dampness that posed a threat to her ancient instrument. "I don't suppose, Kayo, that you know much about caves, but as I've already told you, they're just about as warm in winter as the White House, after you had the president turn down the thermostats."

"How did you know that was my idea?" I asked, astonished. The offhand way in which Nod revealed this knowledge about one of the smallest of my arcane activities made my skin prickle. "That's pretty Allah-damned eerie, that you would know something like that, Nod!"

"I told you that Meg is gifted with extraordinary psychic powers," Nod said, obviously exasperated by my obtuseness. "I expect you to listen when I tell you something, especially something as important as that."

"So you still see her? I thought she and the goats butted you out of the cave for being a spoiled brat or something."

"As death is (or are) the wages of sin, so slander is the cost of fame," Nod said. "Meg and I remain on the best of terms, even though she is an old lady and set in her ways. No, she sent me out into the world because she recognized that I (if not through myself, through my influence on another) was destined to change it and she had taught me all that she could."

I asked guardedly, "Does she say anything about my effect upon your destiny?" Of course, I didn't believe Meg possessed occult powers, except maybe for the way she had come to me when I was both ravenous and asleep; still, that busi-

---

[1]As a general rule, in Kayo's text even the most casually introduced reference to a minor character (or to such a trivial object as a "Zippo" lighter, for that matter) is followed by other references in later chapters; but I find no mention of Sonya Monosovich in any chapter other than the present one. Though the praise of her is put in the mouth of Nod, we must always firmly keep in mind that Kayo himself is our artificer; out of character though it may seem, we must assume that he included Nod's compliments in his book because of his own love of music. I wonder, though, if his taste goes beyond "haunting, gypsylike airs."

ness about the thermostats continued to puzzle me. If Meg read the newspapers (remember Nod saying there was a newspaper tube near the cave, Sid?), maybe she had come across some reference to me (for whatever my low profile, my role as a presidential confidant naturally enough had led to a certain amount of journalistic speculation: Nod, after all, was not the only victim of gossip). Were she to possess some of my own native shrewdness, as no doubt any successful witch would, she might very well have figured out who was behind the White House energy-saving measures. I'm not superstitious in the slightest, but I do have intellectual curiosity, which is the only reason I wondered what, if anything, Meg knew about me.

"Maybe she does, maybe she doesn't," Nod said, infuriating me with such teasing. "Reveal a prophecy, and you so change the future that it can't come true. Anyway, witches know less about what is to come than about what was and is—so to a degree they're like the prophesying ape (Meg won't like that analogy!) in The Authentic Adventures of Kayo Aznap. Surely you recall that famous scene, Kayo?"

"Of course," I said promptly, a downright lie: the Cliffs Notes guide had not mentioned it. Whatever gentle playfulness all that chicken had provided him with vanished in another of those profound sighs of his; and even in his teasing me about Meg's prophecy I had detected a note of sadness. Nod gushed on, as usual; but it was now as if by words alone he would drown a dank melancholy that had pervaded the depths of his own soul. He asked me to imagine him, if I could, not as the elderly, fat slob he had become, but as the slender youth, his head full of fables and whatnot, who had been sent forth from the cave by Meg to find his destiny (how he returned to grandiose formulations about his fated future!), and who had struggled, as all peasants must, for a formal education that was, he insisted, no "higher" than the learning he had gained from Meg's lips.

"Do you speak Gaulish, Kayo?" he suddenly asked.

"Braire," I said at once, a conditioned response. "Present participle, brayant; past participle, brait; future, braira and brairont; imperfect, brayait and brayaient."

"Excellent," Nod said, with subdued admiration. "The various forms of <u>to bray,</u> a defective example of the fourth conjugation of irregular verbs."

"Yes," I said, doing my damnedest to cheer up that O.F. "The one irregular verb successfully drilled into me through constant repetition by the arrogant Vladimir, the butler of my childhood, as proof to him that I was an ass."

All I got for that was another of those dreadful, garlicky sighs, this one right in my face! "As a young scholar infatuated with the Gaulish masterpieces of older days," Nod said, "I spent my first sabbatical in the gay and cosmopolitan center of Gaul, a lovely city, simply to pick up the language for myself, for Meg didn't know it and we had no Gaulish-speaking butler in our cave. I adopted the ways of a <u>boulevardier</u> despite my impecuniousness, and even had a cane and a tight-fitting—dashing, if I do say so—coat, somewhat patched, that I had picked up for a song at the famous <u>flea market</u>—an actual song, for in those days I could carry a tune nicely, and wasn't above singing in public for a coin or two." He made a brave attempt to smile. "So even then, I was something of what the Gauls call (not without admiration) a <u>poseur.</u> Be that as it may, another characteristic, less admirable to the Gauls, sometimes caught me up: I refer to my wholly United-ian innocence, for beyond doubt I was <u>naïf,</u> a condition they deplore. Once, for example, I gave a few <u>centimes,</u> though it was all the money in my possession, to a young lady on the street I thought to be in extreme circumstances; as it turned out, she was a prostitute, considered my gift an insult, and so threw the coins, accompanied by the conventional spit, into my face. In my embarrassment, I walked into a ditch some five or six feet deep. (The sanitation department was digging up a sewer line, and, no doubt because of that insouciance that characterizes the Gauls, had neglected to put up any barriers.) It is to that young lady's credit that she helped me out. And then—but what followed remains a private matter, though one in which I lost some of my innocence. Well may you ask, Kayo, why I am confessing all of this to you."

I wasn't asking anything of the sort from him, being occupied with sucking whatever juices I could out of that pitiful collection of bones on the pie plate; all I wanted to know was whether I had to kill this sorrowing creature (his sorrow made me feel guilty enough to wonder if the prophesying Meg actually might have revealed to him my murderous intent) or not, a decision that depended on whether he still believed enough in The Authentic Adventures of Kayo Aznap to accompany me, in accordance with the wishes of that figment Diana, to the Kayo Corral, for a duel to the death.

"In answer to your question, let us jump several years— as much as half a decade, actually—forward in time, and back to that university in this, our lovely Lake District. As a bachelor, I was assumed to be lonely (though I had my precious books!), and frequently was invited by my married colleagues to their family dinners. Some of those dinners could be pretty squalid affairs, with screaming infants and nervous little terriers that darted out from under chairs to bite your ankle, and so on; but on one memorable evening, I attended a dinner of the sort that makes a bachelor envious of the happiness that marriage and children on occasion can bring. The dinner was an early one, out of consideration for me, for afterward I planned to attend a lecture by a celebrated woman novelist from Gaul. I wanted, in part, to see how well my command of her language had held up over the years, and I might as well tell you now that it held up quite beyond my expectations, which, because of the nature of her remarks, delighted me less than you might think.

"The husband and wife were both in their middle years; they had two teen-aged sons. You will simply have to accept my testimony when I say I was in the presence of something that seemed blessed: a man and woman who cared deeply for each other, and two intelligent and sensitive children who obviously loved their parents, respected each other, and participated in the conversation of their parents and guest without showing any desire to be off in their rooms, a phonograph deafening their young ears. I can only say that I was touched, deeply moved by that experience. . . ."

Forewarned by his pained and pensive look, I ducked away this time, to miss a frontal blast from his sigh. To save you from suspense, Sid, let me summarize what he said about the lecture, and about the events of the following morning, when he was heading into the library to pick up one of the novels by the celebrated foreign author of works in the latest fashion, the <u>nouveau roman.</u> Though she was stylishly dressed and spoke in a most cultivated and agreeable voice, she was, in Nod's memory, one of the <u>hobgoblins,</u> precursors of those enchanters who, in denying both the soul and its truth, make us simply <u>the juncture of a series of interpersonal systems.</u> The essence of her lecture was that the individual self had become, for various reasons known to all people of culture, nothing but a bore to writers; human personality was simply <u>banal,</u> and hence authors had to seek something other than people and their always predictable behavior as a center of whatever "stories"—or whatever one would call fiction without characters or plot—they chose to tell. It was her assured manner, and convincing delivery, that sent Nod to the library the next morning, to see how well her practice fit her theory.

Now, I must report another of those coincidences that (as my words have already demonstrated) are far more numerous in life than any novel dares to emulate. As Nod was climbing the library stairs, he met (and I have no reason to doubt the veracity of his account of this encounter) his host of the night before, rushing headlong down those same stairs, having been summoned from his carrel by a librarian with the news that his wife—driving the little sports car that had been one of the topics of conversation the previous night—had within the past hour skidded into a truck on the icy highway, on her way to a nearby skiing resort, and been killed.

You should know, Sid, that Nod (the dearest and kindest friend a man could ever have)[2] began to sob as he told me this, his own anguished face a far better image than any his words could provide, as he attempted to describe the ravaged look on his colleague's face while the latter briefly told him that he had lost his wife. How obscene (Nod said) any notion, however genteel its expression, of the banality of the individual self, of human personality, when one is forced to see the

---

[2] Kayo himself is so obviously overcome by this tragedy, known to him only through Nod's narration of it, that he here at last reveals the full depth of his own love for the man whose death by Kayo's own hand was foretold in that initial message for Professor Duck that I intercepted and decoded, <u>DEAR FRANK WHY CONTACT ME I TOO AM A MURDERER SANCHO.</u>

intensity of such love, such bitter loss! He regretted the impulse that had sent him to the library, and returned to his office without the book; and yet (for such was the nature, Sid, of this greathearted and thus vulnerable companion of mine) the glimpse he'd had into the suffering of another made him wonder if he himself was truly alive, wonder if perhaps he was nothing more than the youthful poseur, somebody whose own idealism was part of a prideful illusion and the Unitedian cultural molasses, and who actually was motivated by nothing more than his biological appetites. (Here you have a prime example of why I tell you to be wary of your own idealistic tendencies, Sid!) That is to say, he wondered if he wasn't as banal as the French novelist declared all individuals to be, and if that by and large she might not be reflecting a truth about nearly everybody on our planet. . . .

I don't know why such revelations moved me so, maybe because my sucking of all those bones had not satiated my hunger, and hunger is something that always makes me receptive and alert when it doesn't make me sleepy; all I know is that he talked on and on, until even the skunk gave up, and the raccoon as well—or maybe it was almost dawn by then, and they went off by instinct to find their dens, skunks and raccoons being nocturnal animals, as you probably know. "Listen, Nod," I interrupted him to say, "I am telling you again, with all the honesty I'm capable of and for the sake of your very own and precious life, that Diana—yes, Diana, that figure you adore—truly implores you to save Jean, within whose shape she has been imprisoned, from the gamblers at the Kayo Corral, however much you may think they have been replaced by newer enchanters. If you don't fight a duel with the Desperado, your beloved mistress will be lost forever! Have you completely lost your belief in The Authentic Adventures of Kayo Aznap, the most universal text of them all?"

Once more, that enormous sigh! "Ah, Kayo, the new enchanters say that Diana is but a reflection of my own male ego, another illustration of the false values through which the male sex dominates the female, by putting her on a pedestal—even though, or so it seems to me, such an illusion is a characteristic of our species, and women as well as men try to locate their impossible-to-obtain (at least on this planet) spiritual ideals in an equally faulty person of the opposite sex: an idolized cowboy, for example. And let me say that your distant ancestor, the author of The Authentic Adventures, who was indeed the wisest of men, had his obviously autobiographical character admit on at least one occasion that Diana was true only as an ideal for his own contemplation. Now, I grant you that any text, if you subject it to merciless Gaulish logic, is full of oppositions, that indeed it can be said to deconstruct itself, even as I, in perceiving the full extent of another man's genuine suffering, was led to consider its opposite, the banality that denies the preciousness, in love and grief, of every individual alive, especially myself. . . .

"In the years after that encounter on the library steps, I often thought of the fragility of the human soul, intangible quality that it is, yearning always to be one with the infinite, a wisp that declares its home within the stars, within the vastness of the cave that is the cosmos. And yet without that sense of sacred oneness, of what import, really, our Unitedian sense of the worth and equality of each of us? What is the point of an individual per se? Note, too, our Unitedian belief in freedom. Isn't freedom itself finally a metaphysical desire, a wish of that intangible soul to escape all confinement, its imprisonment within our very social identity as well as that imposed by vile totalitarian regimes? And why should it be that this wish for freedom on the part of the soul gives meaning to the very identity it would escape from? Surely these all are oppositions that should cancel each other out, were we to trust to logic and language alone, were we to deny the soul. But if we continue to admit its existence within us, how can we deny it to the raccoons, the skunks, the chipmunks? To the succulent chicken that you and I just ate, with such satisfaction? To those feared viruses that eat our bodies, with an appetite as deadly as our own? Our souls tell us we can't deny a like soul to any living thing, our bodies and logic say we must. . . .

"So let me be the first to admit that I was not impervious to the logic of the enchanters, caught as I am in my own body and mind, within the politics of a world that knows little but hostility and differences and fear. How hard it is to trust to the truth of the soul, to the worth of the individual, when one sees daily proof of what we truly do one to another! That we permit ourselves to be seduced by the likes of Oz and Tommy and Frank; that we apparently must build missiles and Domes to protect ourselves from Idaho potatoes and Allah knows what else. And let me admit, too, that I turned back to the grand old books, especially The Authentic Adventures, in order to escape all terrors and hobgoblins and modern enchanters; but what have I achieved, as Nod? Have I changed the world by being thrown out of a college and a church?"

He cast an imploring glance upward. "I hope, if my dear Meg is attuned to these words, she won't take offense if I say that her prophetic words about my destiny may have been wrong. In reading as closely as I have in these past few days the works of the poststructuralists—of the semioticians and the pernicious deconstructionists—I realized, to my horror, that what I have done, as one who gave up his banal persona of Professor Michael Quexana to become Nod, the grand and quixotic character of a work by an ancestor of yours, is simply to prove I am living in nothing but a text; and that, of course, is the sine qua non of poststructuralist belief. What bitter irony, Kayo! Indeed, I was so carried away by the deconstructionist view of things that I climbed up that tree, in order to saw off the limb I was sitting on, for they say you can do that.

"In beginning this story of my life so many hours ago, I told you I would explain the reason for this act that must have struck you as absurd as it seems dangerous. Let me say that I have determined from my studious concentration upon the works of the deconstructionists that they themselves have nothing of their own to offer, nothing new and original but their sawing away of the centuries-old illusions they have shared with us, for they find that even what seems to be our deepest and most submerged truths, whatever comes to us in dreams or wherever, has its source in our very consciousness and in our cultural ingestions. As one of their clearest and most charitable proponents observes, they are engaged in "a calculated dismemberment or deconstruction of the great cathedral-like trees in which Man has taken shelter for millennia," but even that phrase describing their own activities, like all language no matter how it tries to divorce itself from the poetical, is nothing but a metaphor, a human construct—and

157

this they cheerfully admit! For that matter, the philosophical notion of the "ground" to which one falls, after sawing off the limb, is metaphorical as well. That is to say, not a word we speak or read refers to anything "real" or essential or true in itself, but always to some other contingency or fancy.

"And so, accepting, in fear and trembling and half in doubt, their rules about such matters, I sawed off the limb, and now confess to you my belief that they must be right; for, as you can observe, I survived, unscathed, and so was engaged in nothing but a metaphorical act."

"But that gigantic limb actually <u>fell,</u> Nod: there's no metaphor there!"

"Yes, I regret the damage done to a noble oak. Such damage to cathedral-like structures is apparently desirable, in their view; but perhaps the tree, actual though it seems, is but a metaphor itself, as it is in any number of bad poems. I'm afraid I'm not thinking too clearly."

"Probably because you got knocked unconscious, Nod. My Allah, how lucky you were not to be killed. . . ." (I was the one who sighed then, Sid, for it seemed as if I were destined to be the tool, not that heavy limb!)

"My wind momentarily was taken from me, no doubt because I landed, physically without harm, on some new philosophical ground, and the world no longer looks the same. My illusions are gone, gone with the wind. Yes, the old wonder, the sacred awe, has fled."[3] He shook his head and rubbed his eyes, looking at me without (I thought) truly seeing me at all. Not until that moment did I notice that his binoculars (as always, dangling from his neck) had been damaged by the fall, one barrel bent askew, its lens shattered. My pity was great enough that I didn't want to bring such ruin to his attention.

Who was it who gave that next prodigious sigh, was it Nod or was it I once more? My hand was stealthily moving (I swear against my will, Sid!) toward my shoulder holster. "I

---

[3]Nod's account of the sudden ebbing of a faith that had seemed so staunch has an authentic ring. On our planet, the most fervent deconstructionists once were those most dedicated to the sublimities of the Romantic poets. Poor, enchanted Nod! And yet the <u>use</u> he will make of deconstructionist practices contains a good bit of sublimity, to my way of thinking.

suppose I must assume then, Nod, that you have absolutely, one hundred percent, lost your belief in Diana; that you therefore refuse to believe that she is in thrall to the evil gamblers, and see no reason whatsoever to respond to her appeal to engage in a duel with the Desperado at the Kayo Corral at the thirty-first hour on this very day? You will note that dawn already has come, the journey is long by horseback, and we would have to leave at once, were we to outwit the gamblers."

He gave me the sweetest smile you can imagine, Sid! "Though I may have lost my belief in the universal truth of The Authentic Adventures, Kayo, it is obvious to me that you have not, and that you continue to find a spiritual solace by living within its pages. Since this is the case, and you are my friend, I gladly will fight the duel for your sake, hoping that you manage forever to live within the world of childlike imagination and spiritual illusion; for the loss of it has been a grievous blow to me, I admit."

At that instant I dropped to my knees to offer a silent prayer of thanksgiving, trusting that at least the witch, gifted as she was with extraordinary pyschic powers, would hear it.

CHAPTER IX. *Back at the Kayo Corral*[1]

And so, just as the brilliant sun reached us through that gap in the majestic oak made by Nod's sawing, we set out, he on Tammy and I following on Smoky. We barely reached the Kayo Corral on time, for Nod dallied in the departure, carefully arranging his mildewed books in his saddlebags (and got himself immersed, despite my protests, in one volume after another, while in the process of stuffing them in their proper

[1] So at last we are to reach the event with which Kayo opened his story! As it turns out, he began less in medias res than near the end—but whether the delay is a result of craft or his hesitancy to reveal the humiliating truth of what actually took place, no mere scribe can say.

order). Finally, he buckled the bags and lugged them under the shelter of the oak, where he tucked them within a sheet of plastic that contained so many rips and holes it wouldn't have offered much protection against the weather.

"For Allah's sake, Nod," I said impatiently, "it's not going to rain—look, there's not a cloud in the sky."

"Who knows the hour or the day of my return?" he asked (and indeed he was never to come back to this campsite again: did he suspect this might be the case?). "A _man of letters_ must always see to the welfare of his books: for even though to him they may have lost their universality, there may be others, such as yourself, who eventually will find them of redeeming value." And then, he had to saddle and bridle the horses, but it seemed to me that he fussed inordinately over that sorry pair of animals, not only cleaning out their hoofs with a little pick he kept for that purpose, but grooming their coats and pulling stray burrs from their manes and tails. "Don't we want them to look their best on this day, Kayo?" he responded to my continuing protests that he was wasting the hours. "And certainly a _man of letters_ who also is a _lover of animals_ would not refuse the care he gives to his books to his faithful beasts."

Actually, it was lucky—given the age of the animals and the proclivity to talk that on occasion made Nod so forgetful of his surroundings that he permitted Tammy to take the wrong path—that we reached our destination at all. I was nervous the entire way, constantly imploring him to make haste—even though Smoky's infrequent trottings caused me, an inexperienced horseman, to bounce up and down so severely I would lose the stirrups and be forced to cling desperately to the mane to keep from falling off.

Now, Sid, you might be wondering why I would be going through with an elaborate pretense at a certain risk to my own life, given the fact that Nod had fallen to a new philosophical ground that caused him to disbelieve in so many things—including Diana, the figment in whose name he had engaged in so many preposterous acts. Was he not now as thoroughly _gelded_ as the beast I was straddling, whose capacious belly, you may be assuming, may have been a pain to my thighs, but whose behavior was totally predictable?

Well, let me tell you something, to wit: Smoky and Nod

alike were, if generally moody, still mercurial, given to violent changes in disposition. That horse I rode sometimes tenderly nipped the tail of his companion, but sometimes (however I kicked at that blubber protecting his ribs) loitered on the trail, picking leaves from the trees with his great and yellowed teeth, or grazing upon daisies and wild clover. And yet if Tammy vanished from his sight around a bend, he would neigh hysterically, circle three times, and gallop toward his mate with the speed of a three-year-old thoroughbred.

As for Nod, I actually did have the temerity to ask him if maybe he was too dispirited to go through with the duel or to engage in any future antics (whether in the name of the sublime Diana or not) directed against administrators—say, his former chairperson or dean or university president, the archbishop of a cathedral, or for that matter our nation's top leader; but just the mention of <u>administrators</u> so stirred him that his eyes flashed in anger, and you would never have thought he had lost the glorious battle with the <u>new enchanters,</u> the devious deconstructionists.

"Listen to me, Kayo," he said sternly. "I may look old, in fact I may <u>be</u> old, but by that very fact alone I am younger than your chairmen and chairwomen or most of your other administrators—though not younger than the deplorably naïve <u>Teddy,</u> president of many identities, whose flaw is a lack of imagination—"

I gasped. "Then our inept DSP agents were as wrong about what you know as they were about everything else? You know about <u>Teddy?</u>"

"Are you completely deaf, Kayo?" he thundered in his rage. "<u>How many times</u> do I have to tell you that Meg is a witch <u>gifted with extraordinary psychic powers,</u> especially about what <u>was</u> and what <u>is?</u>"

I was so struck by that thunder I might have died at that instant! "How many presidents does Meg think Teddy has been, Nod?" I warily asked.

"It is possible, I suppose, that Meg may have been engaged in figurative talk," Nod said reflectively, the storm gone. "<u>Teddy</u> may be some dark metaphor of her own deep and inscrutable mind. Who can say? Nothing is what it seems, anymore."

"Yes, no doubt he's only a metaphor," I agreed. "Oz, of

course, is our one and only legal president, being democratically elected to serve our country, as everybody knows."[2]

"Oz may be as much a figment as anything else," Nod said. "But, as I was saying, I am younger by far than most of your administrators, younger too than the devious whippersnappers who have so enchanted my own poor brain that it has become only a cesspool for metaphors of metaphors itself. And certainly I am younger than you, my beardless friend."

"Why would that be?" I asked, glad to pander to this strange turn in his deranged thoughts.

"Because I was born first, you numskull! Born to a younger and more innocent time, when it still was possible to trust to the soul, when idealism was still the proper frame of mind, when the future of our species was brighter. . . . Don't you know that each generation is older than the one preceding it, bearing from its birth the weight of everything that comes before? Young as they seem, your present administrators (by and large) and all of your deconstructionists are older and even more disillusioned than I, Kayo!"[3]

While our steeds ambled onward, and Nod himself ambled along in his own disjointed way from this to that, I reviewed my game plan for the afternoon. The thought that if my scheme worked as well as I hoped it would, I would never see Nod again—this poignant awareness gave me a moodiness much like his own, I confess. . . . As the clock struck the thirty-first hour, Nod would ride Tammy from behind a building at one end of the downtown block of the frontier town, and I would ride Smoky from behind a building at the other end. I would have substituted a real gun—my family heirloom—for the starter's pistol that Nod believed he was carrying in his holster, though my own weapon would be such a harmless one; for it was the essence of my planning that Nod

---

[2] I confess to a lack of dexterity with figures; but according to my reckoning, Teddy must have been reelected as "Oz" for at least as many terms as was Franklin D. Roosevelt.

[3] Must one be both old and deranged in order to possess such insight into the youth of the elderly? Not Meg but Nod himself here bewitches me with his understanding of a clear but generally unacknowledged truth.

be convinced that he had truly killed his dearest friend, and so his weapon would have to go off with the roar and kickback that only a genuine blunderbuss could provide. The television crew would be there to record the event not only for the general public but so that Nod would carry to his grave every action of the deed. I had not the slightest doubt that the fat and frightened fugitive from justice would search the newspapers and surreptitiously peer from his position behind a bush in the lonely dark through the golden panes of farmhouse windows at the flickering blue glass of television sets in order to separate fact from fancy, to convince himself that my death was not just another metaphor of a mind given to unreliable images. (One has to build all the authenticity one can for a killing in which the victim's body vanishes—even though events like that are a commonplace in your late-night murder mysteries.)

How was I to make sure (1) that Nod didn't <u>really</u> kill me while (2) making it appear to the spectators, the television camera, and Nod himself that he had? Throughout my entire narrative, I have stressed, perhaps sometimes to your annoyance, Sid, the degree to which my political advancement depended upon what underachievers in life would sneer at as an obsessive, even a neurotic, concern with the minutest of details. I grant you that my strategy for the duel might have involved an excessive amount of detail, and that perhaps I might more successfully have achieved my ends by less elaborate means. But when your intention is to save somebody from dying at your own hands, you try pretty damned hard! Every scheme I've ever engaged in has been useful to me, as a <u>learning experience</u>; and I suppose what I learned from carefully planning the duel—and then executing it to the best of my native ability—is that it is far more difficult to do a devious <u>good thing</u> than to do a devious <u>self-serving</u> one that by its very nature avoids moral questions. And there are certain schemes that nobody concerned wholly with his personal welfare would even begin to dream up!

Be that as it may, I was using belt and suspenders alike to keep the trousers of my scheme from slipping toward any embarrassing disclosure. The main street of a frontier town is characteristically dusty, but I had ordered truckloads of unwashed sand and gravel to be spread on this particular main street, so that the prancing horses would raise obscuring clouds. Furthermore, since the television van was to follow me as I advanced toward Nod, I had arranged for a member of the camera crew to toss a smoke bomb at the proper moment—thus permitting me, after my mortal wound (in my final paroxysms, I would squeeze a plastic bottle of tomato ketchup concealed within my jacket, that vile stain spreading from the region of my heart), to vault into the saddle, gallop Smoky into the nearest alley, and make my getaway in the leased car (certainly not one of your Rent-a-Wrecks!) waiting for me there.

As for my safety, everything depended on the distance between Nod and me—on the point at which we halted our horses, engaged in vile curses or reasoned indictments suitable to our respective roles, and began firing; and naturally I had selected positions far enough apart that Nod (and, of course, he wasn't a sharpshooter like that cute <u>Diana</u>) would miss me by a country mile.

To make it abundantly clear that I was no <u>fruitcake</u> like Nod, but remained pretty much the same sharp cookie who at age twelve had won my president's affection and admiration, I would stress here that everybody in the unavoidably large cast of this carefully staged extravaganza had the profoundest of reasons to be loyal to me. As you already know, all of the employees of the Kayo Corral but one (Teddy's ever-inebriated cousin, Freddy) were relatives of mine—unless you're a stickler for unadorned facts and insist that Dilsey, the most faithful woman I knew, the one who more often than not was mother to me, was not "family." All of them had been instructed in their easy-to-perform roles, and had in fact patiently rehearsed them, with the customary Desperado (Freddy) and the customary Good Avenger (Mirabelle's illegitimate son, John Wayne Mammalia, who was always called, in good southern fashion, plain "J.W."), playing me and Nod on the Kayo Corral's nags, and with the public television crew in attendance.

I didn't have to worry about the fidelity of <u>that</u> little troop of professionals, since it had been made quite apparent to them that the whole matter of either a tripled federal subsidy or <u>no subsidy whatsoever</u> for that impoverished network hung in the balance.

Chatting on in his desultory fashion while I anxiously reviewed the above scenario, Nod at last preceded me into the main street of the Kayo Corral, under a sun that dazzled our eyes after the sylvan shade. Now I fear it is my embarrassing responsibility, Sid, to correct some misconceptions that may have arisen from my initial account of the duel. Out of my desire to win at once your admiration, I may have misled you with my opening words, and so must admit to having been something of a <u>poseur</u> myself, one who assumed a greater pride in physical appearance (however reasonable such pride might seem) than was entirely justified, and a greater arrogance than was absolutely necessary (even for a very clever person).

What, exactly, went awry that blazing afternoon? As I say, everything had been prepared, including new costumes for Nod and me, since J.W.'s white buckskin was much too small for Nod and alcoholic Freddy's black suede (glittering with its many little mirrors) much too baggy for me. Before donning my outfit, I briskly entered the saloon, to pay my respects to that oil painting of my dear <u>Papa</u> in its ornate frame, which Dilsey had hung above the mirror in the bar. "I hope, <u>Papa,</u> that this day I will justify your faith in me, and likewise prove how wrong Vladimir was when he cried out at me his fateful 'Dolt!'," I said to myself, almost a prayer; for I was so taken up by my forthcoming role that I didn't question its bold, spiritual significance. My heart pounded, much as it had on that day of my childhood triumph at the White House; right was unquestionably on my side, and it seemed that nothing could possibly go amiss!

But I suppose when you're working with such a large cast, however loyal its members (my triumphs, it is worth noting, have always been solitary ones), you're bound to have some kinks. First of all, and for the only time in her long life, Dilsey <u>was faithless.</u> She caught one glimpse of Nod and me in our costumes, and simply refused, as a matter of personal dignity, to be the gorgeous cowgirl <u>Diana</u> in the guise of the brilliant female scientist <u>Jean</u> who has been forced into a life of prostitution by the unscrupulous enchanters, the gamblers now on tour at the Kayo Corral saloon. (The gamblers, I'm glad to say, were played to perfection by some pretty shifty-eyed members of Mirabelle's clan.) So Mirabelle herself, bleached hair and all, became a last-minute substitution as <u>Diana-Jean,</u> even though she was no match for Dilsey, who, until she let me down, was to my way of thinking a pretty fine spiritual ideal, and certainly, age-wise, would have made a perfect match for Nod. You should have seen the crestfallen look on the Good Avenger's fat face (not to mention that on my own lean-er visage) when, as we were astride our respective horses in front of the saloon, ready to take our positions, Mirabelle coyly called out to Nod, "Hi y'all, good-lookin'? You gawna rescue little ol' me from a life of depravity and sin? Oh, my goodness me!" (Dilsey never would have been guilty of such poor taste.)

And in my first version, Sid, I neglected to tell you that my pants (bought by that same thoughtless Mirabelle whose entire clan had me for benefactor) were much too tight (shouldn't she have known enough about male vanity to allow a few more inches than I gave her as my waist measure-ment?). They split, the moment I tried to vault into the saddle with the reckless abandon that marks any true Desperado—something that caused some pretty fancy contorting of the body to prevent my red bikini-type shorts from being dis-played to the whole nation via film, after I fell to a ground too hard ever to be considered philosophical. Furthermore, that same mindless Mirabelle, in contradiction of my specific order, had bought that brand of ketchup the makers are so proud of—I mean, the gluey kind that doesn't want to come out of the bottle. I really bruised my chest by pounding at the plastic bottle before it splurted out in one vast glob, the way the same brand does on a hamburger or hot dog.

By this time, I'm afraid, things had already gotten pretty far out of hand. Let me back up a bit by saying we managed to get Smoky and Tammy at opposite ends of the street only by enticing each of them with rubber buckets filled with oats, which I understand is normal policy for horse owners with beasts that have minds of their own. What I hadn't foreseen was that Smoky wouldn't budge until he'd licked the final oat from his bucket—or that, having had his fill, he would sud-denly notice he was separated from his dearest companion, whirl about three times, and then, in an ears-back and furious gallop, oblivious to any "Whoas!" or any pulling back of the reins, dash right past that place where he was supposed to stop, while Tammy herself would be the unmoved mover (a female prerogative, perhaps), whatever Nod's coaxing. My initial version faithfully records the horrid explosion (while the two horses were nuzzling each other) that very nearly brought my life to an untimely end.

You can say that fortune was giving me at least a sad, small smile, and not only because Nod's bullet missed. Sullen because Nod had taken his role on the one day that it was being televised, J.W. had joined the equally unemployed Freddy under a tree near the spot where the confrontation unexpectedly took place, and both of them had been drinking something stronger than beer. J.W. was the "accomplice" who lurched toward the camera, ogling into it in his attempt to be a star; and it was the same J.W. who at the opportune moment blocked the lens, as he was grabbing for any support to keep him erect.

Nearly (but not quite) everything else, you should know, worked precisely as planned. That is to say, the smoke bomb went off, when the van finally caught up with us; and the astounded Nod, having observed my bleeding torso, scrambled to Tammy's back in a panic, which as a shrewd judge of character I had expected him to do, and galloped off. At this juncture, it seemed more than time for me to leave, too, and so I leaped to the saddle of my already moving Smoky, intending now to find a back route to the getaway car before the dust and smoke settled.

I suppose I should have realized that no rider, however skillful, could have made Smoky do anything other than pursue his beloved. Nod directed Tammy in a smart turn around the corner of the last building; Smoky, in making the identical turn, half flung me from the saddle. It was clear that both of those old horses could travel pretty Allah-damned fast when they wanted to; thickets and trees flew past with such incredible speed that those horses, plump as they were, seemed even more like Cuban cigars than Idaho potatoes, I tell you! A branch (how much better it would have been had the deconstructionists sawed it off, or turned it into a metaphor!)

whipped my skull. Stunned by the blow, reeling in the saddle, I believed that Tammy and Nod had truly vanished from the planet, for all at once they were gone. And then Smoky and I disappeared as well; I mean, I couldn't see a thing, and only knew I was still riding a horse from the jolting of the saddle against my posterior.

For perhaps the first time in my life, I felt the consternation of a man who has bungled things badly and now hasn't the slightest idea as to where he is, or where he might be going. Even the blunderbuss that I had worn next to my skin so long that it was part of my identity had been left behind, as further evidence for the ballistics experts that a murder had been committed. I was following Nod as if I were bound to him, and everything was a source of great astonishment to me. I painfully confess that in my fright I whispered to myself, "Verily, Kayo, you must be in the hands of some <u>pretty powerful enchanters.</u>"

CHAPTER X. The Mystery Explained

Those horses couldn't have experienced such a strenuous day in years (nor, of course, had I!), and it didn't take long for their mutual gallop to drop to a trot and finally to a slow walk. Not on the darkest of nights had I felt such a suffocating sense of blackness: here was no cave that (metaphor or not) was one with the starry universe. Afraid to speak, I let Smoky follow what I could only assume was his Nod-bearing mate (one might as well consider that one can permit the inevitable), for I could hear the clopping of other hoofs before us. We had proceeded a considerable distance—a half-mile? a mile or more?—before I heard Nod speak gently to his horse, praising her for her endurance and valor. What an enormous comfort, to hear that kind voice!

"Nod!" I cried. "I'm here, right behind you! Where are we, my dearest friend?"

Nod moaned, an eerie and echoing sound; he must have

thought me a ghost, for his soft praise of his animal turned suddenly into rough "Giddaps" and into rude slaps administered (I thought from the sound) to that long-suffering beast's rump.

"Don't make that poor horse burst her gallant heart in obedience to you, Nod," I said. "It is I, your Kayo, riding behind you. . . . I've never known such darkness! Where are we?"

"Kayo? Is this some final and most cruel trick played upon me by the new enchanters? Has everything in the world been reduced to the reverberating deceptions of language in the dark? It must be so, for Kayo, my beloved Kayo, is no more, killed by the gun in my own hand, and at point-blank range!"

Those words revived my spirits, Sid, for they were proof enough of how close my scheme had been to success. In short, my confidence in myself began to return, and I realized that I no more than Nod himself had been tricked by the enchanters, and that apparently I had been led into a tunnel whose entrance no doubt had been disguised by vines and shrubs. "Tell me, Nod, where this tunnel is taking us to. I really don't like darkness without a ray of light, without a single star to see by."

I hadn't realized he had dismounted from his horse until I felt the hands patting my leg, as Nod gingerly tested to find out if I was anything more than slippery and deceiving words. The touch of his palms scared me so much I let out a scream that sent him scampering off; I heard the thud of his body in collision with Tammy's rear. If that old horse hadn't been so tired, she probably would have kicked him senseless, and then have bolted, with Smoky and me in hot pursuit, leaving Nod to wake up alone in the dark.

Do you remember the Zippo used by "X" so long ago, when I arrived at the White House for the first time and he took me into the closet for my briefing and to present me with the Aznap-Cola slug that signified my election to the secret order of presidential advisers, Sid? Well, "X" was so well heeled that he was always leaving that particular Zippo, one with a fourteen-karat cover, carelessly around, as if expensive objects like that were a trifle to him. What is simple and much-to-be-regretted forgetfulness on the part of the needy or the abandoned (as I was then) is pure ostentation on the part of your typical business tycoon become confidant to presidents, and on the day he was smugly telling me that <u>of course</u> my new job, being an honor, carried no weekly paychecks, I snitched his gold Zippo when he wasn't looking, and a good thing I did—for Allah knows what Nod would have done had he not seen that little torch brighten up the familiar human countenance of an equestrian statue in the pitch-black tunnel!

Only a few adventures separate me from the tragic but unavoidable conclusion of my long narrative, Sid, and I have slowly been gathering the courage needed to face that. Certainly by now you see that I'm not your common murderer, as uncouth as he is insensitive—that common murderer is your <u>banal type</u> if I'm any judge! I hope that I have presented myself to you as one with a genuine depth of character—with a wispy bit of soul, perhaps, but I wouldn't overdo that—and as somebody you can understand, and (is this a vain wish?) toward whom you even feel a certain empathy, separated though we may be by an infinitude of stars. . . .

You may recall that I shy away from descriptions of sentimental greetings and the like to the best of my ability (note how I bypassed my reunion with Teddy, for example, and avoided bathos through understatement in describing the much more emotional reunion with Nod!), and here I'm not going to waste time describing Nod's overjoyed face, how his tears glistened in the light of the Zippo, etc.—or, for that matter, rehash with you the lengthy dialogue in the tunnel during which I explained to him, as best I could, how I had tried to save his life from my own hands by convincing him he was a killer who as such would never again have the idealistic heart to go around doing and saying things that would make Teddy envious and discontented. Of course, to explain all this to him, I had to reveal part of what I had sworn never to reveal, my membership in the Order of the Oval Token, and then it seemed that for his understanding of all my activities I had to tell him that Meg had been right, whether she was simply being metaphorical or not, and that, yes, Tommy and Frank and all the rest were figments as much as <u>Diana</u> had ever been, that Teddy had been our president for generations, and that the greatest obligation of the OOT was to prevent forever the <u>new and wonderful</u> from ever happening, for it was up to that little but stalwart band to protect the stability of our nation by a vigilant enforcement of <u>conservative time.</u>

I don't know why, Sid, that my reneging on all my vows of silence didn't seem to matter at this moment in which I had made Nod so rapturous simply by the fact that I, his bosom pal, was <u>alive;</u> it made me feel good to say what I did, to have no falsities separating us—though I guess I was to pay for my betrayal of these most important of our national secrets, at the bitter end. Since you're already privy to everything I had formerly withheld from Nod, what I said to him is of no interest to you, and you probably would prefer it if I would satisfy your curiosity about this long and mysterious tunnel instead. So be it.

As a native of our Lake District, I had known, of course, of the vast deposits of salt left by a sea in prehistoric times— salt buried far beneath our many freshwater lakes and beneath much of the land separating those once pure (and even now only slightly contaminated) bodies of water. And I had heard reports of the tunnels, some still in use but many not, made by the miners of that salt—some of these tunnels, it was said, were burrowed beneath even the deepest of these deep lakes, the subterranean passages connecting hamlets and villages many miles apart, and separated by mountains as well as by water shining in moon and sunlight. What I knew only from hearsay Nod knew from his own experiences, both as a vagabond and as one led about in his childhood by a witch with a divining rod.

"Never fear, Kayo," Nod said cheerfully, after explaining to me that we were in such a salty and boneless catacomb— and just as the Zippo expired and the darkness seemed more impenetrable than ever. "These tunnels have many intersections, but Tammy knows the way even better than do I. By simply <u>giving her the rein</u> we'll come out safely, in one good spot or another; and while we journey through the blackness, I'll meditate on the startling nature of your revelations, and tell you what I think they may possibly mean to you, and portend for me. It is my view, from what you have said, that my <u>destiny</u> indeed may come as Meg prophesied, even though she is more trustworthy about the past and the present than the future—about which in general she has but queasy feelings. I had not wished for destiny to strike so soon, though I can see that it is probably time; I most certainly have cast aside all of those illusions that gave my life its deepest meanings. This entire matter is of such serious import that I will have to consult Meg for advice; for the present, I say no more."

After these grave words, he remounted Tammy, and we resumed our slow, silent, dark journey.

------------------------------------ ⚡ ------------------------------

CHAPTER XI. *Dark Portents*

Nod deliberated in silence for perhaps an hour before releasing me from suspense with a speech. Since his monologue was carried on in the absolute darkness of the long tunnel, I have nothing to report about the surrounding atmosphere other than this simple fact; nor can I, for the same reason, describe the love or perplexity or fear of his changing moods, as one by one they must have traveled across that dear face.

He began with what seemed to me a matter of trivial interest, a literary disquisition about The Authentic Adventures of Kayo Aznap and the myriad texts of the following generations that had been influenced by it—some of them even filching, in the manner of a counterfeit book published before my illustrious ancestor had finished his patient labors on the second part, the very characters of his work. "And this, mind you," Nod said, "despite your ancestor's severe warning, Kayo—a warning delivered by the scribe who took down his deathbed words—that nobody in the future should dare to resurrect Nod, Kayo, Diana, Jean, the gamblers, or any of the other characters that belonged to his true life and dreaming mind alone; for if they did, in however mangled a form, he surely would return to haunt them.[1]

[1]Whether the spirit of a writer can traverse the cosmos is moot; as Kayo's scribe on Earth, one who has violated this last wish of a cele-

172

"Perhaps the reason so many writers have ignored that threat is that they (like humanity in the aggregate) have found themselves written into that original manuscript—if not as a single character, then as a combination of Nod and Kayo; for certainly, though Nod is the hero [let me intrude here, Sid, by hastily saying again that this is certainly not _my_ view, nor that of the Cliffs Notes guide, if you read it with care], he is a caricature without his Kayo. One represents the soul, the other the body—with all of the body's cunning and materialistic desires. To prove that this is the case—that the two are one—the greatest of all the Aznaps (you shouldn't mind coming up short of him, Kayo, for in comparing the two of you I am paying you the compliment of a comparison with the author of the greatest masterpiece ever written!) often has Nod descending into Kayo-like behavior, Kayo rising to Nod's idealistic heights, with an especially important merger between the two taking place as the doughty pair approach their grand finale. Perhaps he initially separated the two as an allegorical device, perhaps so each could argue with the other. The absurdities of that tragicomic text, then, are the absurdities of the human condition itself, of the struggle between these two antithetical aspects that constitute, in the tension between them, the drama as well as the essence of individual personality. When one aspect goes, a shell remains (as is presently the case with me), when the other goes—well, who can say?

"Now, the great Kayo Aznap, in setting his story in the days of the golden West, assuredly was not confusing that glorious period of our youthful nation with the age of gold itself, which was the age (which I now must reckon as nothing but illusion) before man killed man and before he slaughtered the beasts, the age remembered by the soul as the sacred silence that lies behind the dripping to be heard in the

brated author simply by his fidelity to another's account, I confess to a certain uneasiness. Believe you me, it's quite enough to be called up before a review board that is investigating your competency to be continued in a tenure position while your wife sulks in the kitchen because you spend all your spare hours at home before a computer screen, taking down daily messages from outer space—without having questions of this sort to vex you!

deepest pool of the deepest cave; but surely he had intimations of that silence. Remember your ancestor's <u>cosmic slant</u>!

"However long my preamble, Kayo, be silent now yourself and listen, for what I am saying and yet will say represents everything I have learned as a <u>man of letters</u> and has profound significance for you as well as me. Surely, if you're not the numskull I impatiently called you earlier on this exhausting day, you can see from what I've already said why <u>The Authentic History of Kayo Aznap</u> is the archetype[2] that it is, and why it has spawned so many descendants, certain examples of which I now present to you."

What a literary quarry, filled with junk and treasure, that Nod had for a mind, however simply <u>metaphorical</u> it had become! I had no idea that so many Nods and Kayos had been born in emulation of the first cowboy and his more important and aristocratic sidekick, known sometimes as <u>Sir Kayo</u> or <u>Kayo, Lord Aznap,</u> sometimes as <u>Prince Kayo.</u> At one extreme (in my opinion, Sid, these examples are "extremes" simply because both left Kayo out!), Nod was a divine idiot; at the other a foreign scholar of mature years in the Assorted States, one lusting for his Diana in the implausible form of a gum-chewing and television-watching <u>nymphet.</u> (Obviously, you can never tell in advance much about any given man's taste in his passionately spiritual dreams.) Among the more conventional treatments was one in which Nod became a sweet-tempered priest who innocently attends a pornographic movie and spends the night at a bordello (blowing up condoms into balloons!), seduced into both houses by his Kayo, a former Marxist mayor. So wide-ranging was <u>my</u> Nod in his parallels, so far or so loosely did he cast his net, that he declared that a certain opium-addicted detective and his practical-minded companion, a prosaic medical practitioner, were descendants of the first Nod and Kayo—as were, at a further remove (since the novel in question was written in our own period), a learned and semiotically inclined elder member of a monkish order engaged in solving the mysteries of an ever-increasing num-

---

[2] I'm glad to see Nod's casual use of a word coined (at least on Earth) by Jung, a pioneer in psychoanalytical studies who doesn't exist in the deconstructionist view of things.

ber of murders in a fog-enshrouded abbey atop a mountain in the fourteenth century, and his companion (and scribe), a naïve young monk of another order. I won't bore you with any more of this comprehensive listing, except to say that Nod ended it with a reference to a story his enchanters triumphantly upheld, as further proof of their position. It was the story of a man (if you can imagine this, Sid!) who wrote, word for word, whole segments of The Authentic Adventures without ever having read the original, but whose text meant something entirely different, having been composed in a later age.

"All that I've just recounted is but the introduction to something I say only with the greatest hesitation, for I am perplexed and afraid," Nod said. "As the events at the Kayo Corral conclusively have demonstrated, you have chosen not only to enter, but to believe wholeheartedly in, a grand text at a time my own belief in it has faltered; but you have also entered it, as my literary discourse has indicated, at a time that the text has become corrupt, the clarity of its meanings suspect, its transcendent glories tarnished. Will your growing idealism be enough to replenish the values of that text, and (concomitantly) does it still contain enough of the original to nourish you? A most serious question, one that not even Meg probably can answer, though I must consult her about it; for in donning your suit of mirrors and permitting me to win the combat, you were quite likely foreshadowing a mortal blow to me,[3] and I need to know if I will live on within you, or if all is forever lost."

Here, Sid, he broke off, his emotions too much for him. After a pause, he said, his voice trembling, "Whatever happens, Kayo, know that I forgive you in advance, and that I love you as if you were already the noblest part of whatever I have been. For the present, I say no more." And he was true to his

---

[3] Perhaps Nod is simply referring to the reflection of himself he would have seen in the fallen Desperado's suit of mirrors; but in our own stunning Don Quixote, a giddy but quite minor character, not to be confused with Sancho Panza, dresses up as the "knight of mirrors" and is defeated in a ridiculous combat with Don Quixote early in part two—an event that presages a return combat leading to the hero's own defeat and consequent death.

words for a second time within this tunnel, remaining silent as Tammy and Smoky bore us up a long and gradual ascent, breaking out into a universe of stars against which were outlined a vast series of what seemed large metal ears or dishes affixed to towers. Include Nod's lengthy story of his life and my own dreaming, and you will agree with me that too much had recently happened for me to respond adequately either to what he had just said or what we now were viewing. All I could think was that Nod, having lost his soul, had become madder than ever, in this desperate attempt to live on within me, and the thought added to my numbness.

"In none of my wanderings, either by myself or with Meg, have I come across such strange structures," Nod said pensively, as we looked upon these grotesque ears. "Can such a technological monstrosity have suddenly been constructed, in this, our lovely Lake District? But I know by now, Kayo, that nothing is what it seems; and this no doubt is some strange new intrusion made by your own corrupt and tarnished text."

As we watched, there was a faint and ominous sound, a kind of mechanical buzzing, and all of those metal ears began to turn, as if to listen to our words. The explanation of this last wonder I must leave for the next chapter.

CHAPTER XII. At *the* SETI *Facility*

We tethered our horses to a high metal fence in a place where they had a luxuriant stand of grass to graze upon,[1] and

---

[1] No doubt (a detail omitted from Kayo's narrative) Nod and Kayo fetched water for the horses, in addition to making sure they had sufficient grass. One of the many differences between Kayo: the Authentic and Annotated Autobiographical Novel from Outer Space and our own Don Quixote is the greater affection and care shown to all animals in the former work—something I can only hazard to be the case in The Authentic Adventures of Kayo Aznap as well. Animals sometimes are cruelly mistreated in Cervantes' work, which to my mind is a blemish in that masterpiece; my readers may remember that the author is so indifferent to the beasts his characters ride that on one occasion he forgets that Sancho has lost his ass.

walked through an open gate, passing several rows of those strange metal ears as we climbed a hill toward a brilliantly lighted building at the top. "As a highly placed official privy to the deepest secrets of our government, Kayo," Nod said, speaking slowly because he was panting from all that exertion (though I took the hill in stride), "you must have some idea as to why this facility has been built so rapidly. Haste, as is said, makes waste, and the expense must have been astronomical."

I know that it seems out of character that Nod, especially at such a moment, would worry his head about anything so trivial to him as money; so let me say, Sid, that ever since he had lost his soul to the enchanters, he had given subtle indications of a developing practical bent. For example, it was Nod, not I, who had determined our climb to the building, deciding that here I could find shelter for the night, while he journeyed on, by woodland paths and an occasional tunnel, to the cave where Meg dwelt—but don't think he was being simply altruistic. That fat belly of his was grumbling, even though he had eaten (as you will recall) much the larger (and juicier) portion of the chicken that had constituted our only meal in a good long time. He knew there had to be food of some sort in a building as big as this one!

"The sheer volume of funds pouring into the Hexagon in support of The Dome project has been a source of embarrassment even to the generals," I told Nod. "If I recall this clearly"— and I paused, trying to remember details of a life I had so recently been living that now seemed not only mundane but to belong to a far earlier time—"there was far too much on deposit, whatever the spin-offs for missile development; and so a certain sum was designated for a scheme called SETI— an acronym for Search for Extraterrestrial Intelligence. Everybody agrees that the military applications, at least in the early stages, will be minimal; but we didn't want the Bear to get ahead of us, even in this unexplored field."

"So those ears are tuned to the stars," Nod said. "You might have thought, especially since they decided to build it in the neighborhood, that somebody would have consulted Meg for advice on a project of this kind and magnitude."

By this time, we had reached the front door, only to find

it locked. Peering through a nearby window, we saw that people were running back and forth in the corridor, sometimes colliding into each other in their frenzy or haste, suggesting (as Nod observed) that some kind of extraterrestrial contact had just been made. However vigorously he pounded on the door, nobody paid us the slightest attention. Nod looked keenly at the lock that barred our entrance. "A dead bolt, Kayo, so your ordinary plastic credit card won't be of any use," he said thoughtfully. "Look here, though! It's one of those newfangled locks that open to the touch of selected thumbprints—no doubt only those of high officials. Mine won't make it work. Try yours, Kayo—wouldn't it have been keyed to your thumbprint?"

Well, I'm delighted to tell you, Sid, that indeed it had been so keyed, which shows the respect shown even in the scientific community to the powerful Order of the Oval Token! Barely had we entered that brightly lit corridor—the door slid open and shut with an efficient swish—than a disheveled young man (wearing a Dacron jacket with a felt basketball and the name of a basketball team embossed upon it) walked at a quick pace past us, muttering to himself, "A bogey at the edge of the galaxy, not many light-years from Alpha Centauri, hundreds of janskys, frequency around 9.2 gigahertz." He turned around for a second look at us. "Holy shit!" he exclaimed.

Nod stood on tiptoes for the added height, sucked in his belly as best he could, and said curtly, "Take us to your kitchen, boy!" I hadn't known he could show such authority, such arrogance!

"Yes, sir," the young man said quickly, leading us through an incredible confusion of noise and bodies, as people rushed this way and that, calling out to each other, "No, it's not a transmission from a secret military satellite, that's confirmed by the highest authority in G-46," or "It's on the 1420 megahertz hydrogen line and the 1667 megahertz hydroxyl line—all over the Allah-damned spectrum!" But whatever the general excitement, Nod and I attracted a number of curious stares. The young man in the Dacron jacket took aside one of those who had stopped to gawk at us—a young woman in an immaculate white uniform, obviously a technician[2]—and whis-

[2]A computer repairperson, perhaps?

178

pered a few words into her ear, from which was dangling a little golden ornament of a colorfully ringed planet. "Gotcha, Willy!" the woman replied over her shoulder, dashing off.

I suddenly realized how odd we must have looked! I had forgotten completely that Nod was still wearing his now somewhat soiled white buckskin with the fringes on the jacket and that his broken binoculars were still hanging from a strap around his neck and that I was dressed in my tight-fitting black suede costume bedecked with glittering mirrors, and no doubt with my red bikini underwear showing through a ripped seam. Immediately I strode to a position just in advance of Nod, trying to get him to goosestep behind me, to hide that gap; but we got our legs entangled, and sprawled to the flecked tile that covered the floor. "Clumsy ass!" Nod hissed.

Apparently those astrophysicists, if that is what they were, were too dedicated to their scientific mission to eat properly, for their "kitchen" was a small room with a table, its walls lined with vending machines. "We don't have any of your money," Nod said to Willy, for he had perceived much more quickly than I the misconception about us that the young man in the Dacron jacket must have held. Since others had followed us into the room—enough, indeed, to fill it—many hands plunged into pockets for the change needed to load Nod and me down with sandwiches, candy bars, and cola drinks of a brand I see no reason for divulging—that competitive brand whose unfriendly corporate takeover might have removed the name of Aznap-Cola from the supermarket shelves, but never from the nostalgic heart of a single Unitedian!

While we were gulping down those half-frozen pickle-and-olive-loaf sandwiches, a willowy woman, casually dressed, her eyes wide-set in her angular face, her brown hair gathered by a tortoiseshell barrette at the nape of her neck, came briskly into the room; a name tag on her T-shirt identified her (as well as I could read without my glasses: they had been left behind at the Kayo Corral, too bulky for the pockets of my tight-fitting pants) as Ellie Waynarrow or maybe Nellie Wayarrow, though the words of her title, printed beneath that name, were large enough that anybody with any vision at all could read them: DIRECTOR.

Nod gave me a meaningful nudge. "No doubt the brilliant female scientist of your corrupt text, Kayo," he said in a low voice, as the crowd respectfully moved back to make way for her passage.

"Holy Toledo!" she said, giving us first a searching and then an amused glance before turning to the Dacron-jacketed young man. "Now, I know, Willy," she said, while affectionately running her fingers like a comb through his disheveled hair (for she obviously was a woman who could accomplish a number of tasks at once), "that all of us are excited by the latest signals. It's not every day that we get a picture over and over again on our sophisticated model BLT receiver-visualizer of what seems to be a duck, but you know as well as I do that the picture is far from clear, because of all those dots and dashes of energy that disturb it. We'll have to develop a chemical code box, perhaps even one with an atomic breathalyzer, before we can be absolutely sure the duck is not really a quark. The bursts of energy themselves could be, I admit, the message the duck is sending; but the lack of consistent pattern suggests something similar to the wave distortions we get from that nuclear weapons depot down the hill from us, whenever something leaks, or for that matter similar to the wiggles made whenever the Bear tests a new device to penetrate our yet undeveloped Dome. That is to say, we cannot tell whether we're receiving messages from an intelligent extraterrestrial source or not. . . . Let's not get hysterical, boys and girls," she said, now speaking to the group at large. "Not one of our hundred and thirty-one radio telescopes is a transporter, for Allah's sake, capable of beaming aliens from Duckland or anywhere else down to us."

"Then what are they?" Willy asked, made sullen by his embarrassment. Note that he didn't ask Nod or me, Sid, who obviously ought to have known: he asked his brilliant director instead! And she did know, for a fact. She chastised her subordinates for spending their spare hours watching old science-fiction programs, pornographic films, or quiz shows instead of something informative, such as the news hour on public television; for had they been watching that, they would have known that before their very eyes were sitting a hungry murderer and his equally hungry victim. "But since they are both here, both alive, we can assume that even public television can be duped by what undoubtedly is a publicity stunt for a manufacturer of western wear. So <u>let's get back to work!</u> We may—and let me emphasize that word, 'may'—we just <u>may</u> be onto the most crucial and important scientific discovery in the history of the planet. Let's get back to see if that <u>duck</u> is for real!"

That group of dedicated scientists cheered as if in one voice, every one of them obediently running from the room without a single backward look at Nod or me! At first, I had the feeling of a tremendous <u>letdown,</u> from being ignored like that, a deflation that Nod himself must have felt. "While I realize, Kayo," he said sadly, "that your ancestor's depiction of the golden age of the West is not in any sense to be construed as a reconstruction of the <u>age of gold,</u> yet it seems to me that this text you have entered—and I say this despite the scientific and technological marvels it displays—is even more removed from that idealized period than I would have expected from a text of our time, however corrupt. In a story of this sort, there seems no need for you and me at all."

"Perhaps that's why they left so quickly."

"No doubt," Nod said, still munching away. "Still, I advise you to be careful, and to sleep with one eye open while I'm away, for that fellow in the Dacron jacket who told the technician in the white nylon uniform to fetch the director with the tortoiseshell barrette didn't seem to me wholly convinced by the director's words, and it just might be that Willy will call the police or the newspapers." He added kindly, as I was using my thumbprint to unlock the front door for him, "Be forewarned that in one way or another, Kayo, the <u>jig is up for you.</u> As soon as your Teddy finds out the truth, won't he expel you from the powerful secret order of advisers?"

Do you know, Sid, that I had lately been thinking so little about myself that this obvious fact had not even occurred to me? What you might think even more surprising is that, once Nod had said in parting what he did, I felt the freedom and relief one does upon being released from dreadful anxieties, and, despite Nod's advice, I slept like a newborn babe!

CHAPTER XIII. *Morning of the Last Day*

Since the present chapter is a preparation for my grand finale—one taking place back at the White House with some of the earlier, more important, people in my life reintroduced, and with Nod and me still dressed as we had been for the duel at the Kayo Corral—my first priority is to explain to you how we managed to get there (beyond the obvious wherewithal for the plane tickets, which was provided by my handy and tax-exempt federal credit card, that smallest of fringe benefits for members of the OOT).

At the dawn following my night at the SETI facility, I woke from the couch I had been slumbering upon to see everywhere about me, in chairs and in sleeping bags scattered about the sterile tile floor, scientists and technicians still soundly sleeping after their hectic night. Peering through the glass door of the control room with its array of computers, I saw on dozens of display screens the clear image of a duck flashing off and on without any dot-and-dash energy distortions. No wonder the workers slept so soundly, having achieved this crucial part of their decoding! I caught sight of Ellie Waynarrow (or Nellie Wayarrow) in that control room, still fiddling at the giant computer keyboard, still hard at work; her tortoiseshell barrette had become unfastened, and her hair flowed down and past the nape of her neck. Diligence like hers is rare, and to be applauded. I clapped my hands and waved at her, and she waved back; and then, yawning, I walked out for a look at the sunrise.

Before me lay the hill that Nod and I had climbed, and in the opposite direction the series of radio telescopes continued— perhaps for miles. I took deep breaths of the misty air, reveling in my new freedom. . . . But if I continue to dramatize these little events, I'll never get us to the White House in time! Behind a screen of trees to my right, I heard some high-pierced curses and screams, and of course I had to find out what all that was about. The brilliant and driven Ellie, or Nellie, had mentioned the previous night the nearby nuclear weapons depot, and it is true that such a depot exists in our Lake District, close by one of our most beautiful lakes; the depot is surrounded by a large fence, with many wild animals, including a herd of albino deer, living within those parklike grounds, browsing even on the shrubs and thickets growing on the ominous mounds that rise up at regular intervals in the vast open spaces. (I mention all this to you, Sid, so that you will realize that I knew from the director's passing remark precisely where I was, whatever my first confusion about the newly constructed SETI facility; and furthermore that I understood at once not only what the commotion was about—but that in a sense I was responsible for it!)

Acting upon my orders, the federal <u>Bureau of Theme Parks</u> had already made a theme park of a portion of the nuclear weapons depot, so that interested citizens could view, in the subterranean storage areas, examples of some of our older missiles, ready for sudden transport despite their rusted surfaces. Just outside the theme-park fence, a group of feminists (to whom our missiles old and new were and are phallic representations of the destructive and male-dominated world they want liberation from) had constructed a <u>women's encampment,</u> a picturesque shantytown from which they could make their peaceful protests, such as cutting large holes in the fence for them to step through in order to hang their wash or the thickets covering the mounds, stomping on the Unitedian flag while nursing their babies, chaining themselves to the gate, etc.

Since they were getting far more attention than was the theme park, I had decided on a typically shrewd course of action. I told the bureau chief (my appointee, of course) <u>to include the women's encampment</u> within the confines of the theme park itself—something that would provide the women, through their percentage of ticket sales, with money to wash and dry their clothes at a Laundromat, for example, while subtly <u>defusing</u> their own volatile and unpatriotic activities by making them part of the larger picture. Foreseeing possible trouble with those strong-willed females, the bureau chief had sent a truck with a crew and fencing material to get the new fence installed before the women were awake on this very morning, but to no avail: the women were awake, having been alerted by their night sentry, and, unlike our more pacific religious organizations, were stoutly resisting both fence and the cash it would bring them.

Even now, Sid, I have difficulty understanding my emotions that morning! What I did was to rush to their aid, right into the heart of that encampment, to help them repel the crew from the Bureau of Theme Parks! Using my authority while I still had it, I told the crew and the women alike that the order to install the fence had been <u>mine alone,</u> as a close adviser of the president, but that now I was rescinding it. Would you believe that neither the women nor the crew thought I was telling the truth? I suppose it was because of that cursed suit of mirrors, with the rip in the seat of the pants. One of those <u>harridans</u> (if I can safely generalize from a single example) searched through her sewing bag for a big safety pin (a diaper pin, actually), saying she wanted <u>nothing more</u> than to protect my modesty; but when I bent forward, to permit her to fasten the pin, she jabbed it viciously into my posterior. "Just to pay back you male chauvinists for all the p___s in the ___ you've given us," she howled.[1]

At that (for me) opportune moment, Nod came riding up on Tammy, with Smoky, of course, trotting behind; on Smoky's back, a couple of topcoats were strapped. (Nod had filched them from the hooks of a motel coffee shop, a theft that surprised me, but that certainly came in handy when we boarded the airplane, what with our peculiar and perhaps recognizable western wear.) He talked with such restraint, such courtesy, to the women that not only did they show him how to get Smoky and Tammy through a gap in the fence so that they could graze happily, and in full security, with the albino deer, but even drove the pair of us in an old car to the nearest airport, the banner of the Women's Liberation Force gaily fluttering from the radio antenna!

Collars up, coats fastened to the top button despite the stewardess's worry that we were shivering and perspiring from

---

[1] The censorship here is Kayo's, not mine; the attack wounded his sensibilities as well as his buttocks.

some contagious disease, we jetted to our nation's capital, Nod explaining as we flew the reason for our hasty flight. "Be it known, Kayo, that my destiny is imminent. Meg has read in the newspaper that your childhood butler, Vladimir, and the mother that abandoned you, Emmamae Mammalia Aznap, are being feted this day at a White House tea, in honor of Vladimir's forthcoming appointment as our ambassador to Bearland. No doubt on this occasion you will discover the fact that long has concerned you—namely, the identification of the man who fathered you—even as I have just learned from Meg the names she has so long withheld of both my parents."

"Who are your parents, Nod?"

"My mother is Miranda, Teddy's wife when he was Frank, and whom he exiled to a desert island—"

"And then your father is—?"

"Exactly. Teddy himself. It was Meg who gave me the name of Quexana—or, in her forgetfulness, Quixada, etc."

"But Teddy looks younger than you!"

"Recall how long he has been president. A lack of imagination preserves one's youth. And, of course, the plastic surgeons—"

"What did you discover about your destiny?"

"Only that it will come after I confront Teddy with my new knowledge."

"And you really think I may find out the name of my true father?"

"Play your cards properly, Kayo, and you'll find out. After all, Emmamae must now believe you dead, and when you suddenly confront her, while I confront Teddy—"

"I see your point, Nod. You are a pretty shrewd one, today, at least."

Add this information I learned on the airplane, Sid, to everything else that had happened to me recently, and you can see the reason I was glad to be wrapped up in that topcoat while aboard the plane and while the taxi took us to the White House: given such a mental overload, how could I not be shivering and delirious, suffering from the sort of headache that produces hallucinations? I even wondered at the truth of what my always honest friend had just revealed. Could he have invented this entire scenario for some devious ends that had something to do with his notion of his <u>destiny,</u> even as I had invented the Kayo Corral scenario to save his life from my own hands? Did Meg really exist, or was she another of those many figments now cluttering my brain as well as Nod's? Or another, even madder, thought: Were Meg and Nod and this very trip he (or they) had planned really <u>part of some greater text</u> than the one of mine that Nod had entered, when he agreed to play the role of the <u>Good Avenger?</u>

I displayed my special Aznap-Cola slug to the White House sentry while he was arguing with me that I must be some <u>look-alike</u> of Kayo Aznap, who most surely was dead. "Do I look <u>dead,</u> Sammy?" I asked, letting him have his fill of that sweating and possibly haggard but still-handsome face he had known so well. "Yes, I am Kayo, adviser to Oz, and in fact I am bringing him his missing son, lost since infancy, as a glorious surprise. You know that only <u>Kayo Aznap</u> is capable of things like this, Sammy."

"Holy shit <u>and</u> Holy Toledo!" Sammy cried, twin exclamations I'd never heard him make in the past; and in his eagerness he actually shoved me and then Nod through that revolving portico door. And so it was, Sid, that Nod and I entered the White House sitting room, dimly lit by the bulbs of small wattage in the great chandelier, just as tea was being served.

CHAPTER XIV. *Late Afternoon of the Last Day*

In addition to being poorly illuminated, the sitting room had majestic proportions, allowing us to enter without being immediately observed. Nod and I stood with our backs to the wall, hands in our topcoat pockets, he looking eagerly toward Teddy, his alleged father; while I (to prolong the delicious suspense before I saw my <u>Maman</u>) coolly took in Vladimir, sitting at the table as in the days of old, wearing something that looked much like his former butler's outfit and sipping tea while speaking (in <u>Gaulish,</u> as I could tell from his pursed lips) to somebody leaning back in his chair with one oafish foot on the linen on the table—probably a member of the <u>Bear</u> legation. Before I looked at <u>Maman,</u> I could smell (was it simply the memory of that fragrance, or did it waft to me now?) her exotic perfume, and hear (certainly this had to be memory) the clatter of the many bracelets on her slender wrist.

Before this last, sad, and inevitable drama unfolds, Sid, I want to correct some misconceptions you might be holding.[1] Although in an excess of love my <u>Maman</u> may (or may not) have fondled me as an infant in a manner your psychologists would frown upon, I don't believe my devotion to her, whatever her abandonment of me at an age at which I was able to take care of myself (something I've proved beyond the shadow of a doubt I was capable of doing)—I don't believe that this devotion of mine is any different from that felt by any other wholesome and well-balanced Unitedian son for his mother.

If you think I foolishly idolized my <u>Maman,</u> please bear in mind that never did I consider her an impossible-to-attain, rifle-toting <u>cowgirl.</u> And if you think that the hostility between Vladimir and me was a rivalry between father and son over the most beautiful of mistresses and mothers, think again: <u>as events soon proved,</u> Vladimir was not my father, though I am a prince!

All right, you may be saying, I am willing to grant you all that, Kayo, so far as you and Emmamae and Vladimir are concerned, but how about the undeniable resentment and envy that Teddy has shown toward <u>his</u> son, and Nod's own irrational rage at all <u>administrators</u>—those authority figures who represent, according to the "experts" who presume to know more about us than we know about ourselves, the father to the son? To despise or even to heartily dislike <u>any</u> administrator—doesn't this imply, <u>ipso facto,</u> an Oedipal disorder?

The flaw in this line of thinking is that it requires both Teddy and Nod to have known of their family connection for a good long time; and yet Meg seems to be the only one who

---

[1]How glad I am that Kayo makes it <u>absolutely clear</u> in the following paragraphs, digressive though they may be, that in <u>no way whatsoever</u> are we to reduce Nod and our narrator (or other characters we have come to know) through a crabbed Freudian analysis of their rich personalities!

all along has known, at least with any certainty. But let's be fair to the conjecture. Given Nod's long and intimate relationship with Meg, it certainly is within the realm of possibility that at some time in the past she inadvertently dropped some shadowy hints about an unnamed father who had cruelly mistreated Nod's mother, hints enough to prejudice Nod against all people in power, especially male ones.

Since we are dealing here with something that is no more than a supposition, we are free to respond to it with suppositions of our own. Even if Teddy—kindhearted though we know him to be—actually <u>did</u> exile his spouse Miranda to some sheik's island, do we know for sure that such an exile constituted "cruel mistreatment" of her? Isn't it possible that on the island she led a comfortable life, attended always by courteous servants? And how do we know for a fact that she opposed such a fine new life? Might she not have put the idea into his head (and how easily Teddy assumes the ideas of others to be his own!), as discontented wives have been known to do, because of her personal longing for warm climates and sunny beaches as well as young and more ardent lovers?

As for the benign Teddy, I seriously doubt that he ever would have made that unconscious slip of the tongue ("Let a sleeping dog <u>die!</u>") had he known the dog in question was his <u>own son.</u> I consider it likely that he believed his infant son had been taken by Miranda to a life of ease that both would share. I conjecture that Miranda saw the child as an obstacle to the romances she was dreaming of, and so left him in the <u>obviously capable</u> hands of the witch, Meg. (I would cast aspersions on neither Miranda nor Teddy, Sid!)

Gossip, slander, and the indiscriminate use of modern psychoanalytical jargon can do irreparable harm even to a leader who has labored so long and so patriotically for his country as Teddy, and whose golden voice has won the admiration and acclaim of the multitudes. In truth, I have irrefutable proof that Teddy bore Nod malice <u>only before</u> Nod told him (rightly or not, I can't say) that he was his son. When I was about to murder Nod (which in a few moments I will do: does my narrative strike you as suddenly disjointed, distracted? With good reason!), Teddy, seeing the revolver leveled, raised his hand, mutely crying, "No!"—even though later he was to come to see the absolute political necessity of that act, for the recoupment of his golden oratory and the consequent stability of the nation, and begged me to remain a member of the OOT as well as his most valued adviser, whatever my deviant behavior.

If I have left you holding your suspenseful breath once again, it has been, you may be assured, for the last time, and (as always) for good reason. I want you to know that even though I am the prince that part of me always somewhat guiltily dreamed of being, I continue to share the egalitarian notions of the man whom I will always think of as my dear Papa, accenting the final syllable. I hold to generous and forgiving sentiments about everybody (except Vladimir!), trusting they will feel a reciprocal kindness toward me. I praise Allah (and indeed if He knows everything, as is rumored to be the case, He must forgive us for what we do, with the possible exception of what Vladimir did to me) for letting me learn the truth of the diamond shape from the man I was destined to kill, one as small and as plump and as dear to me as Papa himself!

Having said all that, Sid, I permit the last act of my drama to unfold. Teddy, sharp-eyed as ever (unlike me, he has never had to resort to reading glasses and then bifocals: but glasses or not, I was to shoot on target this day), was the first to perceive Nod and me, lounging against the far wall, hands in our topcoat pockets. "Newly arrived guests?" he called uneasily. "Welcome, tovarishes"—and it says something about his personal feelings about Bears in general that at once he took our no doubt to him sinister images to be those of comrades of the one drinking tea with a foot on the linen.

Nod gave me a gentle poke. This whole scheme was of his doing, but I had to make the first response! Taking one hand from my pocket to muffle my voice, which I lowered to the huskiest level I could, I said, "No tovarishes we, but patriotic Unitedians, both of us carrying information of the most important sort."

"Speak openly then, Unitedians!" Teddy said, adopting the regal tone he used when he was scared shitless and had

189

no trusted adviser (like me) to turn to. (It pleased me, Sid, that, although "X" was one of the tea drinkers present, Teddy totally ignored him.)

Once again, Nod poked me. Was he scared at least witless himself? I had to take but one more look at that disdainful face of Vladimir to know what I wanted to say first! Like many another butler risen in social esteem and visibility through success in the advertising business (or something like that), he wanted the ceremony and glory that an ambassadorship would provide, and clearly wasn't above fudging his past to get such a post. I decided to toy a little with my victim, by asking a few questions of Teddy that would make Vladimir squirm.

"Isn't it true, Mr. President," I asked in my muffled and deep voice, "that it goes against government policy for our ambassadors to be fluent in the language of the country to which they are sent?"

"That is generally so," Teddy responded. "By and large we don't want them to compromise our national policy through the sympathy with the natives that conversation usually brings. But such a policy is not unique with us. For example, nobody in the entire <u>Bear</u> legation knows a word of Unitedian; we've had to hold diplomatic discourse with the <u>Bear</u> at this tea through the use of <u>Gaulish,</u> which both he and our new ambassador to <u>Bearland</u> speak. I must say, friend, that you interrupted some <u>pretty serious</u> talk."

(At this point, the <u>Bear</u> diplomat showed enough knowledge of the Unitedian tongue to remove his foot from the table, sit up straight, and listen intently to the conversation.)

"What," I asked, "would be your response, Mr. President, if you knew that your new ambassador speaks the <u>Bear</u> tongue like a native?"

(Here, of course, Vladimir showed alarm!)

"One of absolute surprise."

"Did you do a thorough background check of your new ambassador?"

"Most assuredly I had the Democratic Security Police—"

"An inept outfit!"

"Listen, fellow," Teddy said, beginning to get angry, "it's a pretty damned good thing this conniving <u>Bear</u> can't understand a word you're saying." (I noticed that the <u>Bear</u> scowled at the insult.) "Loose talk like that can get this nation into a great deal of trouble."

"What if I told you that your new ambassador is <u>a native of the land you're sending him to?</u>"

(You should have seen how Vladimir squirmed!)

"I would say, '<u>Impossible!</u>' At one time, he was, like many Unitedians, a menial, I grant; many were the days (or so I remember from watching television) that he came to this very White House as a retainer of one of our finest families."

"Ah, but you never liked him then!" (This was an unfortunate slip on my part, one that put Teddy himself on the alert. I couldn't toy with the panicky Vladimir much longer.)

"Listen, fellow, whoever you are, all <u>Unitedians</u> are capable of growth and change, both personally and in terms of wealth and party choice. . . . But what makes you think that I didn't like him?"

I ignored that question, to ask the last one of my own: "And what would you say if I said your new ambassador is not only a native <u>Bear</u> but an <u>illegal immigrant alien?</u>"

Now both Vladimir and <u>Maman</u> simply had to know that I had come back from the dead! I would like to think my slow dispersal of hints (beyond my uncontrollable desire to toy with Vladimir) was an attempt to save my <u>Maman</u> from a shock that might have sent her into a swoon, and perhaps unconsciously that was what it was. As for Vladimir, of course he would try desperately to force me into silence and servility, a last wild leap by that hooked fish! He rose, pointed a tutorly finger at me, and imperiously demanded, "Conjugate, in <u>Gaulish,</u> the various forms of <u>to bray!</u>"

"<u>Braire,</u>" I immediately began. "Present participle, <u>brayant . . . Mais non,</u> Vladimir, I'm not the ass this time, but you are instead, <u>certainement. Mais oui,</u> old butler, I am the pupil you so despicably mistreated many years past; <u>Maman,</u> I am your dead son, returned to life; and Teddy, I am your once trusted confidant, <u>Kayo Aznap!</u>"

What a pleased look Nod gave me, for that performance! "And I, Mr. President," Nod said, "I am your own lost son," a somewhat overly climactic revelation, perhaps. Together, we threw aside our topcoats, and stood revealed (at least for a

191

brief moment) for what we were, the doughty pair who according to my ancestor's old text were one, Kayo and Nod—however corrupt the newer text that had us dressed as the Desperado and the Good Avenger! And then Nod rushed toward Teddy, arms wide, and I in like manner advanced toward my Maman—though my wits were not so madly joyous they neglected to note that Vladimir was using the confusion to slide with uncharacteristic self-effacement from that room.

Would that the day had ended soon after my Maman's admission that neither Papa nor Vladimir was my true father, and that I was the result of an early and impetuous liaison "in a ramshackle roadside diner on the rarely traveled Old Dixie Highway"—a phrase you may recall having taken down, Sid, quite early in this rapidly concluding account! I was, she went on, the true son of one Prince Everest of Faro, Faro being that "small but romantic island kingdom" or "princedom," and Prince Everest the one who had given her, in addition to me, the "objet d'art," the delicate crystal bell that (whatever my eleventh rule of conduct) rings forever in my mind as my dead Papa summons the family to yet another of his Sunday breakfasts. So despite what Vladimir may have suspected, it appears that I am a prince of another lineage—more modest than his, but one that suffices for me. Of course, the fact that I was not Papa's begotten son means that the early Kayo Aznap, the great author, was only my ancestor by adoption, but this, too, is enough for me, and someday I will conscientiously read every word of his book in two parts, however long each part may be.

But, alas, on to unhappier matters. After some rapturous kisses, Maman turned a little sullen, having dreamed of the grand parties she would give as an ambassador's wife (she had bought the formal dresses, she said, as well as a darling little fur cap for winter excursions via sleigh to the Bearland shopping malls!); and, noting that Vladimir was gone, rose herself, her bracelets tinkling, and left more curtly than I would have thought she might.

Meanwhile, Nod and Teddy were off in the presidential study, effecting what I presumed to be their reconciliation. Was such a reconciliation to be what Nod had darkly referred to in speaking of his destiny? It didn't seem to me that such

a common experience as making up with one's father, however nice it might be to do that, could qualify for a word bearing that much weight. I tried to engage in small talk with the
oaf from the Bear legation, but he obstinately refused to speak
Unitedian, hiding diplomatically behind that Gaulish tongue
he soon saw I couldn't understand, given his heavy accent.
"X" had been in and out of the room, no doubt eavesdrop-
ping on Teddy and Nod. Obviously he considered me untrust-
worthy, beneath his contempt; and yet on several occasions
he bumped into me, trying unobtrusively to hand me something.

"What in Allah's name are you up to, 'X'?" I asked him,
rightfully angered.

"I don't know if you're competent enough to have it back,"
he whispered. "Still, take it; a friend of yours from the DSP, a
young woman, brought it here this morning. You left it on the
ground at the Kayo Corral."

It was, of course, my family heirloom, that deadly blunderbuss! "How do you expect me to hide it, fool?" I whispered back. "My costume's too tight."

"That should have been obvious to me from your red
bikini shorts," he said with a sly bark of laughter, to cover up
his own inadequate thinking. He picked up one of the linen
napkins from the table, surreptitiously wrapping the revolver
in the cloth. "Pretend you have a cold, hold it to your nose
like a handkerchief now and then," he instructed. "Damn it,
Kayo, you've simply got to be a man and salvage your reputation today."

I was about to ask him what he meant when an ashen
Teddy came back into the room, Nod at his side. . . . Oh, Sid,
I thought by one dodge or another I'd manage to get through
all of the last moments of Nod's life in this chapter, using
every excruciating detail to dramatize the final event in this
history, the one that all along has been its seed, its prime
motivation. I imagined that finally I could reveal the tragedy
openly and easily, having prepared myself by admitting again
and again, if in general terms, that yes, I killed Nod, I murdered him in cold blood in full view of his own (presumed)
father! Still, I find that I must collect myself, I must get some
rest with a tranquilizer or two before I stagger to the end.

CHAPTER XV. *The Last Event*

Before reaching the violent act that ends my story, I should tell you something you perhaps have an inkling of, in consequence of the shrewdness I displayed in the previous (and I swear the penultimate) chapter. While I have no doubt that Nod will have a lasting influence upon my life, that in some trifling way I am irrevocably changed, I am (though a prince) still pretty much the old Kayo Aznap, the one whose <u>formative years</u> I described in convincing detail. I admit to some pretty giddy moments of liberation, especially on the morning following my sleep at the SETI facility; and ever since the night I had my dream in the leafy bower while Nod droned on and on about his life, I've had a certain <u>thing</u> about the stars. I mean, it's as if they could tell me something if I would only let them, or if somebody like Meg would recite their stories to me. Whatever this <u>thing</u> is, Sid, it's what made me snitch Nod's broken binoculars from his still warm body, and keep them in my room, in the same Lake District wine carton that holds the weapon that took two lives dear to me. Furthermore, my communication with you depends upon the combined efforts of Ellie or Nellie, the brilliant director of our planet's most sophisticated facility devoted to the search for extraterrestrial intelligence, and Meg, the witch whose extraordinary psychic powers are related to her rapport with, and her dwelling within, one or more starry vaults. It's obvious, then, that I owe a debt to the stars.

But enough of grateful acknowledgments of this sort. Thanks to the tranquilizers, I've just had a very soothing sleep, and what I want you to know, Sid, as we're about to say goodbye to each other forever, is that down deep I'm the same Kayo Aznap who gave you the sharp lessons about the need to avoid excessive idealism and stargazing, while stressing the importance of <u>conservative time</u> to all of us Unitedians. As an adviser who has selflessly devoted his career to maintaining that time, who has worked behind the scenes to bolster an older and flakier Teddy in his allegiance to it whenever he wanted to do something new and wonderful, how could I, at the crucial moment, have permitted Nod to destroy all my handiwork? And perhaps, through his ruthless stranglehold on Teddy's vocal cords, to send our nation into disunity, perhaps into the claws of an uncouth Bear, however dead that animal's ideology?

Understand me at this hour of our separation, Sid, by seeing my commission of a murder in its mitigating context: that's all I ask of you, my distant friend, as I give you the end of my story.

An ashen-faced Teddy, as I said, stumbled out of his study, Nod in close attendance. You've really got to hand it to that Teddy! He had difficulty talking, the same difficulty that in a few moments was to make his cry of "No!" a mute protest, a mere pouting of the lips, as he foresaw what I was about to do. And yet, as ever, Teddy wanted nothing more than to meet the obligations of his office. You recall his mild chastisement of me for interrupting some pretty serious talk he was having with the diplomat from Bearland. Well, he had broken away from Nod's fierce hold on him simply to finish that!

"Wh-where's Vladimir?" he asked. And then, shaking his head as if to clear it of mist or molasses, he said sharply to us all, "Do I make myself clear? Do you understand what I'm asking?"

"Of course, Oz," I said soothingly. "You want to know where Vladimir is. Well, he's gone."

Teddy choked, his Adam's apple rapidly rising and falling. Finally he blurted out something that sounded pretty incoherent to me, about needing an interpreter even though he realized that all "interpretation" was—well, as old hat as it was suspect. I thought that he was confused, as well he might be, by meeting somebody who had declared himself his son. (Wouldn't you be confused by something like that, Sid, if you were in the presidential shoes? Especially if that "son" turned out to be Nod, for Allah's sake? I mean, an Old Fart in thrall to dark enchanters who were using that poor deluded guy—

195

shrewd as he recently had seemed to be—to cast a spell on you? Wouldn't you be a little <u>distraught?</u> If you already had, as maybe you actually do, a tendency toward flakiness?)

Bravely if squeakily, Teddy declared that he needed somebody to communicate to the man from <u>Bearland</u> his own firm resolve to achieve a peaceful world; the <u>Bear</u> diplomat showed at least a scowling interest in this remark and said, pointing to himself, "Spick Unitiddy some. You spick me. I spick my great leader, what you spick."

Teddy smiled benignly, choosing his words with the care of a man determined not to stutter or flail verbally about. "Well, then, tell him that we are firmly resolved, as part of our sincere quest for peace, to build a secure <u>Dome</u> for our people; and that, after we have achieved that, we promise to share our technology with <u>Bearland</u> and every other nation, however criminal, that may want to build the same."

"You build <u>Dome,</u> we build skinnier and stronger <u>Cuban cigars.</u>"

"<u>Come on,</u> fellow!"

"Underlying physical law of <u>chaos</u> make <u>Dome</u> no damned good, no damned how."

Teddy gave him a suspicious look; something else you may recall is that the head mathematician on Teddy's scientific team had told him about this stumbling block. "You got a mathematical stool in my scientific team, fellow?"

"We long know about chaos!"

"Well, tell your leader that if you don't stop manufacturing <u>Cuban cigars . . .</u>" Here Teddy ceased talking, which had become so clearly painful to him that I wondered if he had a severe sore throat, to whistle a few bars of "Home on the Range," the tune that, as again you may recall, was always a nostalgic reminder of his childhood days on the range—and, as such, a help to him whenever the frustrations of his office became too great. "As I say, if you don't stop manufacturing them, why, we'll build a <u>Dome</u> on top of our <u>Dome</u> to protect it from cigars as well as chaos; and tell him that if I don't have his promise by midnight, I carry this resolve to the Unitedian people in a press conference tomorrow. I'm sure your leader knows· something about"—and he cleared his throat, trying his plucky best to retrieve his dulcet tones—"about my ability to get one hundred percent support from my people."

While the <u>Bear</u> glowered at him, Nod, who had been listening closely to the exchange, reached for Teddy's arm. "Dad," he said, "aren't you forgetting? Surely you don't mean—"

"Mean?" Teddy echoed. "What is meaning?" I'd never seen him so flaky, Sid! At once he lost the small confidence he had gained; his cheeks, which had put on a healthful-looking blush, became as ashen as before.

"Shouldn't you tell everybody the party's over?" Nod coaxed.

"The party's over, folks," Teddy said obediently, permitting Nod to guide him back to his study. Soon "X" and I were alone in the great room; his heels echoed against the mahogany parquetry of the polished floor as in his nervousness he paced back and forth. "Now, Kayo, it's time," he finally said, giving me another of his unfriendly nudges, this time in the direction taken by Teddy and Nod. "It's time for you to hear what you must hear, and time to do what you must at last do—whatever your new and surprising moral squeamishness. They'll be far enough along so that you can tell with absolute certitude how that <u>Good Avenger</u> of yours is brainwashing our Teddy right out of his golden voice!"

On tiptoe we approached the study door; stealthily, and with the success born of long practice, "X" turned the knob and soundlessly opened the door just enough for the two of us to see and to hear.

Teddy was sitting in the presidential rocker, the one with the homely corduroy cushion and the great seal of the nation.[1] Nod was standing before him, in the pose (which I won't describe) of one of my old university teachers. "And now, Dad," Nod was saying, "let's try our lesson on your favorite song."

"Which one is that?" Teddy asked, obviously too bewildered even to remember something like that!

[1] At this point, time being more essential to me than apparently it was to Kayo, I implored him to forgo all such by now unnecessary details. Remember how eager he was to confess everything, at the beginning of this second part of the story? Now that the dread and final event is upon him, how he stalls!

"The one you whistle, to get back your confidence."

" 'Home on the Range'?"

"Good! Very good indeed, Dad! Now, if you'll <u>sing,</u> not whistle, the first line?"

In that new and cracked voice of his, Teddy sang out, " 'Oh, give me a home—' "

"Thank you; that'll do for the moment, Dad. . . . Now tell me, if you will, to whom you are addressing this request for a home?"

"I suppose it's just <u>a manner of speaking,</u> isn't it? Or should I say <u>manner of singing?</u>"

"Let's not bluff or dodge around, Dad," Nod gently rebuked. "Either you're asking somebody for a home or you're not." He gave Teddy an encouraging smile. "What's the point of singing for a home if you're not singing to a particular person who could help you get it?"

"I guess you might be right."

"You could be addressing, say, a man at the bank. You want to buy a home, something more than a house, and you need a good-sized loan, perhaps?"

"That must be it."

"But, on the other hand, it might be a real-estate agent. You could be in a car, singing to that woman; in general, I think, real-estate persons are female. Isn't that a more likely hypothesis?"

"I hadn't thought of that! Yes, of course, I would be in a car, probably hers, because real-estate agents, for the sake of their commissions, like to drive you about, instead of having you go by yourself—"

"But we haven't absolutely determined whether it's a bank official or a real-estate agent or somebody else, have we? So let's leave that unresolved, remembering only that you're asking somebody for a <u>home,</u> not for a house. What's the difference between the two, in your opinion?"

"A house, I guess, is simply a <u>physical structure,</u> something to live in, whereas a home presupposes . . . Well, a hearth and <u>family life,</u> a place where one lives with those one most cherishes."

"Very good again, Dad! Now, will you continue with your

song, please?"

"I'll have to start at the beginning, to get it right. 'Oh, give me a home, Where the buffalo roam . . .' "

"Continue, please."

" 'Where the deer and the antelope play. Where seldom—' "

"Again, let's stop, trying this time to find out what you're really asking for. It seems to me you have a different concept of what makes a house a home than your average prospective buyer does."

"Why so?"

"Apparently your idea of a <u>home</u> is something of a zoo, I would think. Given your obvious affection for animals, have you ever considered that you may have made an improper career choice? It's not too late; there are examples of many people who, late in life—"

"I certainly was fond of my little pony, name of Joeboy."

"Do you want Joeboy in your home, too?"

"Why not, son? How do you go about buying zoos, I wonder?"

"Before we do that, Dad, let's continue with our analysis of your song. You got as far as the word <u>seldom,</u> which to my mind is ambiguous and may raise some very interesting oppositions. That little word even may work to <u>deconstruct</u> everything you've already said you wanted, including the zoo. Continue with the song, please."

"I'll have to start at the beginning again." (Let me interrupt here to say that poor Teddy's voice had begun to rasp like that of a parrot with pneumonia. Have I <u>now</u> convinced you of the <u>absolute necessity</u> of my act, Sid? "X" was nudging me again and again in that nasty way of his that in any other but these desperate circumstances I would have assumed to be a clue that he knew who had stolen his Zippo and was trying to be as mean as he possibly could.)

" 'Oh, give me a home,' " Teddy began, not even in the right key this time, and then his vocal cords became paralyzed, producing the muteness that kept him from crying "No!" as I entered the room as I had to, cast off the concealing napkin from the heirloom, aimed the weapon, and pulled the trigger. The explosion terrified me as much as anybody else.

For your sake as well as my own, Sid, I leave out all the subsequent details, except to say that my dear Nod died as gallantly as he lived, meeting his death without the slightest fear. The only tears on his face were mine, as I kneeled over him to kiss his cheek and to catch his last words. He wanted me to remember that he had forgiven me in advance, but he also had some last words about the <u>new enchanters,</u> for in his dying moments he had broken free (so he wanted me to know) of them.

"In certain ways, Kayo, we must admit they are right; for words have lost the purity of their first meanings, if ever they possessed them, and are used for reasons that have nothing to do with truth or even common sense. And, as a man who has always believed in the <u>diamond shape</u> that unites us all, I can gladly embrace a view that makes each of us part of the <u>same cultural text</u> and refuses to value one expression of it over another. Here you have a sentiment consistent with the most profound religious attitudes, as well as with your own egalitarianism. Indeed, such a sentiment appears to me to be mystical in nature, especially in the degree to which it hints at the cessation of sound as the only truth. Beyond question, the obsessive concern of these enchanters with cultural entrapment is a result of their denial of the soul, that faculty within us attuned to a freedom and cosmic union that logic can never apprehend. You see, nothing is missing from the deconstructionist outlook but a simple belief in the soul, and the subordinate beliefs that spring from it. I refer, of course, to the belief in witches like Meg, and in caves that are the starry universe, caves that contain a silence beyond the liquid dripping to be heard in the deepest pool of the deepest . . ." His voice trailed off; I could almost swear he gave me a wink, and made a pun of some sort, before he died.

But if he thought it his <u>destiny</u> to silence Teddy's golden voice for all time, Nod most assuredly failed, as he failed at every other absurd task he undertook. Here are a couple of last references from my text I ask you to remember: Meg told him, you will recall, that he might find his <u>destiny,</u> if not in himself, then at least in one whom he was to influence. Given

200

his failure with Teddy, I believe she must have meant me, and I don't think she could have meant that Nod would silence me, for he obviously hasn't. My other reference—about how Nod expressed the hope that his noblest part would live on in me—really points the finger of destiny in my direction. I confess to certain dreams, Sid! But what I can do (other than communicate my story across the vast interstellar regions to somebody like you—that is, to somebody still responsive to the cosmic slant and the universality of texts) is presently beyond my understanding.

And with that, Sid, I end my story. As to any discrepancies, in logic or in fact, that you may have found in my rich, tragic, and necessarily complex nest of narratives, I say that I [. . .]

A Note on Our "Scribe" and His Text

Kayo: The Authentic and Annotated Autobiographical Novel from Outer Space (an absurd title, containing within it oppositions that suggest in advance that the manuscript is bound to deconstruct itself) was found by me, at the touch of a button, in the hard disk of a long-humming home computer—its author (or supposed scribe) having left in such haste for unknown parts that he neglected to turn it off.[1]

At the second or third suggestion of the now retired chairperson of his and my former university department of "English," I and other concerned colleagues of the missing professor (in deference to his desire for anonymity, as well as to protect him from unnecessary ridicule, let us call him Professor "M.") visited his wife one pleasant Sunday afternoon (a nice jaunt into the country) to discover what we could about

[1] As to whether haste or mad cunning prevented him from completing the last sentence he was "transcribing," I can say that internal evidence suggests that the two prologues and many of the footnotes constituted his final labors.

the mysterious disappearance that had left his classes devoid of a professor for several weeks—until a student's chance remark let the cat out of the bag, and a substitute was hastily found.

The bemused wife brought our attention to that hot and humming computer, her own hostility toward it such that she had refused to come near it. Preoccupied with her own career in addition to her domestic anxieties, she could tell us only that Professor "M." for months had been far too engrossed with his new toy—engrossed to the extent that, according to her testimony, he actually felt it contained a kind of magic.[2] The reader who has completed Kayo already has discovered the helpmeet it was to him in the encouragement of those delusions long apparent to his alarmed acquaintances at school.

I refuse to enter any debate as to whether the narrative just possibly might be the work of an intelligence on another planet; were I to tell you what I really feel, I would be forced into a strong evaluative judgment of the entire contents of a "literary" work—something my particular specialty has the wisdom to shun, although of course it honors texts (like Freud's) that powerfully deconstruct widely held beliefs over those that merely parrot them. No, whatever Professor "M." 's narrative may imply, deconstructionists do rank certain selected texts, and always in accordance to the degree that these texts (in addition to Freud's, those by Nietzsche and Heidegger and the ever-fruitful Saussure come readily to mind) support the most advanced critical and philosophical thinking of the day. But why should I worry that the intelligent and attentive reader might be led into error by Professor "M."? By now, that reader will have learned for her-or-himself much about Professor "M." 's state of mind from his footnotes, particularly as the story gains momentum. Whether that momentum is as hysterical and hallucinatory as it is full of the wildest and

---

[2]A clairvoyant of rustic repute (as the reader is aware, she occupies a brief space in Professor "M." 's text) has advanced the curious theory that he was actually transported, via that computer, to another world—possibly as a reward for his faithful transcription of a lengthy message!

most improbable of adventures is for the reader her-or-him-self to ascertain.

I would be remiss, however, were I not to give my well-buttressed opinion about the true relationship between this work and my specialty (become a discipline in its own right)—especially since Professor "M." uses deconstruction as a convenient "whipping boy" for any number of the wrongs he finds on a planet that supposedly is a mirror image of our own.[3]

Above all, I would point out a telling irony—the degree to which Kayo proves the validity of what it sets out to discredit. Whether the reader is a deconstructionist or not, she or he will perceive that indeed, just as its title foreshadows, the narrative contains oppositions within oppositions that work to deconstruct themselves without the slightest help from that selfsame amused reader! Concealed by disguises as various as those of his factitious "President Teddy," Professor "M." even manages to deconstruct the better part of himself, with a big bang at the end.

Perhaps the greatest part of the irony stems from the fact that the author unintentionally has built with his Chinese boxes as good a model of the self-contained, self-referential text as any deconstructionist could. In reference to the crude satire on "domes," particularly the fantastic linkage of "Star Wars" to advanced critical theory, can there be a reader so be-witched by the madcap adventures that she or he failed to perceive the "hermetically sealed world" that Professor "M." himself has spun from his indulgent fancies and dreams as well as from his alleged "real-life" professional and domestic experiences?

Too, while Kayo takes advantage of what (taking a hint from a couple of savvy Italians, one of them a renowned se-miotician who happens to be a pretty fair novelist in his spare

---

[3]Some readers may feel indignation over his depiction both of con-servative time and of a president elected again, again, and yet again, under a variety of disguises, by an innocent populace. Here, they may rightfully think, is a case of that willful, disgracefully flaunted, socio-political alienation that comes from a dangerous addiction to the nar-cissistic "universal truths" of the "soul"!

moments) we can call the <u>Snoopy factor</u>[4] to give freshness to outmoded conceits and banal expressions, by that very strategy alone it shows the strength of the cultural web from which its author thinks that by wile he has escaped. Beyond all this, <u>Kayo</u> relies on two of the hoariest conventions of all—I speak of the <u>Bildungsroman</u> (or developmental novel) and the old narrative of the heroine's or hero's search for her or his true parents.[5] I leave unmentioned <u>Kayo</u>'s dependence upon a countless number of specific earlier texts, of which <u>Don Quixote</u> (a book unread by me) is but the most blatant example.

Professor "M." is so simpleminded in his description and understanding of poststructuralist thought, particularly of the subtleties to be found in deconstructionist theory and methodology, that a reader requires no previous training to follow his every quirk. (Don't worry that you might have missed something!) The reason I persisted in my cajolery of Ms. "M." to permit publication of a manuscript that ostensibly denounces my own specialty will be obvious at once to my delighted confreres—who must be imagining my sly wink as I compose a customary "last note" that simply <u>augments</u> the conventions riddling the text. (As for Ms. "M.," she ignored my repeated requests for several years, though whether from stubborn loyalty or simple uncaring I don't know.)

It is my guess that the prideful professor fled both school and spouse because of what he took to be his forthcoming disgrace—although, in actuality, the committee investigating his competence to continue in his teaching role never had the slightest thought of booting him out any more than it would have dreamed of firing any <u>tenured</u> professor who had served, however erratically, our great university for most of her or his professional lifetime. In fact, that committee (of

[4]I.e., having a dog say certain things you'd cringe like a dog to say yourself.

[5]I can't resist noting here that such a search is conducted not by one character, but by a <u>pair</u> of them in the text, and that neither is female. Is the author of <u>Kayo</u> oblivious to the sexual equality that deconstruction by its very nature supports?

which the undersigned was a member) already had decided to follow conventional policy in such cases—i.e., to recommend his appointment to an administrative post (a minor deanship, perhaps even a position as fifth or sixth vice-president of our burgeoning central administration) at a heartwarming increase in salary!

And let me say that his former colleagues, no matter how rudely he had treated us, did everything in our power to discover Professor "M." 's hiding place. Certain clues in the manuscript led us to a secluded and delightful little chapel many miles away—a chapel that belonged to no apparent denomination and had neither congregation nor pastor. We found it immaculately maintained by an elderly caretaker who was waiting, as she told us, "for the day that the light will shine again." She was apparently as mad as Professor "M.," but gave no sign of being a "witch" and was angered when we asked her if she lived in a cave—both of these misconceptions having come to us from that dubious document contained within the hard disk of a computer. (One wonders, incidentally, at the confidence of an author who apparently never even printed out a copy of his work to take with him in his suitcase!)

Finally, I should note that the quixotic battle that Professor "M." (now presumed dead, at least to this world) was waging against the new research was lost long before he entered the fray, which gives a charmingly antiquarian feel to our book. There have been many changes in structure and attitude at the grand old school since his departure. What once was an exotic bundle of foreign ideas has become thoroughly assimilated into the everyday scholarly commerce of a number of disciplines that formerly took pride in their "humanistic" heritage. Who today would accept the pretentious claims of our discarded "English" department that "literature" is (or ever was) a guide to life; that it has an organic form; that it is quite distinct from, and inherently superior to, more popular cultural artifacts ("Life Styles of the Rich and Famous" on television, the Harlequin paperbacks at the supermarket, etc.); and (more preposterous yet!) that it contains "spiritual values"—an apparently unanalyzable mix, or witch's brew, that puts us in touch with something in our "psyches" lying <u>beyond language itself?</u>

In general, I would say that deconstructionists—at Corinth and throughout America—are far less likely to carp at things-as-they-are than were the more romantic of the old guard, we still-youngish French-speaking Turks being willing (for example) to tolerate certain commercial requests or slogans as necessary compromises for the giving of generously endowed chairs by our right-thinking corporations. And to think that Professor "M." considered <u>us</u> the alienated ones!

John ("Jack") Jones

Bartlett ("The Tree Surgeon People:
See Our Ad in the Yellow Pages")
Professor of Deconstructionist Criticism and
Head, Department of Poststructuralist Thought
CORINTH UNIVERSITY

About the Author

Born in Lakewood, Ohio, James McConkey has been the recipient of numerous honors, including the Eugene Saxon Literary Fellowship, a National Endowment of the Arts essay award, a Guggenheim Fellowship, and the American Academy and Institute of Arts and Letters Award in Literature. He now lives near Ithaca, New York, and teaches at Cornell University.